ALSO BY
AKEMI DAWN BOWMAN

Starfish

Summer Bird Blue

Harley
in the
sky

AKEMI DAWN BOWMAN

SIMON PULSE

New York London Toronto Sydney New Delhi

This book is a work of fiction. Any references to historical events, real people, or real places are used fictitiously. Other names, characters, places, and events are products of the author's imagination, and any resemblance to actual events or places or persons, living or dead, is entirely coincidental.

SIMON PULSE

An imprint of Simon & Schuster Children's Publishing Division

1230 Avenue of the Americas, New York, New York 10020

First Simon Pulse hardcover edition March 2020

Text copyright © 2020 by Akemi Dawn Bowman

Jacket illustrations copyright © 2020 by Sarah J. Coleman

All rights reserved, including the right of reproduction in whole or in part in any form.

SIMON PULSE and colophon are registered trademarks of Simon & Schuster, Inc.

For information about special discounts for bulk purchases, please contact Simon & Schuster Special Sales at 1-866-506-1949 or business@simonandschuster.com.

The Simon & Schuster Speakers Bureau can bring authors to your live event. For more information or to book an event contact the Simon & Schuster Speakers Bureau at 1-866-248-3049 or visit our website at www.simonspeakers.com.

Jacket designed by Heather Palisi

Interior designed by Mike Rosamilia and Tom Daly

The text of this book was set in Adobe Caslon Pro.

Manufactured in the United States of America

2 4 6 8 10 9 7 5 3 1

Library of Congress Cataloging-in-Publication Data

Names: Bowman, Akemi Dawn, author.

Title: Harley in the sky / Akemi Dawn Bowman.

Description: First Simon Pulse hardcover edition. | New York : Simon Pulse, 2020. |
Summary: Eighteen-year-old Harley dreams of quitting school to join
her parents' Las Vegas circus and when they refuse, she joins a rival circus
where she must learn hard truths and face consequences.

Identifiers: LCCN 2018052707 | ISBN 9781534437128 (hardcover)

Subjects: | CYAC: Circus—Fiction. | Aerialists—Fiction. |
Family life—Nevada—Las Vegas—Fiction. | Dating (Social customs)—Fiction. |
Racially mixed people—Fiction. | Las Vegas (Nev.)—Fiction.

Classification: LCC PZ7.1.B6873 Har 2020 | DDC [Fic]—dc23

LC record available at https://lccn.loc.gov/2018052707

ISBN 9781534437142 (eBook)

To the ones who chase the stars,
and to Penny, for helping me find the way

CHAPTER ONE

*N*ot many buildings can rival the bright lights and vibrant colors of the Strip at night, but the big top of Teatro della Notte certainly holds its own.

The black-and-gold-striped building is blanketed by an explosion of twinkling white lights. Built to look like a vintage carnival tent that practically bursts with nostalgia, the structure is impossible to miss—even against a backdrop of Las Vegas casino hotels.

A circus is an attraction, after all. And Teatro della Notte *attracts*.

I slip through the overflowing parking lot and keep my fists tight around the strap of my bag like I'm trying to contain my excitement. I can hear "The Minuet of Ghouls" playing from inside—the arpeggio of a violin, the trill of an oboe—and my heart beats a little faster when I realize how close I am to missing the final performance.

But there's still time.

I've probably seen the show more often than anyone on the

planet—I know the music, and the routines, and the truth behind the magic—but it hasn't changed the way I feel.

I love the circus. I love the mystery, and the wonder, and the way every act transports my soul into another dimension. I love the way it makes me feel as if the world is in reverse and upside down all at once—like there's starlight beneath my feet and the ocean above my head, and every impossible dream can come true with a single whisper.

Mom says I have a romantic view of the world, and maybe I do. But I don't know how anybody could watch an acrobat dance across a tightrope or twist into the most perfect contortions or swing from the ceiling like a bird ready to fly and *not* find it utterly beautiful.

A pair of spotlights flash across the entrance like they're pointing the way, but I hurry to the back of the building and make my way down a set of stairs. I knock on the door rapidly, bouncing on my heels because the tension inside me needs somewhere to go, and my second favorite doorman appears.

Second favorite because he once told my parents I was watching the show when I'd promised them I'd stay home to study. Even though he swore he hadn't meant to get me in trouble, I haven't entirely forgiven him for it yet.

"Har-leeey," he says, dragging out the last syllable like a college dude-bro. Something else I'm not sure I can forgive him for.

"Hey, Billy," I say with raised eyebrows. "Is it okay if I catch the last performance?"

"Of course." He swings the door open so I can squeeze past

him. He's dressed in black from head to toe, which is a stark contrast to the glitter bombs and feathered ensembles of the performers. "Cutting it close tonight, huh?"

I let out an exasperated breath. "Mom sent me all the way to Summerlin to pick up Janie's costume because her cat ate a bunch of the beads. She needs it fixed for tomorrow." I peer up the nearby stairwell and point. "Is anyone in the skyrise?"

"It's all yours," Billy says with a chuckle, and suddenly I'm racing up the steps two at a time, very aware that the contortionist act is coming to a close.

I hurry across a metal walkway that circles around the height of the big top. We call it "the skyrise," but it's mostly used by the theater techs to adjust wires and lighting, and for the occasional photographer to get a good close-up photo of the aerial acts.

It's also my favorite place to watch Tatya's final performance, because when I'm this high, I don't feel like a spectator. I feel like it could be me out there, sitting on the static trapeze, performing to the music my father composed—the extra layer of magic that breathes life into every act.

Traditionally, the trapeze has always been the closing act of the circus, and I couldn't imagine anyone *but* Tatya closing out the show.

Except maybe me. One day.

An artist performing on a trapeze—the strength, and the movements, and the story, and the *sparkle*—it's the very heart of the circus.

I want to be that heart.

I reach one of the many transparent windows in the darkest

3

part of the hall and look down toward the center of the ring. Teatro della Notte boasts an incredible moving stage, surrounded by an impressive collection of dining tables circling around the room like a spiral. Each is decorated in black cloth and its own unique centerpiece representing the seasonal theme of the show; the tables flourish with guests, wineglasses, and confetti from the juggling act that appears during dessert.

Teatro della Notte combines a unique circus performance with a fine dining experience, and most of the guests turn up in suits and gowns. It's the warmth of a vintage postcard combined with the decadence of 1920s glamour, with all the twists and turns of my parents' imaginations.

I smile like I'm a child seeing the circus for the very first time.

Lights flicker all around the ceiling like an enchantment of stars, and I watch Tatya make her way to the center of the ring. She does a piqué turn and moves her arms through the air with the grace of a dancer.

I look at the faces in the crowd, lit up by the lights of the stage. They're already enamored by her, and she hasn't even started yet.

Tatya takes a seat on the static trapeze and flashes a wide smile toward the audience.

Dad's beloved "Bird of the Night" begins to play from the live wind orchestra showcased at the back of the room. Each musician is dressed like they're part of a haunted masquerade, and when the music erupts from their instruments, I picture my dad in his office, humming to himself and striking at the air like he's conducting an orchestra of ghosts.

Even though sometimes it feels like he's a ghost too.

Tatya grips the ropes as the trapeze lifts higher, and suddenly we're at eye level, though she'd never be able to see me through the one-way glass. Besides, Tatya is never distracted when she performs. She's too busy existing in another world.

A world I desperately wish I were a part of.

She pulls herself up, tucking both feet around the ropes and stretching her legs out in perfect form. With every shift of her body, she holds each pose, keeping in time with the music like it's nothing more than a dance.

I know the moves—the monkey roll to sit, the mermaid on the bar, the lamppost, the drop to half angel. I know them because I rehearse every pose in my head while I count the days until the next time I can spend an afternoon at Teatro della Notte's backstage gym. Usually there's time when my parents are too busy counting numbers and going over expenses for a business they seem determined to suck the magic out of.

When they aren't paying attention, I feel like I can be myself.

When I'm on the trapeze, I feel whole.

When I'm in the air with the ropes between my fingers, I feel like I'm everything I ever want to be in the world.

Tatya does a barrel roll over the bar, and I hear clapping when her body stills into a perfect horizontal split. The silver gems on her costume flicker like she's covered in glass, and there are so many white feathers exploding from her skirt and braided hair that she really does look like an ethereal bird lost in a graveyard, ready to take flight.

It's funny to think she had the same dream as me when she was my age—because *look at her*. She's out there, living in the very same clouds a thousand people probably told her weren't even real.

Tatya does a plank in the rope, and I can see the joy erupting from the crowd below.

This is what I want. It's all I've ever wanted.

I only wish my parents could see what this means to me.

What it would mean to hold a dream in my palm, press it tight against my heart, and never let it go.

I find Tatya backstage when the show ends. She's sitting at her dressing table, the mirror in front of her lined with big, round light bulbs and gorgeous white flowers. She spots me in the reflection and smiles, just as she removes the fake lashes from her left eye.

"Fancy meeting you here," she says with a laugh.

I half skip toward her and fall into one of the empty chairs. "You were amazing. Like, I haven't had chills like that since Zelda's big reveal in *Ocarina of Time*."

Tatya unpins the feathered crown from her hair and sets it on the table, patting at the stray red strands that come loose. "I hope you'll still visit me even when you're busy with classes. I'll miss your weird little compliments too much if you don't."

I hide my grimace. She still thinks I'm going to college in a few weeks. She doesn't know about my change of plan.

Not yet, anyway.

Tatya turns to me and purses her darkened lips. "How did you grow up so fast? What happened to the little kid that used to sit backstage reading comic books while trying to get Bobcat to teach her magic tricks?"

"Bobcat." I place a hand over my chest. Mom hired a brother-duo of acrobats from Spain two years ago to replace Bob Catalotti when he retired. He was only thirty-one, but circus performers don't always have a long shelf life. The wear and tear on a person's muscles takes a toll, and more often than not, there's someone younger and more talented waiting to take over. At least Bobcat got to make the decision for himself. "Do you still keep in touch with him?"

Tatya nods. "He opened a circus arts school for kids in Seattle. It's doing really well."

Even retirement sounds like a dream.

I sigh into the bunched-up yellow sleeve I have clutched in my fist. I'm always resting my head against my hands, but Popo—my grandmother on my mom's side—once told me people break out when they touch their faces too much. Using my sleeve as a barrier feels like a decent compromise for my hard-to-break habit and Popo's voice in my head. "I wish I'd trained as a kid. You've been working at this since you were six years old—I feel like I have so much catching up to do, and not enough time to do it."

"There's plenty of time. You're only seventeen," she offers, pulling out some of the makeup removal wipes from her drawer.

"Eighteen," I correct, and I can't hide my grin.

She smiles at me in the mirror, half of her face pinkish-white, and the other half still painted with a decorative silver-and-black mask. "I almost forgot—happy birthday!"

"Thanks," I say, before twisting my fingers together awkwardly. This is my chance—the first move on the chessboard of my new life. A mini battle before facing off with the boss-level baddies that are my parents. "That's actually what I wanted to talk to you about. Do you remember when you said you could train me? If my parents said it was okay?"

She nods. "I do."

"Well, is that offer still available?" There's so much hope in my voice, I can hardly sit still.

Tatya's bright blue eyes widen. "Wait, you're not going to school? Delilah and Kenji are really going to let you take up an apprenticeship?"

I hold up a hand and rotate it in the air like I'm not *entirely* sure. "Maybe? I'm going to talk to them tonight. I just wanted to make sure you would still be okay with it."

"Of course I am," she says with a smile. Then she turns and waves a finger at me seriously. "But only if your parents say it's okay. I can't do anything to upset the bosses, got it?"

I nod too many times. "No, yeah, totally, of course."

Tatya plucks one of the stray jeweled feathers from her table and sticks it in the messy topknot on my head. "Our little bird is all grown up and ready to fly."

She goes back to removing the rest of her makeup, and I look at my reflection in the mirror. Next to Tatya, I look like a shadow. An unrealized dream.

I know my parents will never really understand, but I'm going to try to make them.

8

This place is home to me, and it always has been.

And if they didn't want that to happen—if they really thought pushing me toward an education I don't want was ever going to work—then maybe they shouldn't have opened a freaking circus in Las Vegas.

I'm never going to change my mind, no matter how much it disappoints them. I don't want to go to school—I want to train here, at Teatro della Notte, instead of going to university in a few weeks for a degree I have no interest in.

Mom and Dad keep telling me I need a "real education," but university doesn't feel real to me. *This* feels real. Being at the circus. Feeling like I'm my own person.

They'll just have to understand.

I close my eyes and take a breath.

Everyone gets a birthday wish, right?

CHAPTER TWO

*D*ad's in his office when I get home, which isn't surprising because he's *always* in his office. And it's not just because he's a workaholic—I once found him and Mom holed up in there at midnight playing video games and eating gourmet jelly beans like they were still in high school.

They're annoyingly cute when they think nobody is watching. I mean, how many people genuinely marry their childhood sweetheart? I know it's not realistic, being as there are over seven billion people in the world, and how could you *possibly* be sure the one you met at a performing arts camp when you were twelve years old was going to be the right life partner for you? But it's still kind of adorable.

I didn't have a childhood sweetheart—or a sweetheart at all, for that matter—but it's nice to think it's possible that you could fall in love once and have that be it. No more awkward dates, or messy breakups, or bad kisses—it just clicks together the first time, followed by the Disney-style happily-ever-after.

Some people don't care about love, or life partners. And that's great for them, but not for me.

I want the epic love story.

But only as long as it doesn't get in the way of my dreams. I won't give up the circus for a life partner—and anyone who would expect me to wouldn't be the right person for me anyway.

Dad doesn't seem to notice me when I walk into the room. He's too busy playing a broken melody on his clarinet and jotting down notes on a piece of paper every other second.

I'm not surprised he spends so much time in here—it's the coolest room in the house. The walls are cluttered with nerdy artwork, framed sheet music, and awards he's won over the years. Lined up at the back wall is a collection of instruments—a flute, a violin, a guitar, a piano—and so many tech devices I don't know the names for. There are vinyl figurines all over the office, and behind his desk is a row of all his diplomas. His bachelor's, master's, and doctorate—all for music.

Dad thumps his pencil against the music stand, his dark brows furrowed and his hair slicked back and parted at the side. He's wearing a collared shirt rolled up to his elbows, a sweater-vest, and his signature khaki pants. He always looks and dresses like he's straight out of a Fred Astaire musical, even though I can't remember any movies from the 1930s starring a half-Japanese leading man.

"I didn't hear you come in." Dad's eyes widen in surprise, but his voice is like a calm stream. It carries his words, but the cadence hardly ever changes. He sees his office the way I see the circus—like it's a place where time freezes, and anything is possible. The problem is that he rarely notices anything going on around him when he's in the zone. "Where've you been all day?"

"Mom needed me to pick up Janie's costume." I trail my fingers along the edge of his desk, trying to think of the right way to bring up my change of plan.

The right way to tell him that I'm going to disappoint him.

"How was the show?" Dad asks without missing a beat. He doesn't always notice what's going on right in front of him, but he seems to notice *everything* that goes on when he's not looking.

I smile sheepishly. "Incredible, as usual." I take a step toward the music stand and peer down at the scribbled notes on the page. "Is that for the new winter set list?"

Dad nods, placing the clarinet in his lap and leaning back against the chair. "Just a few adjustments before rehearsals start next week." He pauses, his eyes the color of warm topaz. "The clarinet solo is for the new trapeze act."

My heart feels like it's being tugged by a puppet string. Teatro della Notte does a complete revamp twice a year—once for the summer-autumn season, and again for the winter-spring. There are new performances, new costumes, new music . . . and everything is kept top secret until the opening night of the new show—or, in my case, the first night of rehearsals.

The anticipation is torment.

I have no idea what Mom and Dad have been planning for next season, but I do know Dad's clarinet solo is whimsical and catchy, and I've seen a crapload of colorful fabric samples being shuttled in and out of the house over the last few weeks.

When I ask Mom to give me hints, she just winks and says, "All in good time," which always sounds more ominous than she means it to. But it's better than Dad's reaction, which basically involves ignoring me. He has a good poker face.

I don't know if it's the bliss in knowing the circus will soon be transformed all over again, but I suddenly feel a burst of confidence filling my soul. I feel invincible.

The words pour out of me before my brain gets a chance to process them. A side effect of wanting so badly to be heard.

"I saw Tatya backstage earlier," I say, watching Dad's careful eyes drift back to his sheet music. "She offered to train me. If it's okay with you and Mom."

Dad looks at me for a split second and then jots something down with his pencil. "Mmm. That's very generous of her. Just remember you've got classes, and she has a career—it might be harder than you think to fit in extra training once school starts."

"Actually, I was thinking more of an apprenticeship-type situation? Something more . . . serious?" My heart tugs a bit harder.

"Why do I get the feeling you're asking me for a job?" he asks, setting his pencil back down and meeting my gaze.

"Because I am," I say firmly. "I wouldn't expect you to pay me or anything while I'm training. But if I get really good, maybe you and Mom could think about letting me perform sometimes?"

"Does Tatya know you intend to replace her?" he asks seriously.

"I don't want to replace her," I say quickly. Defensively. I brush my palms against my pants because they're starting to feel clammy.

"But even Tatya takes time off, and you've always had Nina as her second. Maybe I could be Nina's second. Like, a last-resort backup plan. For emergency situations only." My hopefulness feels like it's wedged in my throat—it hurts to get the words out, but it would hurt even more to swallow them back down and bury them in the pit of my stomach, where they'd fester for an eternity because some dreams refuse to die.

Dad's face is emotionless. "How do you intend to take up a full-time apprenticeship and keep your grades up?"

I raise my shoulders like I'm trying to hold up the weight of this conversation. "I—I've decided not to go to college."

Silence. A heartbeat. A twitch on the right side of Dad's mouth. And then all the words I don't want to hear.

"Out of the question."

"But—"

"This is not up for discussion."

"I just want—"

"You're not quitting school."

"I'm not—"

"It's worse than quitting—you're giving up without trying."

"It's *better*," I practically shout, and clamp my mouth shut when Dad narrows his eyes. I can barely hear myself over the pounding in my chest, the ringing in my ears, and Dad rejecting my dreams without even listening to me. I breathe the cold air through my nostrils and try not to cry. "I don't want you and Mom to waste a bunch of money on a degree I don't want. And so many acrobats retire in their thirties," I point out. I can feel the fire in my eyes—

the hunger for him to just *understand*. "If I don't start training now, I might never get the chance."

Mom speaks from the doorway like she's been waiting to jump in for a while. "Why on earth would you trade your education for a career in acrobatics that's only going to last you ten years?"

I turn around. Her arms are crossed against her chest, and her short bob is pushed mostly to one side. She doesn't look Chinese like Popo or Irish like Grandpa Cillian. She just looks like her—like she's content sitting exactly in the middle.

I don't feel like I'm in the middle of anything. I feel like I'm on a thousand different points of a thousand-sided polygon.

I twist my mouth and find my words. "It's not a trade—I don't want to go to school. I don't even *like* school," I say.

"You love school! You took all those extra classes and graduated early from a magnet school with a good GPA—" Mom starts.

"Yeah, so I didn't have to stay there for an extra year," I interrupt. "And my grades were only good because I turned in all my homework and could fake my way through an essay. It's not because I actually learned anything."

Dad sighs. "That's because you're easily distracted. If you spent less time daydreaming and more time—"

"That's not it!" I bark too loudly.

Mom makes a noise that sounds halfway between a growl and a "hey." It's a warning—a yellow light. A sign to tread carefully. She and Popo don't always see eye-to-eye, but they do agree on one thing—children should respect their elders.

And I don't necessarily agree completely—I mean, there's a

gray area to everything, right?—but something tells me now is not the time to argue.

I try to slow down my heart rate by thinking about balancing on the static trapeze twenty feet in the air. "I'm not good at school. Information just doesn't sink into my brain the way it does for most people. I have to reread things a hundred times, and even then, I rarely comprehend any of it, unless there's a movie to go along with it or some kind of visual chart. It takes me longer to learn stuff, and it's frustrating. It makes me feel bad about myself, okay? Like I'm not good enough. And I'm a good aerialist—I can remember routines and positions and terms and everything else. It just makes sense to me, the way music makes sense to Dad or math makes sense to you."

"Not everything is supposed to be easy. In real life, things aren't just handed to you. And even if you *do* get lucky and someone gives you a break, it can be taken away from you like that." Mom snaps her fingers like she thinks she's proving a point. "That's why it's important to have a backup plan." She looks at me seriously. "It's hard enough to get a job these days, let alone get one without a college degree. You need an education. You need a safety net."

I press my lips together tightly. It's so hard not to shout when my chest feels like it's about to burst. Not because I want to yell, but because volume control just doesn't work when my emotions are running high.

I am losing this battle, and I don't know what to say to change course. What can I do to change their minds? What can I say to make them understand that my dreams are worth something?

Dad shakes his head. "You always have these big ideas. When

you were seven, you wanted to own a farm. When you were ten, you wanted to be a magician. When you were twelve, you wanted to move to France and run a vineyard. And it's great to have an imagination, but you can't make big decisions off an idea you just thought up in the night."

"This is different. I've wanted to perform in Teatro della Notte since the first time I watched the show. It's all I've ever really wanted to do. I didn't just dream this up overnight—I've dreamed this up over a lifetime," I say. And it's *mostly* true, because I'm leaving out the part where performing with Maison du Mystère was also part of the dream.

Even though my parents are ignoring everything I'm saying, I'm pretty sure talking about my childhood obsession for a rival circus would make things exponentially worse.

Mom clasps her hands together. "Then you'll still have the same dream after you finish school. But at least you'll have a backup, too."

It's pointless to fight the tears falling down my cheeks. I'm not usually a crier, but confrontation with my parents always makes me feel so out of control. It's like my face is malfunctioning.

I try to be the perfect daughter, but their idea of perfect isn't the same as mine. And shouldn't it be more important to be my perfect *self*?

Even if that means being imperfect to everyone else?

Mom reaches out her hand and pats my arm. "Not everyone has parents who can afford to send them to school. I think you need to appreciate what we're trying to do for you."

I spin around, part of me already prepared to bolt out of the room. "Neither of you are listening to me. *I don't want to go to school.* That doesn't make me ungrateful or unappreciative. But this is my life, and I should have a say in what direction I want it to go in. I'm eighteen—you don't get to tell me what to do anymore."

Dad stands up suddenly, and I know it means the conversation is at an end. "You're right—you're an adult now. And do you know what else adults do? They get jobs, and pay rent and bills, and cook their own food. If you want to stay in this house, you follow our rules—you go to school. But you don't get to have the best of two very different worlds. You don't get to pick and choose which privileges you want in life. That's being an adult too." Dad looks at me with so much sternness, but so much heart, too. And that's the worst part—that he thinks he's somehow doing the right thing.

Mom gives me a tired smile. "Come on, Harley. Let's not fight about this, okay? We've still got presents, and birthday cake, and—"

I don't wait around to let her finish, even though I can hear Dad shouting at me for being rude. But I can't listen to them anymore.

Not when they won't listen to me.

There's a knock at my door long after the streetlamps turn on and the diluted stars appear in the sky—stars that can't compete with the city lights, no matter how hard they try.

The first time I realized how truly beautiful the night sky was,

I was at Mount Charleston on a camping weekend with some kids from school. I'd never seen the sky like that before—like it was filled with shattered bits of crystal. Like I was staring up at a billion tiny windows all leading to a billion new worlds nobody on Earth even had the imagination for.

That's when I realized how small our own world is, and how minuscule I am in comparison.

But I don't want to be small. I don't want to be a blip in time.

I don't want to just get through life doing the "right" thing, or the "responsible" thing.

I want to experience excitement, and beauty, and love, and every other bit of magic in the world.

Why should I have to settle for ordinary?

"I don't want to talk to anyone," I say toward the door. I don't know who's there, but if I had to put money on it, I'd say it's Mom. She's the fixer—she mends feelings the same way she mends faulty costumes.

The door opens anyway, and Mom walks in with a piece of cake and a candle in the center. She keeps one hand curved around the flame to keep it from going out.

"Happy birthday to you," she starts to sing.

I sit up against the cushiony purple headboard of my bed. "You can't fix this with processed sugar and artificial food coloring."

Mom pushes out her bottom lip but makes her way toward me anyway, setting the plate of cake on my nightstand. "Won't you at least blow out your candle before the wax melts everywhere?" That's Mom—always trying to keep the world neat and tidy, like she thinks she can wrap everything in a bow and call it "perfection."

I blink back at her, shake my head, and blow out the flame halfheartedly.

She waves at the smoke. "Did you remember to make a wish?"

"Is this a joke?" I cross my arms over my chest and look up at the ceiling. There are still glow-in-the-dark stars up there from when I was ten. Another change I need to make. "I don't need a wish to make my dreams come true. I need you and Dad to stop standing in my way like you're the Iron Fist guarding K'un-Lun."

"Okay, well I don't know what that is, but I'm sure it's very important," Mom says softly.

"It *is* important. Not the Iron Fist part, obviously, but the part about my dreams. Why can't it be important to you, too?" I ask.

"Look, honey, I know you're excited about this . . . this idea you have. And that's great. But it's not realistic," Mom says, sitting down on the edge of my bed. "Your dad is right—you get these wild notions in your head all the time, but you never think about the work that goes behind them. And we care about you and your future, and we just think you need to grow up a little. Learn what it means to stick to something even when it gets hard."

"I can do that—just let me pick something I'm actually interested in," I point out.

"You picked computer science," Mom offers.

"No, *you* picked it," I say. "I just went along with it because I hate disappointing you."

"How about this—how about you go to school for a year, and if you really hate it after that, we can revisit this conversation?" Mom says.

My shoulders stiffen. "Why can't I train for a year with Tatya, and if it doesn't work out, then I'll start school next year? I mean, I graduated early—this one year is basically a free pass, if you think about it."

"Absolutely not," Mom says. "You're already signed up for classes—you need to give college a chance first. You're so young— your dreams might not look the same twelve months from now, and that's part of being a teenager."

"I'm not going to change my mind." I bunch my sleeves in my fists and wrap my arms around my knees. "I feel like I'm just moving through life in spaces where I don't ever feel like I really belong. But the circus—being on the trapeze—that feels real to me. It makes *me* feel real."

"I'm sorry you feel that way." Mom brushes the hair from my eyes. "You're real to me, you know."

"That's not what I'm talking about," I say stiffly. I feel like I'm suffocating beneath the weight of Mom and Dad's expectations. I feel like they're flicking my dreams away like they don't mean anything at all. "I'm tired. I don't want to talk anymore."

"Okay." Mom gets up to leave but stops halfway and glances back toward my nightstand. "Are you going to eat the cake, or should I take the plate back downstairs? I don't want the ants to come up here."

Cake and ants. *That's* what she's worried about. Not the fact that I'm sitting in bed and my chest feels like it's going to explode and I feel like all the color is being sucked out of the room.

There's frustration and anger and irritation running through my veins, and if I were a dragon, I would literally set this entire room on fire. "I don't want any cake," I manage to say.

She takes the plate and closes the door, and I stare at the street-lights until they go blurry.

CHAPTER THREE

*T*eatro della Notte's gym is tucked away behind the big top. The building feels so mechanical and practical in comparison to the main stage, with the ceiling resembling the inside of a warehouse.

Chloe, who's been my best friend since the third grade, looks over her hands gingerly and makes a face. "My skin is blistered and I've done, like, half of a pull-up." She holds her palms up.

I'm balanced on a large hoop that hangs six feet above the ground, attempting to do a one-handed candlestick. Chloe doesn't care at all about acrobatics, but she's usually happy to tag along and be my spotter. Though, I use the word "spotter" lightly—I'm not sure Chloe has the upper-body strength to ever save me from breaking my neck. She's slender, and clothes *always* look good on her, but that's not necessarily synonymous with strength.

I have curves—maybe a few more than most acrobats—but I'm also really proud of how long I can stay on an aerial hoop without getting tired.

"You get used to it after a while. You build up calluses," I say, grabbing the bottom of the hoop and doing a forward roll until my toes are just above the floor. I let myself drop and hold my hand up to Chloe. "See?"

She pokes a finger against my palm and winces. "That's disgusting. Your skin literally feels like a tortoiseshell."

The amount of interests we have in common has definitely dwindled over the years, but maybe that's also a sign of a good friendship—that we can be different and still care about each other.

"Oh, crap," I say suddenly, catching my reflection in the wall of mirrors opposite the trampolines. I look down and find a tear in my leggings that's at least twice the size of a quarter. "This is the second pair I've ripped this month."

I'm lucky in a million and one ways for having parents with a solid income and minimal pressure when it comes to food, bills, and presents at Christmas. But Dad always wanted me to know the value of money, which meant no allowance, and Mom wanted me to have all my time to focus on school, which meant no part-time job. Basically, all my funding for leggings and sports bras arrives in birthday cards every August or comes from the occasional odd job my parents are willing to give me.

And even though my annual family birthday dinners are usually filled with awkward microaggressions between four different parts of my family tree that otherwise *never* interact with each other, I'm grateful I'll at least be able to buy some better-quality gym attire.

Chloe lifts her curly blond hair off her neck and sighs toward the air-conditioning. "I feel like it's a million degrees in here. Want to get Pink Drinks at Starbucks?"

I pretend I'm distracted by the hole in my pants. If I have to choose between fancy five-dollar drinks and new leggings, I will always, *always* choose the latter.

Chloe wouldn't understand. We have different priorities.

"I have to get home," I say eventually, grabbing my oversized *Star Wars* T-shirt off the floor and pulling it over my flimsy tank top and sports bra. "My mom needs help setting up for dinner."

"Dun dun dun," Chloe sings in a deep voice, which makes me laugh. We might not be on the same wavelength when it comes to money, but she's my best friend for a reason. We get each other, even if we don't always agree. And I think that matters more sometimes—loving someone even if you both have different ideas of perfect. Because everyone has a different idea of what's good and bad. Perfect is overrated—it's our flaws that make us human.

I don't want to be perfect. I want to be vulnerable and messy and free and wild. I want to experience all the crooked edges in the world, and make mistakes, and grow from them. I want twisty roads and dark corners and big, wide bends.

And I know my parents won't ever agree, but I wish they could at least see my version of the world as a *possibility*.

I force the thoughts from my head and smile at my friend. "As long as nobody brings up anything to do with politics in front of my grandpap, the dinner will be fine," I say, walking beside her toward the exit. Grandpap has strong opinions, and one of those opinions is that *having* opinions means he's entitled to share them.

The warm blast of the Las Vegas sun hits me when I push the metal door open. Everywhere has air-conditioning in Vegas, so the first few steps back into the heat always feel good.

But then you reach the furnace that is somehow your car, burn yourself on the seat belt, and remember why you *loathe* the long summers times infinity.

Chloe shoves a pair of exaggerated cat-eyed sunglasses onto her face and turns to me seriously. Except it's hard to take her seriously when she looks like a villain out of an old James Bond movie. "Promise me we'll still do this after school starts."

I scrunch my face in surprise. "What, come to the gym?" Chloe cares about physical fitness as much as I care about AP Calculus.

"No, not the gym." She clicks her tongue against the roof of her mouth like she's scolding me. "I mean this." She moves her finger between the two of us. "You and me, hanging out like we're still kids, even when we're not. Promise me that you going off to college won't be the end of us."

I feel sulky just thinking about school. I'd hoped an aerial workout would distract me, but I'd forgotten what it's like in the weeks leading up to a new academic year. It's all *anyone* talks about.

"It's not like we haven't gone to different schools before. It doesn't mean our friendship is in jeopardy," I point out, and the words taste sour, like an underripe lie.

Because I'm not sure what the future holds, but it can't contain school. It just can't.

She hums into the sunshine, oblivious to how there's anguish and desperation creeping around in the pit of my stomach. "You say that, but you've never gone to college before. I have three older siblings—it's a different world."

A world I don't want anything to do with.

"Not to mention you've always had that look in your eyes, like you were going to fly away at any moment," she says with a grin, and I can't tell if she's joking or not.

I force a smile. "You don't need to worry. We're like Ash and Pikachu—nothing is going to break us up."

Chloe pulls her lip up like she's snarling. "Can we be Thelma and Louise instead?"

"Way too obvious. Besides, they have the most depressing ending ever."

"Ash Ketchum has literally spent over two decades trying to become a Pokémon Master. *That's* depressing."

"You're missing the entire point of his journey, but okay."

Chloe's laugh is all bubblegum pop. Light. Happy. Carefree. She stops in front of her car and pulls her keys out of her bag. "If you save some birthday cake, I'll come over in the morning and we can eat it for breakfast."

"Deal," I say.

She waves before ducking into her car, and I walk across the parking lot to the white Toyota Yaris Mom and Dad bought right after graduation. They made it very clear it isn't *my* car—it's just on loan while I go to school because my university is in-state and they're way too busy to chauffeur me around the city.

I wonder what will happen if I don't show up to class. Will they take the car away? And how will I get to the gym to train? And will my parents really kick me out of the house and make me figure out a way to pay rent, and bills, and whatever else?

Sometimes I feel like there are so many strings attached to everything they do for me that it makes it impossible to break free. Because I owe them too much. I *rely* on them too much.

And even though I hate to admit it, not going along with their plans feels like such a deep betrayal.

I'm either making them proud or disappointing them—there are no other options when it comes to my parents.

When I'm in the car, I leave the door wide open, turn on the AC, and lean back in the seat while the air starts to circulate. Tracing my thumb along the steering wheel, I think of all the things I want to say to Mom and Dad. The things I wish I could tell them, about them holding me back, and about feeling like I have so much pressure weighing down on my chest that I can hardly breathe. I think about how much I wish they would hear me, instead of talking over me because they still think being a parent makes them automatically right.

And maybe they are right. But maybe I'm right too.

Why can't they just give me some room to be *me*?

I'm already starting to get goose bumps on my right arm, so I pull the door shut and click my seat belt into place. I'm about to press the brake pedal when I glance into the rearview mirror and see Tatya near the gym doors, talking to someone I don't know. A tall, broad-shouldered man with a tidy beard and tattoos up and down his arms.

And something about her posture—the way she keeps looking toward the parking lot like she's hoping someone else will turn up, and the way her arms are folded in front of her like she's putting up a barrier between them—makes me feel like she doesn't know him either.

I yank the keys from the ignition and jump out of the car. When my foot hits the sidewalk, I use my loudest voice. "Hey, Tatya!"

When she sees me, her shoulders relax. She smiles—the kind of smile a friend gives you when you save them from being hit on by a pushy stranger.

The man's head snaps to the side like he's a spider sensing a vibration in his web. And that's when I notice his eyes—one bright amber, the other mossy green. I've never seen eyes like that on anyone before. I mean, I know what heterochromia is because Professor Xavier talked about it in *X-Men* once. But seeing something so uniquely beautiful for the very first time makes me do a double take.

The man lifts his eyebrows, and I realize I've been staring way too hard.

I focus on Tatya. I need a lie—an excuse to get her away from him, whoever he is. "I'm glad I ran into you. I wanted to ask you some questions about the new act." I point toward the gym doors. "Do you have a minute to talk inside?"

She hesitates before letting her face soften into understanding. "Oh. Oh, right! You'll have to excuse me." She gives the stranger an apologetic look. "The circus is full of secrets, as I'm sure you know."

I force an awkward laugh. "Dad would kill me if I ruined the big surprise by blabbing about the new set list in public."

The man tilts his head. His dark brown hair is peppered with gray and combed flat against his scalp. "You're Kenji Milano's daughter?"

He's familiar with the circus. Maybe I have this all wrong. Maybe Tatya *does* know him.

I nod. "You know my dad?"

"Only by reputation," he says with a short laugh before dipping his head toward Tatya. "I should go. But please call me if you change your mind." He procures a thin black card seemingly out of nowhere. The silver letters glint beneath the sun, but the name is unmistakable.

So are the words underneath.

SIMON TARBOTTLE

MAISON DU MYSTÈRE

RINGMASTER

My heart hammers. And hammers. And hammers.

I once dreamed of running away with Maison du Mystère when I was a little girl, way before I knew how much my parents despised everything about Simon Tarbottle's business practices.

A circus that travels all over the country—that transforms a quiet, forgotten place of the world into a theatrical extravaganza for just a few nights—was the epitome of magic to me.

Tatya hesitates before taking the card from him.

"I look forward to seeing the performance tomorrow," Simon says with a smug grin. And then he disappears around the corner as his footsteps fade away.

"Was that—" I start, but Tatya waves her hand quickly.

"Don't say it. If you say it out loud, it will only make it worse." She sighs and looks around me as if to make sure nobody is coming. "Please don't tell anyone. I swear I'm not doing anything sneaky behind your parents' backs. He just showed up here out of nowhere. But I know what it will look like, and I don't want the drama."

I frown. "What did he want?"

She bites her lip. "He offered me a job. He says his aerialist keeps threatening to quit, and he wants to replace her with someone better."

"Well, that's quite a compliment. I mean, Maison du Mystère is the most famous traveling circus in the country," I say.

"And also the shadiest," Tatya points out almost accusingly. "Everyone knows Simon travels around poaching performers and stealing ideas. He gets away with it because his show is always on the move, but trust me, people in the industry hate him with a passion. Which is why I don't want anyone to know he approached me. It'll just upset everyone, especially with all the stress of getting ready for a new season."

"I won't tell anyone," I promise, "but—do you *want* the job?"

"No!" Tatya practically barks. "Not in a million years. I love it here—this is my family." She sighs. "Will you do me a favor? Throw this away for me?" She holds out the card toward me. "If I throw it away here, someone might see it. And I don't want it in my bag—I don't want you thinking that I'm even for a second considering his offer."

I shake my head quickly, sensing the genuine worry in her eyes. "That's really not necessary. I believe you."

Her arm doesn't budge. "Please. It will make me feel better."

I take the card from her and hold it in the air. "Fine, fine. I'll burn it when I get home, okay?"

Tatya laughs. "Okay. Thank you. And thanks for coming to my rescue, too."

When I'm back in the car, I tilt the card and watch the metallic gleam move across the words like a magical wave. And when I flip the card over, I find a phone number on the back.

I hate that the thought even crosses my mind—I hate that I'm so desperate to chase my dream that I could even *imagine* it—but it occurs to me that Simon Tarbottle is looking for a new aerialist, and maybe that aerialist could be me.

And then I force the horrible desire from my thoughts and shove the card into my glove box.

Hidden in the darkness, where bad ideas belong.

CHAPTER FOUR

*H*arley! Can you get the door? It's probably your grandpap," Mom shouts from somewhere in the kitchen.

I close the lid on my laptop—and the unfinished document listing all the reasons I need my parents to support me—and make my way downstairs.

The next half hour is a blur of hugging one family member after another. Grandpap arrives first, like Mom guessed, but Aunt Adeline, Uncle Henry, and my three very loud cousins turn up before I've even closed the door.

Aunty Michiko and her new boyfriend follow soon after, and then Aunty Ayako, Uncle Jesse, my older cousin Matty; his girlfriend, Taylor; and their toddler, Isabella. Popo rings the doorbell last, and I'm really not surprised—she likes to make an entrance.

"Happy birthday, Harley Yoshi." Popo coos like I'm still a little kid. She's the only one who ever uses my middle name—which is a family name and doesn't exclusively belong to a Nintendo character. Having to point out to people over the years that I was named after my late grandmother and not a famous green dinosaur has been the bane of my childhood.

My middle name is also pretty much the only part of me that reflects my Japanese heritage, even if it is a quarter of my blood.

I'm a quarter Chinese, too, but I have no name to show for it. Even Popo's first name is Jane, so sometimes it feels like there's this dormant part of me I've never had a chance to learn about. It doesn't fully make sense—belonging to these different cultures, but not *really* belonging.

You know those refillable soda machines at fast-food places? When I was a kid, I used to add a little bit of everything in—7UP, Dr Pepper, Pepsi, raspberry iced tea—whatever they had, I'd mix it all in. But when it was all mixed together, it wasn't really 7UP anymore, or Dr Pepper, or Pepsi, or raspberry iced tea. It was everything, and nothing.

It was something new that didn't have a name.

I feel like that sometimes—like something without any history. Like I don't quite fit in.

An Italian last name, a Japanese middle name, a splatter of freckles across my nose that Mom insists are from her Irish father's side of the family. And a Chinese grandmother whose face I've searched a million times for little bits of me that I was never able to find.

I'm American, but that only explains my passport. It doesn't explain all the other pieces of me that aren't easily labeled.

Not to mention how Chloe calling herself American and me calling myself American get *very* different looks from people.

Sometimes it feels like if I call myself American, people will only ever follow up with, "But what are you *really*?"

But if *I* lead the conversation? If I tell them everything I am? If I point out all the pieces of my heritage to explain why I have my name, and my face, and my culture? Then people tell me I don't get to be all these other things—I only get to be American. Like the rest of me is suddenly erased. Like my heritage isn't import-ant. Like all the pieces that should mean something don't mean anything at all.

And in all honesty, I'm really tired of other people thinking they have any authority whatsoever on what I'm allowed to call myself.

Popo gives me a gentle hug and hands me a red party bag stuffed with yellow tissue paper. She has the happiest eyes of any-one I know, even though her mouth rarely breaks into a smile. The weight of the bag surprises me because it's too heavy to be clothes.

And Popo has never bought me anything that *wasn't* clothes.

Popo loops her arm around mine and leads me into the kitchen to join everyone else, so my curiosity has to take a back seat.

Bunches of blue and yellow balloons are positioned around the room, and glittery silver streamers and stars dangle from the walls. With the exception of my youngest cousins, who've already found a comfortable spot in front of the television, most of my family members are hovering over Mom's Brie and honey appe-tizer, and the rest are digging through the beer cooler.

Mom shoves a cheese-covered cracker in her mouth and

hurries across the kitchen to check the oven. The moment I set Popo's gift on the counter, Mom's head lifts back up like a deer sensing danger.

"Not on the counter, please. I just wiped it down," she says with gentle-scolding eyes.

I really want to point out that this is probably the best time *to* put objects on the counter, being as it's clean, but I keep my words stuffed in my brain where they belong. I still want to believe there's a chance I can change her mind about school, and arguing with her over silly things will only hurt my cause.

"Popo is still spoiling you, I see." Dad eyes the gift bag as I pick it back up and set it on a table in the hallway instead.

"Grandmothers are supposed to spoil their grandchildren," Popo retorts from around the corner. When I'm back in the kitchen, her head is tilted to the side and she's staring at Mom. "You look tired. Do you have a cold?"

Mom sighs the way I do when Mom overanalyzes everything about me. Maybe it's a mother-daughter thing.

"No, Ma, I'm fine," she says. "I hope you're hungry. I made pumpkin ravioli."

Popo walks past her and presses her cheek to Mom's in a weird almost-hug. They've never been good at showing emotion with each other, even though they show *so much* to everyone else.

Twisting her mouth, Popo says, "You should've asked me to cook. I could've made chicken stir-fry."

"Harley likes ravioli," Mom says calmly. She pulls a tray of garlic bread out of the oven. "So does the rest of the family." She means Grandpap, mostly, because he's the only one who turns up his nose when anyone cooks anything that isn't his own idea of "American." We're expected to treat Italian food like it's totally ordinary, but if Mom ever served up ramen or Spam fried rice, it would be treated like it was something unusual. Something *exotic*.

I wonder sometimes if Grandpap defaulted to his own ways when Grandma died. Dad says he can't remember very much of her since he was so young when she passed away, but since he and his siblings all have Japanese first names, she must've been trying to teach them *something* about their heritage.

But then she got sick, and since her family still lives in Japan, Grandpap pretty much raised three kids all on his own.

I think that's why Dad feels more tethered to his Italian side than his Japanese side.

Both my parents are biracial, so family gatherings have always been—as Popo calls it—chop suey. *Mixed.*

And it's not that everyone doesn't get along, because they do. On the surface, anyway. But sometimes it feels like there's another layer that doesn't quite fit right—like four different colors that won't blend. And maybe that's fine for my grandparents, who don't necessarily *have* to blend, but it's different for me. Because I'm parts of all of them.

And I wish I could feel like I was all four parts at once, instead of different parts at different times.

For the record, this is one of the reasons I hate Halloween. People get understandably upset about people dressing up like they belong in another culture, but honestly? I've felt like that my whole life. Like I'm pretending. Like I'm wearing a costume from someone else's background. Like I have no real claim to all the different pieces of my family's heritage.

Mom motions for everyone to sit down at the table, and there's so much talking over the entire meal that I start to get a headache. Grandpap keeps telling stories about his time in the army. Popo gushes about how tall I'm getting—even though I stopped at five foot four sometime during freshman year and haven't grown a millimeter since. My cousins won't stop fighting over the Nintendo 3DS they have hidden under the table. Aunty Michiko keeps trying to ask me about school, but Isabella is sitting next to her and crying about not being able to fling pieces of ravioli onto the floor, so it's too hard to hear.

At some point Uncle Jesse makes the mistake of talking about politics, which sets Grandpap off into Ultra Nightmare mode. They spend the next thirty minutes in a heated debate about everything from taxes to gun control to paternity leave. Grandpap insists Italians are "passionate speakers," but it really just sounds like he's yelling from across the table.

After everyone's had a piece of cake, Mom ushers them all into the living room to relax while I help her and Dad clear the table. Popo lingers in her chair, sipping a glass of water. Her movements are always so delicate and careful. I think it's because she spent so many years as a dancer.

"Well, I'm officially exhausted," Mom says, tucking her hair behind her right ear. She chopped most of it off at the beginning of the summer, and it's still too short to tie up. She nudges me away from the kitchen sink. "Come on, it's your birthday. Go sit with the family—your dad and I can wash the dishes after everyone goes home."

"Technically my birthday was yesterday," I say, but I move aside anyway.

"Always so literal," Mom says with a smile. "Every time I look at Isabella, I remember what you were like at that age. It goes by so fast."

"You were better at eating, though," Dad points out almost proudly.

I try to smile, but I realize whatever I'm doing with my mouth feels mega-unnatural. I'm not good at pretending I'm happy when I'm not. Mom and Dad seem determined to act like yesterday never happened, but that's not going to make my feelings disappear.

Orientation day will be here soon enough. How much trouble will I be in if I don't turn up?

Dad grabs another beer. Mom pours herself a glass of wine.

I count the seconds it takes for one of them to notice me.

Mom frowns. "What is it, honey?"

"I was just—" I start. *Thinking about not going to school. Thinking about chasing my dreams. Thinking about how I wish you would try to understand me.*

Mom and Dad watch me like I'm a mild curiosity in a museum. And I know that look on their faces too well—the look that says, *Don't say it. Don't disappoint us. Don't be disrespectful.*

And the sinking feeling in my gut tells me that they're never going to listen. It doesn't matter if I say all the right words, or fill every hole in my argument. They're never going to agree with me because we don't see the world the same way. We don't see my *life* the same way.

I pull my lips in and shake my head like the hope in my heart is splitting down the middle. "It's nothing. I was just thinking about the new set list, that's all."

Mom's shoulders relax. "I think you're going to really love it. Rehearsals start next Wednesday, if you want to watch."

I force a weak, flimsy smile.

Dad holds up his beer bottle. "Speaking of which, I'm sorry to disappear, but I've got work to do." He kisses Mom on the cheek and nods toward me and Popo. "I've got about a thousand photocopies to make of all the new sheet music, and if I don't start now, I'll be up until three a.m."

He vanishes back into the hallway like he was hardly here at all. Mom motions toward the living room. "Are you coming?"

I'm trying so hard not to cry, that Popo's hand on my wrist makes me jump.

"We'll be there in a minute. I want to talk with Harley first," she says with the raspy, adoring voice I'm so fond of.

When Mom's gone, Popo pats my arm. "Why don't you go and get the present I brought you?"

The bag is still in the hallway, and when I get back, Popo is looking out the window like she's remembering something from a long time ago.

I sit down next to her, and when Popo nods at me, I pull the contents out onto the table.

It's a rectangular photo album, covered in bright red leather with gold flowers embroidered along the edges. In the center are some characters I'm not familiar with, but I am pretty sure are hànzì.

I run my finger along the metallic words. "What does this say?"

Popo's eyes are fixed on me. "It's our family name. Soong. From Taipo's side of the family."

Our family name. Like Popo thinks I have just as much of a right to the name as she does.

I turn the cover and find an old black-and-white photograph on the first page. It's of a little girl wearing a short dress with her hair in a blunt, straight cut. She's frowning at the camera like the sun was too bright, and there's a woman standing behind her with her hands on the girl's shoulders.

"This is my mother, Chin Choy. Your taipo." She points to the little girl—a great-grandmother I've never seen before. Popo looks at the photo with heavy creases beside her eyes and points to the woman next. "And my popo."

Curiosity sweeps over me. "Were you close?"

Popo doesn't take her eyes away from the ghosts of her past. "She worked very hard, especially when my mother was younger. She was born in China, and her family was very wealthy. But then the war happened. . . ." Her voice trails off, and she lets out a sigh. Popo doesn't like to dwell on the negatives of the past, even when they're from someone else's past. "She took a boat all the way to Hawaii and married when she was only sixteen. She worked at a factory and would send all her money back to the housekeeper in China, but she found out many months later that the Communists had been living in her family's home. They would give the letters to the housekeeper but keep all the money that was inside. After she found that out, she never wanted to go back to China. I know she missed home—but I know she loved Hawaii, too."

"I never knew any of that," I say, staring at the photographs.

"It was a long time ago," Popo says. Sensing the end of her story, I turn another page. Her eyes light up with joy when she sees a photo of another small child, standing in front of a horse with flowers draped around its neck. "This was me when I was a little girl. I remember this afternoon very well." She chuckles. "We had just finished watching the King Kamehameha Day parade. On our way home, a fire ant bit the bottom of my foot, and by the next day I had a blister the size of a half-dollar. Ma had to use a needle to break it open. I was so scared."

I flip another page. And another. Popo tells me so many stories about her childhood, and her teenage years, and the day she met Grandpa Cillian, who passed away in the nineties from lung cancer. She tells me about the day she went into labor with Mom, and how Grandpa Cillian was so determined to come into the room when he heard Popo screaming that he fought off four nurses and a doctor to get through the door.

"The second he looked at me and saw all the blood, his whole body went wobbly and he hit the deck like a sack of rice." Popo laughs until there are tears in her eyes.

"Do you miss him?" I ask quietly.

She nods. "Every single day."

I turn a few more pages, soaking in the photographs with faded colors and clothing from the 1970s. Grandpa Cillian's hair is so unmistakably orange, and I can almost see the freckles Mom is always telling me about. And Popo is beautiful, lithe and graceful as ever.

She taps her finger against the book. "You can finish looking through it later. I don't want to be greedy with your time when you have so much family in the other room. But I wanted you to have this—I wanted you to know where you came from."

I look back at my grandma with confusion at first, and then resignation that I'm not as good at hiding my feelings as I sometimes wish I was.

"My history is your history," Popo says. "Don't ever forget that."

"Thanks, Popo," I say, and I lean over and give her a hug, breathing in her soft perfume and lemongrass soap.

When I pull away, something occurs to me for the first time in my life. "What made your parents name you Jane? I mean, it's a great name—Jane Austen is my literary hero—but do you ever wish they had given you a name like theirs?" When people see my name on paper, I know they've already erased half of me in their heads. A girl named Harley Milano isn't supposed to look like me.

But Harley Yoshi Milano—I feel like it's proof that a quarter of me exists. Even if it's not fair, sometimes names feel like a statement.

Would I have less of a right to my family's cultures if I had a different middle name?

Would being called Harley Jane Milano somehow make me less Asian than Harley Yoshi Milano?

I want to believe it wouldn't, but sometimes I don't know. Sometimes I feel like I'm at the mercy of racially judgmental purists who are forever finding reasons why I can't be in any of their clubs.

"I was born in a time when people thought a name could make the difference between standing out or blending in. Back then, people wanted their children to have the best chance in a world that was not always eager to accept them. Names were lost, and so were languages." There's life dancing behind Popo's eyes. "Names can change, Harley Yoshi, but your family—and where you come from—that can never be taken away from you."

Popo gets up to join everyone in the living room, and before I put the photo album back in the bag, I trace the lines of Popo's family name once more, and I hope that if I do it enough times, it will feel like my name too.

CHAPTER FIVE

*T*he late-afternoon sun casts an apricot hue across the skyline, and the parking lot is still empty. I'm early for a change.

Billy is standing outside talking on his cell phone when I approach the back door of Teatro della Notte. When he notices me, he leans the phone against his shoulder and tilts his head toward the door.

"Just a heads-up—it's tense in there today," he offers.

I pause in front of the entrance. "What happened?"

Billy shakes his head and sighs like there's too much to explain. He settles for a single word. A name. "Tarbottle."

My stomach drops like I've lost my grip on the silk ropes fifty feet in the air. Billy lifts his phone back to his ear and says, "Yeah, yeah, I'm still here," and I'm already halfway through the door.

Everyone is either hiding their awkward grins or nervously keeping their eyes to the floor. It's clear the gossip has already made the rounds backstage, but Tatya isn't in her dressing room. I wonder if she knows what she'll be walking into tonight.

Whispers fill the hallway, and I catch a snippet of conversation coming from one of the other rooms.

"I can't believe she'd leave us."

"I hear Maison du Mystère pays well."

"But where's the loyalty? I don't care how much they pay. I couldn't do it."

"I just can't believe she didn't tell us."

"Do you think Kenji and Delilah know?"

When I pass by the doorway, I don't have to look inside to know it's Elise and Katy, the two halves of a contortionist sister act. And I don't blame them for taking part in the gossip fodder—they don't know the whole story like I do—but I'm in a hurry to get to my parents, and I'm not interested in giving them more information than they already have.

They notice me, as evidenced by the hushed whispers of embarrassment that follow.

My parents' office door is slightly ajar, and I catch a glimpse of deep burgundy carpet from the hall, a pair of shadows strewn across the floor.

Mom looks surprised to see me. She's sitting behind her desk, one arm across her chest and the other folded up toward her shoulder. It's the way she always sits when she's thinking hard about something.

Dad shifts his gaze to look at me. He seems flustered, almost like they've been arguing, which would be strange. They *never* argue.

The words fly out of my mouth before my brain has the decency to think. "If you're fighting about Tatya, the rumors aren't true. She's not joining Maison du Mystère."

Mom leans forward so her elbows rest on the desk. "How do you know about that?"

I throw a thumb over my shoulder. "I mean, anyone walking through that hallway right now would know. But I saw Simon earlier—he basically cornered Tatya outside. She didn't even keep his business card."

Mom looks at Dad, who shrugs, like maybe it's true, and maybe it isn't.

"You don't believe me?" My voice carries a sting. They never take me seriously—even when it doesn't have anything to do with me.

"We believe you," Mom counters, standing from her chair and making her way toward me. She closes her hands around my arms and squeezes like it's supposed to be reassuring. "But there's been a lot of hearsay today, and there's no point in discussing anything without Tatya in the room to speak for herself."

"What I told you wasn't hearsay. I was *there*," I argue. And then my stomach coils. "Is Tatya in trouble?"

"Of course not," Dad says with a sigh. "Any performer has the right to interview with other troupes. I mean, we'd hope she'd at least finish out the rest of her contract, but if Tarbottle is paying her what I hear he pays his current lead aerialist, I don't know if that would stop her."

"I just said she's not taking the job—" I start.

"Her contract ends in December," Dad cuts in, his eyes the

serious woodsy brown they get when he's lecturing me. "Even if she isn't going to take the job now, another job offer will give her grounds to renegotiate her salary. We might not be able to afford to keep her if it comes to that."

I frown. "What are you saying?"

Mom lifts her hands and pushes down at the air like it's supposed to slow *us* down. "We are merely thinking of all the possibilities, and whether we may need to think about taking interviews to find Nina a second if she ends up taking Tatya's place. We'd be halfway through the season, and losing a contract renewal with one of our leads is not something we want to be unprepared for."

Something sparks to life behind my sternum, like the tiniest flame in a cold, dark woodland. A second. For Nina.

Dad moves across the room with a thick folder of paperwork—most likely copies of all the new sheet music. There are folders just like it at home. He stuffs it into one of the enormous filing cabinets against the back wall and spins the combination lock a few times when the door is shut tight.

Mom plucks her pen from her desk and sticks it in the ceramic pot beside her computer monitor. She turns back to Dad, her mouth open like she's ready to fall back into normal business talk, but I can't let her. If I don't say it now, I might never get the chance again.

The hope sears through my words, jolting everything in the room like I'm made of electricity. "What about me?"

Mom and Dad look at me with confusion at first, their brows matching with puzzlement and interest. I think Mom figures me out a moment before Dad does because she's first to tilt her head forward and flatten her mouth. A sign that I've been heard—and am about to be ignored.

I keep talking, hoping I might be able to say something—anything—that will make them understand how important this is to me. "I would work so unbelievably hard. And I already have most of the routines memorized. Some of them I've even practiced when I've been in the gym. And I get along with Nina, so you wouldn't have to worry there'd be any Tonya Harding–style sabotage behind the scenes. And I have the cheapest salary in the world because you literally don't have to pay me a penny. I just want the chance to do this—the chance to learn, and to perform, and one day to do this as a living."

I can see it in their eyes. They're not even considering it. They just think they're being good parents by letting me talk.

I fight the burning tears in the corners of my eyes. "Please. I promise I won't disappoint you. Please—just give me a chance."

Dad clears his throat. Mom crosses her arms and sighs.

Despite everything, I can't stop the first tear from falling.

"It's not going to happen. This conversation was already discussed and closed. You're going to school, Harley." Dad doesn't even blink when he talks to me. It's like he's trying to burn the words into my memory, in case I forget them again.

But I didn't forget them. I just don't accept them.

Mom reaches for me, like this time she wants to give me a hug, but I'm waving my hand in her direction because I don't want her to step a single inch closer to me.

Can't they see how much they're breaking my heart?

Why does it not matter to them?

I yank the door open and storm out into the hallway, but I only make it three steps before I'm face-to-face with Tatya.

All the brilliant charm and light I usually find in her blue eyes has vanished, replaced by something cold and stern.

She shakes her head, her auburn curls flinging from side to side. "How could you?"

My mouth falls open, clamps shut, opens again. What did she hear? What does she think? "No, Tatya, it wasn't what it sounded like. I only—"

"You only want Nina to replace me, so you can replace her. I heard you perfectly, Harley." Tatya pushes her tongue against the inside of her cheek. She's angry, and if I was anyone other than the boss's daughter, she'd probably be shouting at me.

"I know it sounded bad," I start, and now the tears are pouring. "But I told them you weren't taking the job. I told them you weren't going to leave. They were just talking about—"

"I trusted you. I wanted you to trust me. That's why I gave you that card," Tatya says in a dull, hurt voice. "Because family is supposed to have each other's backs."

"I didn't mean—"

But I can't get her to listen to me either, and the next thing I know, her back is turned and she's walking toward her dressing room, and there are so many eyes peering out of their doorways that I feel like I've been set on fire.

Shame is the worst feeling I have ever felt in my life.

CHAPTER SIX

*M*y pillow is a salty wet mess from the amount of tears I've cried since I walked through the front door. I want to text Tatya, to tell her she misunderstood and I'm not after her job, but I'm worried maybe some part of me is, even if it isn't intentional.

I started off trying to make my parents see that Tatya isn't going to leave. But by the end, when I saw an opening—a chance at my dreams—I didn't hesitate. I wasn't thinking about Tatya. I was thinking about myself.

Maybe that *does* make me the bad guy.

I think about calling Chloe, but then I realize I don't know what I want from her. Reassurance that my dreams are valid? Affirmation that I'm not a horrible person deep down? Or hope that my parents might still change their minds?

Right now, I don't think any of it matters. Because everything feels hopeless.

I think I've hit a dead end, and the realization that I've not only exhausted any chances of getting my parents to listen, but I've also forever ruined my friendship with Tatya, really hits me hard.

How can I ever train in Teatro della Notte's gym again?

I can't show my face there. Not after what she thinks I did. What I may have done.

I feel the circus slipping away from me like water through my shaking fingers. Panic sets in, and I don't know how to stop it.

Chloe can't make this better. Nobody can.

I roll to my side, trying to find a part of my pillow that isn't soaked in tears, when a bright red corner of Popo's photo album catches my eye.

Pushing myself up, I wipe my sleeves against my cheeks and pull the heavy book onto the bed.

Family. That's what Popo said I was.

But my real family won't listen to me, and my found family thinks I tried to sabotage Tatya's career.

I break open the pages, continuing from the last picture Popo and I looked at together, hoping to find a scrap of comfort in the many faces of my grandmother.

There are pages of photos from when she was a young woman. The earliest ones were taken in Hawaii, with a backdrop of white sandy beaches and thick banana leaves. And then she's somewhere else—somewhere with tall buildings, streets full of cars, and vintage motel signs in the background.

Grandpa Cillian makes another appearance, his bright orange

hair so vivid, it's almost as if someone turned up the contrast just on his hair. There are photos of him and Popo—some separate, most of them together—and even one of them with Taipo. And then there's Popo at the courthouse, her hair curled to one side and covered in a tiny blue hat, with Grandpa Cillian in a brown suit wearing a nervous smile on his face.

And then there's Popo with a pregnant belly, her hands pressed against her skin like she just can't wait to meet whoever is in there.

After that, there are fewer and fewer photos of Popo and Grandpa Cillian. Because Mom was born, and she's clearly dominated their lives.

With each page I turn, I watch Mom grow up little by little. I see the toys she got at Christmas, the kind of cake she had on her birthdays, the friends she hung out with, the instruments she used to play. I see a few of her at ballet class, and another at a piano recital.

And then Mom's a teenager. There's a picture of her with her prom date. Another one of her driving a car, maybe even for the first time. I see Mom at her high school graduation, her neck adorned with several enormous leis.

And then I turn another page, and a burst of ice rushes through me, making me feel like the entire world has stopped spinning and I'm frozen in a single moment of time.

I forget to breathe.

Mom's hair is up in a high bun. Her smile stretches across her entire face, and she's happier and more alive than I've ever seen her. She's wearing a red leotard with a blaze of golden flames across her chest.

And she's sitting on top of a static trapeze.

"You were an aerialist?" My voice is too heavy to hold up, so my words plummet to the earth like they're bags of sand and rock.

Mom is still holding her purse, and Dad isn't even finished walking through the front door. Mom's eyes widen, but I think it has more to do with not knowing I was standing in the hallway than realizing I know the truth.

A truth she kept from me my entire life.

I don't just feel betrayed—I feel manipulated.

She sets her purse on the table and folds her arms in front of her, her dark bob concealing part of her face like she still has more to hide. "It was a long time ago."

Dad parks himself next to Mom like he's ready to be her backup, and it sends a burst of rage through me. Because it confirms what I already suspected—he knew too.

I try to keep my jaw from shaking. "You both knew—you *knew*—and still you've made me feel like being an aerialist wasn't a realistic dream. And the whole time, you knew it was your dream once too."

"Dreams change, Harley, and if you don't have something to fall back on? It's hard. I don't want that for you," Mom says with so much tension in her face.

"How can you not see how unfair that is? This is *my* life. I should get the chance to make my own mistakes, or take risks, or try new things," I say, and I see Dad take a breath, and I know he's the sledgehammer that's going to break apart any hint of a bridge I'm trying to build here.

"You have a lot of growing up to do if you think parents should just sit back and watch their child make the same mistakes they did. That's not how this works. It's not how *we* work," Dad says.

I open my mouth to say something, but I guess Dad isn't done talking because suddenly he's pointing his finger at me, and Mom's shoulders are curved inward like it's his turn now, and it might be a while.

"We know how hard the circus life is. And yes, we know how magical it is too. But we also know it's unreliable. You could tear a ligament or hurt your back, or maybe someone younger or more talented ends up replacing you. The point is, there's very little stability in a career like this, especially one that most performers age out of before they're even forty years old. And that's pushing it, Harley—forty is *pushing* it. And then what's your plan? Even if you manage to have a decent career until you're out of your thirties, what are you going to do then?" Dad's nostrils flare like he's tired of having the same conversation.

He doesn't see that I'm tired too.

Because I've heard all of this a thousand times before. The difference is that now I know what a hypocrite Mom is for living the life I want, and then telling me I can't have it.

I don't want to listen. I want to be *heard*.

"You both are suffocating me. I can't breathe in this house. It feels like you're pushing me further and further toward the edge of a cliff, and pretty soon I'm going to fall over and there's no coming back. You're trying to kill my dreams, and it feels like you're trying to kill *me*." My fists are balled tight. Inside, I'm screaming.

Dad heaves out a sigh all the way from the pit of his gut. "Why does everything have to be so extreme and dramatic with you?"

Mom takes a step closer, her face softening like she believes she can fix what's happening to the three of us. "Honey, I know you love the circus. But I don't want you to chase the idea of something that might not be what you think it is. I don't want you to wake up one day and realize all the magic you fell in love with is just an illusion." She bites her lip, hesitates. "I don't want your love of the circus to be the very thing that ends up ruining your life."

"No," I say flatly. "That's what *you're* doing."

I turn away despite Dad's thundering new volume and Mom's pleas for me not to leave.

I get in my car and drive.

CHAPTER SEVEN

I don't know what makes me remember it's there, tucked away in the glove box like it's the One Ring calling to Gollum. But when I pull out Simon Tarbottle's business card, its silver words glinting beneath the multitude of streetlights, my heart flutters.

It feels like all the frost and icicles Mom and Dad left in my chest come to life, turning into butterflies that pound against my rib cage, anxious to get out.

I don't think. I dial the number.

Simon's voice is leathery and worn. More indifferent than the show he was putting on for Tatya. "This is Simon."

"Hi." I blink. Am I really doing this? "This is Harley Milano. We met yesterday, outside of Teatro della Notte?"

He grunts. I think it's an acknowledgment that he remembers. "What can I do for you?"

I gulp down the anger and hurt and yearning that's been building in the back of my throat for days. *Months.* "I want to join your circus."

I guess I really am doing this.

There's shuffling, and I think maybe he's sitting up. "Ah. You're calling me for a job."

"I know I'm not as good as your lead aerialist," I say, trying to keep a sense of coolness to my voice that probably sounds more like vulnerability. "But I'd make a good second, especially if you let her mentor me. I've been training on the trapeze all my life. I pick things up quickly, and I don't need to ask a lot of questions. I wouldn't be a burden to anyone. In fact, you don't even have to pay me a salary—just food and a bed. Maybe one day you'll think I'm good enough to hire officially, but for now, all I really want is the chance to train. The chance to improve, with a professional who will know how to push me to the next level."

My parents are forcing me to go to school after lying to me all my life. Tatya will never agree to train me again. And I can't step foot inside Teatro della Notte after what I've done—what everyone *thinks* I've done.

I lost my family—my home—and now I'm desperate.

Simon's voice perks up like he's smiling on the other end of the phone. "You're bold, kid. I like that."

My heart quickens, hopeful.

"But I'm not in the business of doing charity work," he says, and my stomach starts to disintegrate. "However, I do have an obvious issue with my lead aerialist, and maybe a second might put a bit of fear in her. Remind her there's always someone waiting to take her spot."

I start to point out that I'm not trying to take her job while she still wants it, and that I want her to train me—I want her to *like* me—but I bite my tongue because there's a hint of possibility in his words.

The possibility that this might end in my favor.

I don't want to screw it up trying to say the right thing.

"I won't pay you a salary," he says. "An internship, I can get behind. But the food and room? That's going to cost you."

Cost is a funny thing. People put so much importance on monetary value, haggling to the penny just to feel like they got a bargain.

But what about when the cost is loyalty? Trust? Morality?

People don't bargain with morality. Sometimes they don't even hesitate.

A *good* person would hesitate.

I wonder what it says about me that I don't.

"What do you want?"

He doesn't hesitate either. "I want the set list for Teatro della Notte's new season. The music for the opening, the acts—even the theme that gets played in the lobby. I want all of it."

Time goes still, and I feel like a bird frozen in flight.

Betray my parents and buy a place in Maison du Mystère as a trapeze artist. That's his price.

"If you bring me all that, you're in," he says. "I'm at the Desert Garden Motel, room 104. But just so we're clear, at six a.m. tomorrow, I'll be getting into my truck, suitcase packed, and driving back to Arizona to meet the troupe. If you don't show—if you're even one minute late—the offer will no longer be on the table. You understand?"

My voice doesn't shake. "I understand."

I wish I could say it was hard to sneak into Dad's office in the middle of the night.

I wish I could say it was hard to go through his filing cabinet until I found folder after folder stuffed thick with copies of the new set list.

I wish I could say it was hard to pack my duffel bag with my clothes and toiletries, and to leave a note on my bed that says I'm okay, and that I had to do it, and that I'll call when I'm ready.

I wish I could say it was hard to close the front door to my house for what could be the last time for a long time, and to get into the taxi waiting by the curb, and to not have doubts or worries or a change of heart.

I wish I could say it was more difficult to do something so unforgivable to my parents.

But I can't.

Because I feel like a stranger in this life. There's nothing left for me here—just a wasteland of lies and disappointment and stolen dreams.

I can't thrive in this place my parents have built. I won't survive in it—not without the circus.

I had no other choice.

Running away to join Maison du Mystère was the easiest decision I've ever made.

CHAPTER EIGHT

The taxi pulls into the motel entrance, the crunch of gravel beneath the tires reverberating through the car. It's velvety black outside, and the sky is lit up by the stars I so rarely get a chance to see. The motel rooms are spread across two floors, and the building is shaped like a giant square box. I spot room 104 and the massive black truck parked outside, shadowed in the early morning darkness.

My feet clomp heavily on the street, and I grip the box of stolen sheet music tightly to my stomach. I vaguely hear the taxi drive off behind me; I'm too busy staring at the metal beast in front of me. It's not like I haven't seen a truck before, but this feels so different. It's like a sleeping monster—the kind you run into when you're playing an MMORPG. The kind you are under no circumstances ever supposed to face alone.

God, I hope I know what I'm doing.

I take a breath of imaginary courage and walk across the pebbled road. I've only just set the box down and lifted my fist to knock on the motel door when Simon Tarbottle pulls the door open, the end of a cigarette still wedged in his fingers and the remnants of a smoke cloud floating away behind him.

My face recoils when the smell of vanilla and cloves fills my nostrils.

Simon grins through his beard, tapping his cigarette into the ashtray perched on the table next to him. "Filthy habit, I know. That's why I only smoke when there's a full moon." He lifts his chin to the sky, and when I look up, I don't know how I missed something so quietly beautiful.

I can't help but think of all the other things I've never noticed. All the stuff I've never experienced. And I know I'm doing a horrible thing, but maybe there's beauty in it too.

Because I'm finally and truly chasing my dreams.

For me, this is a fresh start.

I bring my eyes back to Simon and cross my arms over my chest to fight the dawn chill. "I brought what you asked for," I say.

He nods. "I gathered you wouldn't be here if you hadn't." He extends his hand expectantly.

I pause, adjusting the bag hanging from my shoulder, before bending down to retrieve the box at my feet.

There's no going back now.

I thrust the container of sheet music in front of me, letting him grab hold of everything that will inevitably break my parents' trust in me forever. Before I let go, I say, "I have one request."

His peculiar eyes flash with mischief. I get the overwhelming feeling he's not usually the type to grant requests, but his smile doesn't fade. "What would that be?"

"I don't want anyone to know who I am. Who my parents are." I burn my stare into his, because this part can't be negotiable. I don't want to be treated any differently. I want to earn this, the way everyone else has.

It's the only way I'll know whether I truly belong.

He raises a brow. "If anyone finds out, it won't be from me." I let go of the box, and he shifts it onto the nearby table, looking quickly through the pages of music Dad worked so hard on. The music he worked so hard to keep secret.

I press my lips together and dig my heels into the concrete.

When he's satisfied, he straightens like he's getting back into character. "Simon Tarbottle. It's a pleasure to officially meet you."

I shake his hand, feeling my insides twist like cotton candy being spun around a stick. "Harley. And . . . thank you for this opportunity."

He chuckles like I've said something amusing, before motioning over his shoulder. "I'll just grab my suitcase."

It feels like my skin is crawling with a billion tiny bugs. Big, ugly green ones. Representatives of my betrayal.

I try to ignore them.

Simon doesn't say a word until we're outside the city limits, the backdrop of Las Vegas hotels shrinking fast behind us.

"I'm guessing you've never run away from home before," he says. He's not smoking anymore, but I can still smell ash and vanilla.

"I'm not running away." My voice clips. "I'm an adult—this is me moving out."

His laugh is coarse. "Whatever you say, kid."

We don't speak for another whole hour.

"You been to Arizona before?" he asks, his fingers covered in silver rings that make a hypnotic clicking noise against the steering wheel every time he taps them in time with the music.

"No," I say, soaking in the red and yellow desert that seems to stretch for an eternity. It's so empty here. Lifeless.

I feel like there's a kind of poetry in me leaving a place so vacant and dead, but I'm finding it hard to be excited. I'm too aware of what I've done—too aware that Mom and Dad are going to notice I'm gone any minute now and my phone is going to explode with angry texts.

Not that I'll get them. We haven't had a bar of signal for miles.

"I left home when I was sixteen," he says suddenly, his chin jutted forward like he's recalling a fond memory. He glances over at me, his amber eye like a hawk's. "It's scary at first, like you're in a dark tunnel and you know there's a monster watching you, and you're just hoping to get the hell out of there before it decides it's hungry. But you get out, eventually, and you'll see you're all right after all."

I pin my eyes to the horizon. I'm not scared of a monster—I'm worried *I'm* the monster.

I'm worried my parents will never speak to me again.

But if I had stayed, my life never would have been my own. Leaving was my only option.

And I'm angry at them for that. Maybe even as angry as they'll be at me.

"My parents aren't bad people." I feel like it needs to be said. "But I needed to leave. Not because of them, but because of me."

"Well, lucky you. My parents were assholes," Simon says, erupting with laughter. He goes back to drumming his fingers to the beat of the music. "But Maison du Mystère is family. And now we're your family too."

We stop for gas once, and again for burgers at some random diner outside of the Mojave Desert. After another couple hours on the road, Simon pulls off the freeway. The truck rumbles onward for a handful of miles, and eventually we enter a large clearing that's part desert, part abandoned parking lot. An outlet mall looms in the distance.

"Just in time for load-in," Simon remarks.

I look ahead and see the flutter of red fabric still lying on the ground and a mess of metal poles, scaffolding, and thick cables, all spread out like an array of puzzle pieces.

A dozen or so men are moving around with machinery and tools, and beyond them is an entire community of trucks, buses, trailers, and motor homes.

It's a neighborhood on wheels, lost in the middle of the desert.

No, I think. *Not lost.* My eyes drift to a sign lying on its side, a row of sleeping bulbs outlining every letter, each painted in vibrant cranberry red.

MAISON DU MYSTÈRE

A tiny flame bursts to life inside me.

Simon drives around the center field where a dozen or so people are setting up the big top. "That's the ring crew," he says with a nod. "We call them the Lucky Thirteen. Good guys, but a few of them will almost definitely hit on you when they realize there's a new girl around. If the phrase 'fuck off' isn't already in your vocabulary, I suggest learning it now. You only need to tell them once, and they'll get the hint, but if they don't—you come and tell me. I don't tolerate harassment of any kind."

I guess my face must have changed, because Simon raises a brow and looks at me curiously.

"That surprising to you?" He tuts, smirking. "I might toe the line between varying legalities when it comes to business, but human nature is a different beast. We have to respect each other's boundaries. That's how you keep a family happy—you draw your lines, and you stick to them."

He parks the truck next to a massive trailer. There's a pot of flowers outside the door, with a pinwheel stuck inside.

"This is my trailer." He motions toward the metal home. "I've got an open-door policy, but I encourage people to talk to Sasha before they come to me. He's my right hand around here, and if you've got a question, nine times out of ten he can answer it for you." He points across the lawn to another trailer, where a few chairs and a grill are set up beneath a white awning.

Sasha must've heard us talking through one of the windows because the door opens and a man in his midtwenties hops down to the grass, bouncing on his toes the way so many acrobats do. Like the entire world is one big trampoline, and they're merely waiting for the next opportunity to perform. He runs a hand through his wild blond hair, his thick muscles visible even through his shirt.

When he speaks, he has a subtle accent that makes his words string together. "Picked up another stray?" His blue eyes dance with laughter.

Simon motions a hand between me and Sasha. "This is Harley; Harley, this is Sasha. He was one-third of the Kosovich Brothers, until one brother had some visa issues and had to go back to the Ukraine, and the other decided to leave our family for another troupe."

Sasha shrugs. "But now I get a big trailer all to myself, and nobody steals my good wine."

"I'd prefer to still have my act," Simon says dryly.

"Are you a performer or crew?" Sasha asks, raising a pale eyebrow curiously.

I look at Simon, not knowing if I fall into either category.

Simon looks like he's not sure either. "She's here for a mentorship—I'll explain later. For now, I need you to show her around, get her settled into a room. I have to check in with the ring crew."

Sasha nods. "You want her in the bunkhouses?"

Simons pauses, scratching at his dark beard. He looks at me like he's considering something, then drops his hand with a sigh. "No. Maggie will want nothing to do with her if I put her there. Give her Tessa's old bed," Simon says, and the *way* he says it makes me flinch.

As if he's already certain the people here might not accept me.

Deep down, I knew the first impressions would be hard. At least half the performers here will have been training since they were children. Some of them will have been to circus school, and some of them will undoubtedly come from generations of performers, all following in their family's footsteps.

My experience seems elementary in comparison.

But still, I was hoping my love of the circus would be enough to prove myself. At least until I could show everyone what I can do on a static trapeze.

"I'm on it, boss," Sasha says, and waves his hand at me to follow him between the row of trailers.

Simon disappears without saying goodbye, and it's just my duffel bag and me, painfully aware that I am severely out of place in this world.

We weave through a maze of motor homes and trailers until Sasha points to one with sparkly stars in the window and the smell of fresh coffee wafting through the screen door.

"This is it," he says, rapping his knuckles against the metal. There's no answer.

He fiddles with his keys—there are at least thirty of them, some of them color-coded with tape, and others wound with string—and unlocks the door.

I follow him inside and am immediately welcomed by shades of fuchsia, teal, and violet. Everything matches, from the teapot to the rug to the throw pillows on the tiny seating nook. A bunk bed sits to the right, with another bed just above the table area. A tiny kitchenette sits on the left, and a narrow corridor leads further back to what I'm assuming is where the bathroom is. It's definitely small—especially for three people. But I don't care.

This is my new home.

Every step further into this world feels like another step closer to my goal. And it makes my heart kindle to feel so close to what I've always wanted. Hope feels like a bubble expanding inside me, pushing against my bones, trying to fight its way out before it bursts.

I won't let it burst.

Because the more I hope, the more I see my dreams falling into place. Dreams I can reach out and brush with my fingertips.

Dreams that are becoming reality.

Whatever Simon was concerned about in front of Sasha doesn't matter. It can't. Not when I've come this far and I'm standing in front of the doorway that leads to the life I've always wanted.

"It might seem small, but you're lucky," Sasha says. "Most of the newbies have to live with the crew in the bunkhouses. They're just stacked-up beds crammed in metal containers, and their showers and toilets are all outside. At least here you've got hot water and a microwave."

"It's perfect," I say, and I mean it.

He motions to the top bunk on the right. "This one is yours. Go ahead and unpack. The top bed lifts up, and there's space under the mattress for all your things. I'm going to grab you some sheets and a towel from storage. Are you hungry?"

I shake my head.

He nods. "Okay, well, the Lunch Box is open twenty-four seven, as long as we're not traveling. It's the big double-decker bus opposite the rehearsal tent. You can't miss it." He disappears back onto the grass, and the door rattles shut behind him.

Being alone makes my thoughts so much louder. Hope fighting with reality fighting with logic fighting with desperation. Too many thoughts, all colliding together until they're tangled and messy and making my head spin.

I'm not sure I want to untangle them, so I unzip my duffel bag and focus on organizing my new life.

Phoenix, Arizona

August—Week 1

*J*here are twenty-seven missed calls from Mom on my phone, and at least forty text messages, which is a lot for her. She's still stuck in that time period where phone calls were apparently "faster." She likes immediate answers and instant results.

So forty text messages without a response means Mom is definitely and without a doubt furious with me.

They vary in levels of anger: **Where are you?**

Call me back.

THIS IS NOT FUNNY.

YOU ARE IN SO MUCH TROUBLE.

ANSWER YOUR PHONE.

I just want to know that you're okay. You're not in trouble. I'm just worried about you. Please call me back.

Are you even getting these messages?

YOU ARE SO GROUNDED.

Running away is not the answer, and I need to know where you are, and if you're safe. Call me back immediately.

IMMEDIATELY.

WHY ARE YOU NOT CALLING ME?

They go on like that for a while, alternating between a string of all-caps rage and short paragraphs that are supposed to sound reasonable but are probably the moments Dad is standing over her shoulder directing her with what to say. Dad likes to lecture and draw out explanations like he's at his own TED Talk. Mom blurts out her feelings without really thinking about them, and then tries to reshape them into something reasonable once all her feelings are on display.

Sometimes I feel like that too—like a balloon with too much air, or a spring with too much tension. I need to pop—to release everything I'm feeling—which usually just sends me in the opposite direction until the same thing happens again.

Mom and me? We have highs and lows, and nothing in the middle.

Dad *lives* in the middle. I think he likes it there, because he doesn't have to show any real emotion about anything, and he can mostly pretend he doesn't know what's going on with the two of us because we don't make any sense to him.

I check the time stamps on Mom's calls and messages and realize she sent them while we were driving, when I didn't have any phone signal. I've just been too afraid to look at my phone since we started getting closer to civilization again.

I type back quickly: I'm safe, but I don't want to talk right now. You don't need to worry about me. I'll call you when I'm ready.

I hit send, and I'm glad Mom doesn't have iMessage like Chloe and I do, because I won't be able to see when she's read it.

A weird part of me hopes she's already typing a response.

The other part of me is terrified of what that response will be.

There's a knock at my door, and I stuff my phone clumsily into my back pocket before hurrying to open it, expecting to see Sasha.

Instead, the face of a young woman greets me. She has bright hazel eyes, warm brown skin, and a lopsided smile that takes over the right side of her face.

She brings her fingers to her forehead in a salute. "Vivien de Vos, reporting for duty." Her laugh bursts out of her like a trumpet. She lets her hand fall back to her side. "You can call me Vivien or Vee, but *never* Viv."

"I'm just Harley." The words tumble out of me too quickly. She must be the lead aerialist—the one person in this world who is finally going to help me realize my dreams. I suddenly feel like every nerve in my body is sparking with new life. "Thank you for agreeing to mentor me—you have no idea what it means to me." I thrust my hand toward her and feel my heart thud against my chest.

She lets out another wave of laughter before accepting my handshake. "Trust me, you wouldn't want me to mentor your left shoe." I must be frowning without realizing it, because she pulls her hand back and waves at me like she doesn't want me to get too worked up. "It's nothing against you; I'm just not who you think I am. You're looking for the Sapphire Peacock." She tilts her head back dramatically. "Madame Wintour! The star of Maison du Mystère!" Her laugh pours into the room like a crash of wind chimes, and when it dies down, I can't help but smile. She talks too fast, all of her words stringing together like they're one big sentence. "I'm not your mentor—just one of your roommates—Sasha says you're an aerialist? I like to think of myself as a weapons specialist. Mainly of the knife-throwing variety. Dexi does the high wire—you'll meet her at the Lunch Box. Are you hungry? I'll walk you over."

I pull the door shut behind me and follow alongside her.

When we turn the last corner, a massive double-decker bus decorated in graffiti comes into view, the smell of bacon and eggs wafting through the air. All the artwork features food in some way—a clown juggling fruit, a flyer leaping off a hamburger, a contortionist balancing on a stack of waffles. THE LUNCH BOX is painted across the side, just below an open window where I spot a cook hovering over an industrial-looking metal kitchen. A few people are standing in line at the window.

Vivien notices me hesitating near the back of the line and shakes her head, pointing toward the doorway. "We're eating in."

As soon as I step foot on the bus, I'm overwhelmed by the smells and sounds of a deep fryer, an enormous extractor fan, and the clinking of silverware and glasses. Vivien leads me up a narrow staircase and onto the top level. There's a black-and-white-checkered path along the center aisle, with cherry-red leather booths up and down both sides of the bus.

Most of the booths are full, which isn't surprising. Fitting an entire diner into a bus is no easy feat. Seating is understandably limited.

The performers and crew members emit a rumble of greetings, ranging from "Good morning, Vee" to "Who's the new girl?" I think it's mostly friendly curiosity, but it's hard to tell.

I know letting a bunch of strangers intimidate me is only going to make things harder, but I can't help it. They're all part of the circus. As far as I'm concerned, everyone here is the *coolest*.

God, I hope they like me.

"Look who I found," Vivien says in a singsong voice, tucking into one of the booths and patting the seat beside her.

I plop onto the leather cushion, meeting the dark brown eyes of the girl sitting across from us. She has pale skin, small eyes, and shiny black hair that sits in a low braid in front of her shoulder.

"So. You're our new roommate," the girl says, her voice like crystal. Beautiful, but easily shattered if you're not careful. "I'm Dexi Liu."

"Harley," I say with a nervous smile.

"Did Vivien tell you the housemate rules?" Dexi asks, but then doesn't wait for an answer. "If you put something in the fridge that doesn't have a name on it, it's fair game. The shower schedule is on the door and is nonnegotiable. No spraying perfume indoors." She pauses, motioning to Vivien. "Vee has allergies."

Vivien mouths, "It's true."

"And if you have a problem with another roommate, don't let it fester. You say something, and we'll hash it out. This is too small of a space to be harboring bad feelings, and people will never know they're annoying you until you tell them. Communication is key." Dexi blinks at me.

I nod like my neck is made of Jell-O. "Okay. Got it."

She looks at Vivien, then back to me, with one of her brows raised curiously. "What's your Hogwarts house?"

"I don't know," I reply. And then more quickly, "I've taken the test before, but sometimes I get Hufflepuff, and sometimes I get Slytherin."

Vivien makes an oohing noise. "Loyal but ambitious. I ship it, even though snakes are the worst." She shudders dramatically, her nearly black hair swaying back and forth.

Dexi's mouth curls into a smile. "There is no shame in Slytherin."

Vivien makes a face. "Says Dexi Liu-strange." And then, brightening, she adds, "Hey, look, we're bonding already!"

The click of heeled footsteps draws near, and a young woman with pale lavender hair appears at the top of the stairs. She's dressed like she was plucked out of the 1950s, with oversized curls, bright red lips, and a short playsuit covered in pink flamingos and ice-cream cones.

Everyone looks up at her as she makes her way down the center of the diner, one hand clutching her phone and the other flattening her collar. Even though there's youth in her face, she doesn't carry herself like someone who might be just out of high school. She's too . . . professional.

Vivien leans forward so her words carry past me. "Hey, Maggie," she starts, and I get the feeling there's a particular way to approach her. "This is Harley. I don't know if Simon told you, but—"

"He told me," Maggie cuts in like a blade. And not a big, chunky sword—she's more precise than that, like the needle of an assassin that reveals itself only when it intends to do the most harm. Her luminous gray eyes snap toward me, making my heart quicken.

Maggie. I remember what Simon said—about her wanting nothing to do with me if I was holed up in the bunkhouses. Suddenly it all clicks together.

She must be the lead aerialist.

I start to stand, to tell her it's nice to meet her, and to assure her I'm willing to work hard.

But she holds a finger up to stop me, pursing her lips. "Don't bother."

I freeze, slowly sinking back into the booth. Heat floods my face, and even though I'm here with Vivien and Dexi, I feel thoroughly alone.

"I don't know what arrangement you made with Simon behind my back, but it's not happening. I hardly have the time as it is—certainly not enough of it to willingly mentor my own replacement." Maggie doesn't blink.

Every word is laced with poison, and my entire body is an open wound.

Shrinking into myself, I try to fight the powerful urge to burst into tears right this very second. "I'm not here to replace you. It's just an internship."

"This isn't a school." Her voice is black ice in total and utter darkness.

At first I'm only vaguely aware the room has gone quiet, but then I hear the sound of my pulse reverberating through my eardrums. Apart from the sizzling of the fryer below us, it's the only sound in the room.

Every single person here is looking at me.

Because I am the thing that doesn't belong.

The rumble of an engine grows outside the Lunch Box. A black motorbike winds around the disassembled rehearsal tent, the rider's face hidden beneath a dark helmet, before zipping between a row of motor homes and toward the back of the camp.

Maggie doesn't glance out the window, but a smile creeps onto her face as the sound of the engine fades. She looks down at Vivien and flutters her lashes. "If you want to surprise someone with your new roommate, why don't you go find Vas? I'm sure he'll be thrilled—especially when he finds out Simon somehow conjured the entire winter set list from Teatro della Notte this morning." She turns to me flatly. "When did you arrive again?"

And then she twists her kitten heels and joins her friends in a booth near the back.

My heart is no longer just hammering—it's a wrecking ball pounding through concrete at the top of a skyscraper.

She knows what I did. And now everyone else will too.

I tuck my arms around myself as I get up and head for the stairs with my head lowered in shame.

Not even Vivien tries to stop me.

CHAPTER TEN

*W*hat was I thinking? *Of course* the lead aerialist of Maison du Mystère doesn't want anything to do with me.

This isn't just my dream—it's hers, too. I'm just some random person who is getting in the way of her job.

Mom and Dad were right. I never think things through.

The realization that I may have made a horrible decision makes me queasy. I made a deal with Simon that he may not have the power to enforce. I mean, he brought me here so I could train with Maggie.

He never said Maggie would definitely *agree* to it.

And he already has the set list—I have no bargaining chips left.

Besides, I'm not sure it's as easy as begging Maggie to change her mind. Not with what she knows. It's not that I *want* to give up so easily, but I'm not sure how to recover from "the girl who stole Teatro della Notte's set list and ran off with a rival company." She already doesn't trust me.

So why on earth would she help me?

Somehow the weight of my phone hidden in my pocket triples. *Quadruples.*

Mom's always been a fixer, but could she fix this?

No, I tell myself. *And she wouldn't want to. Not after what you did.*

I'm on my way back to my trailer when I see a young man wearing a leather jacket unzipped in the middle, revealing a gray V-necked shirt and a silver chain around his neck. At first glance I think it's a cross, but when he gets closer I realize it's a dagger. He looks about my age. Maybe a year older.

I move to the left to avoid him, but he moves too. We move to the right, left, then right again.

He stops in front of me, his brow furrowed and a black helmet tucked under his arm. He has thick, messy hair that curls at the ends. Beneath the desert sunlight, it shines the color of honey.

He must be Vas—the one Maggie was talking about. I don't know why he would care about me or the set list, but I gathered from her tone that this is someone who is destined to hate me when he finds out what I've done.

The hollow space in my throat grows and grows.

And to think—once upon a time, I was good at making friends in the circus.

When he speaks, his voice is stiff, but it doesn't hide the accent that rolls off his tongue. "I'm not all that fond of dancing, I must admit."

He sounds British, and American, and maybe something else,

too, like his accent is multiple colors swirling together to make something new. Something blended.

Chop suey, as Popo would say.

There's plenty of room between both rows of motor homes, but with a stranger this close, it suddenly feels like everything is shrinking around me, like I'm Princess Leia in the garbage chute and the walls are closing in.

I take a step back and hold up a hand apologetically. "I'm sorry," I say, finding his gaze so he knows I'm being sincere. Maybe he'll remember this moment when he hears the news.

His eyes are a muted green and are piercing straight through me.

He pauses, tilting his head to the side. "Do you know where you're going? Because you look lost."

"I feel lost." The words leave my mouth too soon, and my cheeks burn red with the afterthought. My brain and I need to have another talk about processing information before letting me speak, because I'm seriously tired of regretting half the stuff that comes out of my mouth.

I try to think of something clever to say—a way to laugh off whatever it is that I'm feeling—but I can't. There's not enough room to breathe, or time to think, or words to make me pretend like everything is fine.

Everything is not fine.

I push past him and hurry to the trailer without another glance.

Vivien knocks twice at the door before walking inside. There's a small cardboard box wedged in her hands, with a bottle of orange juice balanced on top. Dexi is behind her looking exceptionally bored.

"You don't have to knock—it's your room too," I say meekly from the top bunk. I'm rolled on my side, a pillow stuffed under my cheek and my phone two inches from my eyes. I've been trying to figure out whether to call Mom, and what to say if I do.

Vivien snorts and shuts the door. "I walked in on my last roommate with one of the clowns once. He was in full costume; she was not. Trust me, I will *always* knock first."

Dexi raises a finger. "It wasn't me, for the record. Clown fetishes are not my jam."

A sad whisper of a laugh escapes me, but I'm mostly glued to the bed. Or, as glued as I can be when my brain is going a million miles per minute and I feel like I'm teetering on the edge of a balancing act.

Vivien holds up the box. "I brought you lunch. A crew special. Thought the comfort food might make you feel better." God, she's nice. They both are, even though Dexi is less obvious about it.

I'm not sure I deserve it, but I'm also not about to turn down an offering of friendship. Or food.

"A *what* special?" I perch myself up with my elbow and raise a brow.

She lifts the lid of the box, revealing two thin pancakes, several dumplings, and two small plastic pots wedged in the side. "The performers tend to eat the healthier stuff—egg whites, fish, greens, and all the rest of it. The crew prefers food that is inevitably covered in salt and grease, but *so* delicious. Ergo, a crew special, Russian-style."

Dexi catches the confusion on my face and chimes in. "People join Maison du Mystère from all over the world. The cooks change up the menu every day so everyone gets a turn to feel like they're at home. Keeps the morale high."

Vivien nods gleefully. "We brought you syrniki and blini, with jam, sour cream—I can get you some minced meat to go with it too, if you want it." She hesitates. "Or if you'd rather, the borscht is pretty good. I can't do the soup-for-breakfast thing, but it is tasty, if you like beetroot."

"What you brought is perfect. Thank you." I slide off the top bunk, find a fork in one of the nearby drawers, and sit at the small table that's only a few feet away.

Dexi falls into one of the chairs like a snowflake floating to the ground. Vivien sits down too—more like a lumberjack falling into her chair after a long day at work—and folds her hands under her chin.

"Sorry about Maggie. She can be difficult sometimes. I know it's not fair to say you have to grow thicker skin, because it seems like that's putting the blame on you, but it does help." Vivien shrugs. "Sometimes we all need a little armor to protect our hearts. That doesn't mean it's our fault—it just means we don't want to get hurt."

I swallow a bite of food and wipe my mouth self-consciously. "I think it's too late for armor. I don't know if I belong here."

Dexi frowns, her eyes scanning me like she's trying to figure out exactly what's broken. I get the feeling she's a fixer like Mom, deep down—she just likes to analyze everything first.

Vivien turns her mouth down and drops her hands to the table. "You're not giving up already." I'm not sure if it's a statement or a question.

I set my fork down and stuff my hands into my lap to keep myself from fidgeting when I try to figure out the words I want to say. "I don't *want* to give up. But if Maggie won't train me, I don't know what I'm supposed to do. I came here to learn—to get better. Not to waste time with a circus that doesn't want anything to do with me."

Dexi shrugs matter-of-factly. "Go home, then."

I hesitate, letting the sharpness of her tone fade. Maybe she's not a fixer. "I can't. My parents . . ." I shake my head firmly. "I can't let them be right after less than twelve hours."

She raises a brow and tilts her head back and forth like a bobblehead. "Then stay, and stop pretending like you don't know what to do."

I let out a brief laugh. "You're doing the reverse-psychology thing, aren't you?"

Dexi does a slow blink, like she's telling me I already know my own answer.

I trace my finger along the edge of the table. "It doesn't bother you guys what Maggie said? About the set list?"

"I'm certainly not going to claim a moral high ground when we're all well aware Simon doesn't exactly do things by the book," Vivien says.

Dexi nods. "Maggie is just trying to intimidate you. She's going to give you every reason in the world to quit, but you can't let her win. Not if you really want to be here."

"I do," I say. "More than I've ever wanted anything."

Vivien leans into the table and crosses her arms. "Good. Because if the rest of us ran away every time someone told us what we wanted was unrealistic or impossible or just plain not going to happen, there'd be no circus. This world we live in, that moves from city to city and houses families from thirty different countries, exists in spite of the nonbelievers. We exist because we work hard, we don't give up, and when we hear 'that can't be done,' we find a way to do it anyway. Who cares if Maggie doesn't want to train you? Change her mind, or find another way to train. Not everyone gets a chance to run away with the circus—don't waste yours just because someone tried to dull your shine." She winks, and I feel like the room stills just for her. "Stars shine their brightest in the dark. So take this opportunity, and supernova the shit out of it."

CHAPTER ELEVEN

*V*ivien and Dexi try to make me feel welcome by showing me around the yard and telling me about all the people who live here. I should be grateful—especially after Maggie's inference at the Lunch Box, which I'm sure has already made the rounds.

But every time somebody looks at me, I feel the questions in their eyes. The judgment, too. It makes me feel like I've let the entire world down, rather than just Mom and Dad.

Vivien and Dexi say they don't care what I did to get here, but they don't speak for everyone. There are probably at least a hundred people in Maison du Mystère, if you include the performers, the ring crew, the technicians, the designers, the service members—not to mention their families. That's a lot of people.

And if having a big, diverse family has taught me anything, it's that the bigger the crowd, the louder the opinions.

A person's reputation is like a shadow—it follows them every-where, for eternity, no matter what. We mostly have no say in how we look to other people. Someone could carry themselves a certain way their whole life, but if someone else says one bad thing about them? It catches like wildfire.

I don't know if I'm ready for a hundred people to have an opinion about me. It makes me want to curl up in a ball, shut my eyes, and never look at the world again.

But if I'm afraid of the world, it means I'll be afraid of the circus, too.

Under no circumstances am I ever going to allow that to happen. Even if it means starting off my career at Maison du Mystère with a tarnished reputation.

We pass by a kid practicing cartwheels outside one of the big trailers. Vivien tells me it's pretty normal to see families in traveling circuses, especially since they spend nearly eleven months out of the year on the road. Some of them perform together, like the Terzi Brothers. Others were practically raised by the circus because their parents were once performers, like Dexi, whose acrobat lineage goes back three generations.

And other families found one another *because* of the circus. The costume designer is married to the set designer. One of the Terzi Brothers is engaged to a clown named Anna, who is pregnant.

When I meet Jin Thompson—a juggler who was born in Iowa but has performed all over the world—he tells me he has more exes in the circus than Vivien has knife cuts.

"I rarely cut myself these days," she says, making a goofy face.

Jin's black topknot barely moves during his workout, the swish of the jump rope snapping against the air in front of me. "I'm just glad Simon took away your live target. The thought of you accidentally butchering Marco's beautiful face was wreaking havoc on my anxiety."

"To be *very* clear," Vivien says, her voice dropping low, "Marco was never in any danger." She looks at me, eyes softening into a grin. "But Simon thought my act was too scary for kids."

"Oh, believe me, it wasn't just the kids." Jin tuts. "The only people who enjoy seeing knives thrown at other people are sadists and people who hurt animals."

"Because that's not a sweeping generalization," Dexi notes with the same icy tone that never seems to thaw.

Jin winks. "We are who we are." Something draws his attention behind me, and he gives a halfhearted smile, the rope whipping against the dirt with the rhythm of a metronome. "Which is sometimes so damned unfortunate."

I turn around and see the motorcyclist from earlier walking toward us.

"You're back!" Vivien shouts, giving the leather-clad stranger a hug. "How was your vacation?"

"Fine," he says curtly, his eyes pinned to something in the distance. He looks flustered, but the others don't seem to notice. And if they do, they don't acknowledge it.

My ears burn. I wonder if he knows about the set list.

"Well, there's a face I've missed," Jin says with a smirk.

Dexi's laugh is soundless, but present in the way she crinkles her nose. "One-way road, Jin."

Jin cuts her a look in the corner of his eye, but they're so familiar with each other that I get the feeling it's nothing more than a long-standing joke between them all.

Vas runs his knuckle beneath his brow like he's searching for a distraction. And maybe it's my own ego that's the problem, but I can't help but feel it's because of me.

Especially since I'm the only one he's actively trying not to look at.

"Hey, so you two probably haven't met yet." Vivien starts to hold her hand up toward me, and we both reply at the same time.

"No," I say.

"Yes," says Vas.

We look at each other briefly. *Is that a scowl?*

I clear my throat. "We didn't *meet* meet. We just ran into each other earlier." Almost literally.

Vivien grins, nudging him with her shoulder. "Wow, Vas, it's not like you to be so talkative around strangers." There's a wisp of playfulness hidden at the edge of her mouth, and I realize quickly that she's teasing him.

Maybe they're together.

Vas furrows his brow and glares at her. *Definitely* a scowl. Okay, maybe they aren't together.

Vivien laughs like she doesn't care. "Well, Harley is an aerialist. She's here to train with Maggie."

It's the first time Vas looks remotely interested in anything she's said. He glances at me with dark eyebrows that don't match the honey-brown tones of his hair. "Maggie would never agree to that."

I open my mouth to defend myself, but I realize there's no

point. It's true—she didn't agree to it, and I'm not sure what to do to make her change her mind, aside from, well, begging.

Dexi fights a yawn. "Maggie is a spoiled brat, and she doesn't get to have everything she wants."

Jin snickers, and Vivien's eyes widen. I guess it must not be common to bad-mouth the star of the show.

Vas shakes his head like he doesn't want to get involved, still scowling.

"You're in a mood," Dexi notes. Part of me feels pleased I'm not imagining things, but the other part is bracing nervously for his reply.

"Simon pulled the plug on my set list. Says he has some second-hand stuff he wants tweaked instead," he replies.

Secondhand. Dad would die of rage if he heard his compositions talked about like that.

Vas's eyes flick toward mine for the briefest moment, and it takes everything in me not to look away with guilt.

"I'm sorry," Vivien says, thinning her mouth.

"That sucks." Dexi leans back against the trailer.

My entire face feels like it's going up in flames. The tension is suffocating.

"They've got borscht at the Lunch Box," Jin offers, seemingly oblivious to what's going on. He tosses his jump rope to the ground and stretches his arm behind his head.

"I'd prefer my own set list, but cheers," Vas says flatly.

Jin holds up his hands like he can't believe the lack of enthusiasm. "It's food from your homeland!"

Home. The word tugs at the loose strings in my chest.

"All your sour cream and dumpling amazingness is impossible to resist," Vivien grumbles in a faux-deep voice.

Vas forces the grimmest look possible. "I don't know how that has anything to do with me. I haven't lived in Russia since I was a child." He sighs, uninterested in continuing the conversation. When he reaches for the door, I realize he must be Jin's roommate. "I need to shower. I'll see you guys at the two o'clock meeting."

"Let me know if you want company," Jin half sings.

Vas snort-laughs and shakes his head, disappearing into the trailer.

Jin lifts his shoulders innocently. "What?"

Dexi and Vivien turn to each other, their stifled laughter drawing the attention of a unicyclist nearby. I know I should be used to the circus life since I pretty much grew up knowing nothing else, but Teatro della Notte is a completely different dimension in comparison. It's dark, atmospheric, moody—Maison du Mystère is more like an extended camping trip.

There's a rawness to it. I feel like there are fewer rules, and more crooked edges.

I love it more than I can put into words.

My phone buzzes in my pocket, and when I look at the screen, I see Chloe's name and a photo of her and me from the morning of graduation. Why does that feel like such a lifetime ago?

But the nostalgia isn't what's unsettling—it's the fact that Chloe *never* calls me. We communicate exclusively through texts.

Something must be wrong.

I motion to Vivien and Dexi that I'll be right back and hurry away from them, pressing the phone to my ear.

"Hello?" My voice clips, not knowing what to expect.

"Oh my God, where *are* you? Your parents said you ran away."

Relief floods through me. "Well, that was anticlimactic. I thought you were hurt or something." I let out a short laugh but get no response.

She pauses for enough seconds that it feels awkward. "Did you? Run away?" Irritation muddies her tone.

My defenses go up like I'm Tony Stark transforming into Iron Man. "No," I say almost aggressively. The combination of Vas's weird mood, and the entire circus potentially hating me, and Mom and Dad being royally pissed, and now Chloe, too . . . It's a lot. Maybe a little too much for one morning. "I'm an adult. Adults don't run away—they move out."

"So . . . you moved out? Without telling anybody?"

"I didn't really think about it. I just had this opportunity and—"

"Without telling *me*?" her voice cuts in.

My shoulders relax. Shit. I should've said something to Chloe. I mean, she's my best friend—we've told each other pretty much everything since the third grade. No wonder she's mad.

"I promise it wasn't on purpose. I wasn't trying to keep a massive secret from anybody. But I got in this huge fight with my parents and—" I let out a heavy breath and look up at the sky, which is slowly turning a milky blue. "I couldn't stay there, Chloe. They don't understand me."

"Yeah, well, I don't blame them. I mean, you literally left without saying a word to anybody. You could've been dead, for all we knew!" She's angry. Angrier than I think is fair.

"I left a note in my room," I say tersely. Why is she giving me such a hard time? I know I should've said something, but it's not like I planned this. It's not like she wouldn't have done the same thing if the roles were reversed.

I didn't do anything wrong.

Well, nothing wrong that she knows about, anyway, because if my parents told her about the set list, she'd be throwing it in my face already. She's the kind of person who thinks feeling morally superior makes her immune to criticism. It means she never listens when she's wrong, but she's always the first person to start shouting when someone else is.

"You could've sent me a text." Her voice is like crumpled felt. Soft, but distorted.

"This didn't have anything to do with you. It was about me," I say, wanting to be firm.

"Oh, believe me, I know that," she says, but it comes out like a sigh. Maybe she's going to let this one go. "So where are you?"

I twist my mouth and look around at the desert landscape. "Somewhere in Arizona?"

"Is that a question? How do you not know where you are?" She pauses. "Who are you with?"

"Look, if I tell you, you have to swear you won't tell my parents. I'll tell them when I'm ready, but I need time to figure some things out. So this has to be between just you and me. Promise?"

"Of course I do, Harley."

I take a deep breath. "I joined Maison du Mystère as an apprentice trapeze artist. I'm going to train here, and gain some experience, and maybe even one day perform in the big top. I know it sounds ridiculous, but I'll never get a chance like this again, and I just had to take it. I had to, because my parents don't support me and they don't understand what this means to me and things are just so messy at home and I can't go back there. I can't give up the circus. I need this like I need oxygen to breathe."

Another long pause.

"I'm happy for you. Honestly, I am. But, I don't know. . . . I think you should call your mom. She's really worried," Chloe says. "So was I."

"I'm fine," I say. "There's nothing to worry about."

"Are you sure about that?" Her voice pounds into the phone like a hammer. "Because your mom said the last time you got this obsessive about something was right before November."

November. My heart rate picks up, and I feel my fingers dig around my side. I can't believe she's talking to my mom about November.

She's supposed to be *my* friend, not Mom's. Since when did she start caring whether my parents are worried or not? Since when did she become so . . . not on my side?

Besides, it was one bad month. One bad *day*, really. It's ridiculous that everyone wants to hold it over my head for the rest of my life. Like I'm not allowed to have *one bad day.*

"I have to go," I say thinly. "There's a lot of stuff to get ready for."

"Okay." Her voice sounds sunken.

"Remember, you promised."

"I know. I won't say a word."

"Okay. Bye."

"Bye."

I hang up, shove the phone back into my pocket, and try to push the bubbling feelings of dread from my stomach. Dread that Mom and Dad will never forgive me, that my best friend is turning on me, and that I have no idea what I'm doing but I feel like I'm on a moving train that I really don't want to stop.

This is my journey. Maybe someday everyone else will understand, but for now, I really don't care.

CHAPTER TWELVE

*V*ivien says it normally takes about twelve hours for the Lucky Thirteen to finish load-in, but that's only if everything goes smoothly. It could take up to twenty if there are any issues at all—including bad weather, which thankfully the Arizona skies don't seem to have in the cards.

Though the ring crew is still setting up the big top, most of them visibly sweltering beneath the afternoon sun, the rehearsal tent has already been constructed. It sits a handful of yards away from the Lunch Box, the red fabric as bright and rich as a candy apple.

Vivien and Dexi lead me inside the tent for Monday's roll call, and my stomach twists and turns like it's the first day of school.

The floor is lined with foam padding, but the equipment is still mostly in pieces at the back of the room. I spot a net, silk ropes, a hoop, and a mess of wires in the corner that sets my heart on fire.

Simon Tarbottle stands in the middle of the room, and the rest of the troupe circles around him before settling onto the floor. The sound of electric drills and metal hammering onto metal is too loud to avoid, but Simon doesn't seem fazed, his mismatched eyes darting around the room as he hands out this week's schedules.

My eyes scan the list. Rehearsal times for every act, show times for Thursday through Sunday, group workout sessions on Mondays and Wednesdays . . . It's everything. Everything I'm finally a part of.

I can't stop grinning. *My very first schedule.*

I'm so happy, I could explode.

That is, until Maggie walks into the room, her face void of the excitement that is bursting through my body. Vas and Jin are right behind her, and it occurs to me that they might all be friends. My mind zooms into reverse, retracing words I said earlier, digging up every part of the conversation I had with Jin, and hoping desperately I didn't say something that could make Maggie hate me even more than she already does.

Dexi called her a spoiled brat. Will I be guilty by association if Jin tattles?

I press my lips together, reminding myself I already have plenty to worry about without imagining fake scenarios in my head. I'm on edge. No, scratch that—I'm literally dangling *over* the edge.

She doesn't look at me—not even when she walks right in front of me to find an open space in the crowd.

"Welcome to Arizona, everyone," Simon says with a wide smile and his arms spread.

Everyone claps with mock enthusiasm, most of us still looking tired from the traveling.

"As you can see, the Lucky Thirteen were kind enough to

get us some shade this morning. Now we just need the coffee machine up and running, and we'll be ready to rock and roll." A few people laugh, and Simon dives into a speech I get the feeling he says at every new venue. He talks about rehearsal times and costume checks, and he even reminds everyone about proper protection from the Arizona sun.

I'm trying to soak in every bit of it. The way everyone looks at one another like they're family—some brothers and sisters, others very distant cousins a few times removed, but family all the same.

I hope they'll look at me like that one day too. Because this place—the circus—it's home to people who've never quite fit in anywhere else. It's home to people who feel different. It's home to people who see that magic doesn't strictly exist in fairy tales.

When I look around, I know the magic is dormant in the rehearsal tent, where everyone is wearing gym clothes with their noses buried in the paper schedules. Right now, it's more classroom than circus.

But the *heart* of the circus remains. The work ethic and drive and knowledge that every single person is here to do a job. Every single one of them brings their own unique spin to a show that's going to transform this barren bit of landscape into something *wonderful*. All of them deserving of a place here because they are some of the most talented performers in their field.

Everyone except me, who is here because of a horrible betrayal.

I bury those thoughts down, down, down into a pile of imaginary dirt, and wonder instead how long it will take before they accept me as one of them.

If they'll ever accept me at all.

Simon's eyes scan the crowd, the green mossier and the amber more golden, until landing on me. "And last but not least, I'm sure you've all noticed our troupe has grown by one. If you haven't already, please say a warm and friendly hello to Harley. She's going to be shadowing Maggie, learning all the tricks of the trade."

Shadowing. That's what he's calling it now. Like I'm a ghost and not a mentee.

Not family.

I barely hear the rumble of greetings meant for me. I'm biting the inside of my cheek, hoping my face won't give away the horrible disappointment swarming through me.

Immediately following the meeting, Sasha takes Simon's place in the center of the room and instructs everyone into a group warm-up. I take a place near Vivien and Dexi and try to convince myself that people are definitely *not* looking at me and whispering about what I did to get here.

Even though deep down I know they are.

Dexi swings her shiny black braid over her shoulder and stretches her arms toward her toes, grabbing hold of her ankles like it's nothing. Vivien does the same beside her. I always thought I was flexible, but in comparison to everyone else? I'm practically a giraffe, impossible to bend.

When Sasha switches positions, we all copy him, stretching left and then right, and combining yoga poses with push-ups and mountain climbers.

Maggie never once looks at me, and I hate the way it rattles me. Like I'm someone who should be rattled.

I need her to like me. I need them *all* to like me.

I want to belong here more than I've ever wanted anything.

A ridiculous burst of courage overrides the worry in my head, and I walk a few yards away to where Maggie is—her leg bent forward in a deep lunge—and stop beside her.

"Hey—" I start, hoping to forge some kind of connection. Something beyond irritation, at least. I want to assure her I won't get in the way, that I just want to learn what she knows, and maybe one day have a chance at being truly great at the static trapeze.

But Maggie snatches her water bottle off the mat and moves back to the place I came from, between Vivien and Dexi, like she's making a statement, avoiding me completely.

My face flushes with embarrassment, but at least the people around me have the decency to pretend they didn't see anything.

I fall into a lunge, hoping I can magically blend in and no one will see how it's taking literally everything inside me to fight the hot tears from pouring down my face.

Vas is beside me the entire time, and I know he must hear me sniffling, but he doesn't say a word.

CHAPTER THIRTEEN

I spend most of the evening in the trailer, declining when Vivien and Dexi invite me to dinner. I'm too nauseous to eat—too angry at myself for being silly enough to think this would be easy, and at Maggie for not even giving me a chance, and at my parents for making it so this was my only option to begin with.

I'm mad at nobody and everybody all at once.

I force my eyes closed, hoping that sleep will help dull the horrible sensations rumbling around in the pit of my stomach. But after hours and hours of tossing and turning on the thin foam mattress, briefly falling asleep only to be woken up again because my body won't settle, my brain is basically mush and lead.

Parting the window curtains beside me, I see desert mountains stretched across the horizon, and a dusky lavender sky that suggests it's probably too early to be waking up.

Still, I haven't eaten a real meal since yesterday's lunch. And the hunger pangs in my stomach are definitely not helping to keep my mind at peace.

With my best attempt at being light-footed, I manage to get myself off the top bunk without waking Vivien, who sleeps wearing an eye mask decorated in a pair of sparkly cartoon eyes, which is honestly *terrifying*. Dexi doesn't stir either, though being on the other side of the room probably helps.

Slipping on my shoes, I step outside and keep my hand firm on the screen door to keep it from rattling shut.

The air is dry, and I can smell charcoal and burnt wood nearby from an evening barbecue. It isn't far to the Lunch Box, which has a scattering of tables and chairs in front of the awning. I spot a few of the Lucky Thirteen on the top deck, plus one of the clowns and a tiny girl with oversized clear glasses who I'm pretty sure is a performer's daughter, though I'm not sure whose.

The night cook sets his beefy hands on the counter and leans his neck forward so he can see me through the wide-open window, reminding me of a cartoon vulture. "There's no table service at night, so you have to order from the window," he says, clearly recognizing that I'm new. "What can I get you?"

My eyes dart upward to the chalkboards hung above the window. The specials menu has already been wiped clean, which is a shame because Vivien told me the borscht was heavy, and I'm practically ready to gnaw off my own arm. But there are other chalkboards—the standard ones that never change—with plenty of options for breakfast, lunch, and dinner.

I ask for the maple-syrup-and-banana oatmeal because it sounds like it'll be equal parts filling and fast.

The cook busies himself in the back, and a short while later he sets a generous bowl of oatmeal on the counter before pointing me in the direction of the silverware and napkins. I grab what I need and climb the narrow spiral staircase, packing myself away into the closest empty booth.

I eat in complete silence, the warmth filling my stomach but never quite reaching the outside of my body. My skin feels cold everywhere, the chills forever running up and down my limbs. And I shouldn't be cold—it's August in Arizona, for crying out loud—but my mind is so preoccupied with other things that maybe it's stopped caring what it says on the calendar.

I catch the girl with glasses watching me, but when I look at her, she turns away. The clown and crew members ignore me completely.

And even though I'm prone to assuming people hate me for the million things I probably did wrong without realizing it, this time being ignored *definitely* feels intentional.

I dig my phone out of my pocket, thinking now would be a good time to distract myself by catching up on all the Instagram posts I'm sure I've missed lately, but the notification from Mom makes my chest go hollow.

It's an email.

To: FlightOfTheRedPanda@gmail.com
From: Delilah.Milano@teatrodellanotte.com
Subject: The time I ruined your blanket

We had this beautiful blanket made for you with your name stitched in the corner right before you were born. I thought it would be the kind of thing you'd fall in love with as a newborn and fall in love with again when you were all grown up. Like a memory blanket.

Except those first days were such a blur, and I had baby brain pretty bad. I accidentally put your blanket in the dryer—it was wool, so when it came out, it was practically a burp cloth. I was so upset because I felt like I ruined something that was supposed to be special for you.

I know you think I do that often, and on purpose, but I don't mean to.

I love you. I want the best for you. And I hope you'll call me soon.

Love, Mom

I have to read the email three times because my eyes get too blurry by the halfway point.

It would be so easy to think this was the moment where we'd change—that we'd find a moment of clarity and finally and totally understand each other. But we've been here before, and it won't happen. Not like this.

Because even in Mom's nostalgia, she still thinks she's right. She still thinks wanting the best for me means she *knows* what's best for me.

And then there's the whole stealing their set list, which she clearly doesn't know about yet. . . .

Whatever is happening between me and my parents right now is not going to be fixed with an email about a shrunken blanket. We need time. Specifically, time *apart*.

I did the right thing by leaving, and I'll tell myself this for as long as it takes to start believing it. Because I need it to be true. I need being here to mean something.

I shove my phone back into my pocket and return to my oatmeal.

When I'm finished eating, I set my dish on the counter in front of a sign that reads: BE THE BUSBOY YOU WANT TO SEE IN THE WORLD.

Outside, I hesitate in front of the dining bus, not really knowing where to go or what to do or how to make myself feel better. And because the circus really is the only thing that makes me happy, my eyes drift across the yard toward the now fully constructed big top.

It's patterned in chunky stripes, deep cranberry and velvety violet, with wires upon wires trailing along every seam and stretched out over the empty parking lot—lights that probably won't turn on until the first show on Thursday night. And while Teatro della Notte's big top has a vintage carnival feel about it, Maison du Mystère's is more dark whimsy and twisted fairy tales.

For one, the massive tent has four distinct points, like spires on a castle. It's surrounded by a fenced-in outer ring, where there's room for the acrobats and magicians to perform for guests before the real show starts. Because at Maison du Mystère, the circus doesn't begin when the curtain opens—it begins the moment you pass through the gates.

And then I hear a noise. The scrape of a violin echoes from far away. A single note calling out to the sky. I'm drawn to it, the way I was drawn to the circus lights as a little girl. The instrument breaks into a sad melody, like a ghost wandering aimlessly through an eternal forest.

A ghost with no name. A ghost with no face.

A ghost with no family.

I tuck my arms around myself, fighting the emotions I don't have the energy to sort through, and walk closer to the big top.

It's enormous in every direction. The first opening spills out into a foyer, where mechanical beasts slumber, soon to be filled with popcorn and peanuts and cotton candy. There's a glass counter waiting to be stocked with chocolate bars and licorice, and a soda machine perched in the back. I follow the red carpet to the next opening, where the violin grows louder, drawing me closer like I'm a fish on a hook.

When I peer inside, I know the violin wasn't meant for me. It couldn't be.

Because the violin and its beautiful music belong only to *him*.

Vas stands in the center of the ring, surrounded by over a hundred empty chairs. The lights above him are dimmed. Moody. And he's facing away from me, his dark wooden instrument tucked under his chin.

I watch his fingers dance across the strings, vibrating when he holds the long notes that make my heart ache.

I feel myself swaying without really thinking, and I realize it reminds me of when I was a child hanging out in Dad's office.

He was always practicing—always writing something new. And usually he was fine with me listening, as long as listening was all I did. Under no circumstances was I ever meant to make a sound.

But I stayed anyway, because Dad's music was beautiful. *Is* beautiful.

And I stole the thing that means the most to him to trade it for the thing that means the most to me.

I wish there were a way to make that sound less selfish.

How much longer will it take for Dad to realize I broke his heart?

Regret tethers itself to my heart, spilling through my veins like Venom taking over Spider-Man. I don't want to let it in. I can't—not when I've risked so much to get here. I need to see this through. I need to prove myself before I make sense of what I've done to my parents.

But the music rips through me anyway, and all I can see is Dad in his office, smiling at his little girl.

I blink, tearing myself away from Vas and his violin before he has a chance to realize I'm there.

CHAPTER FOURTEEN

*A*s the afternoon wears on, it becomes more and more apparent that people are avoiding me. They're not outright rude about it, which I guess is nice. But they either avert their eyes or pretend they don't see me at all.

This morning I asked one of the magicians if they'd seen Dexi, and they got so flustered I spoke to them that they turned around midway through their answer and walked off.

It feels unfair. Like maybe what I did doesn't deserve this kind of reaction. At least not from strangers who don't even know me.

But even though this isn't the fresh start I imagined, the battered piece of hope that's tethered to my heart urges me to keep going. To *adapt*.

I can't force people to like me. But maybe if I keep myself busy enough, I'll stop noticing when they don't.

I spend a lot of time wandering around, trying to get used to the layout of this place, and to understand how it works—what the rules are—so I can avoid ignorantly stepping on any toes. But most of the performers are on such a strict rehearsal schedule that not having anything to do makes me feel even more out of place.

I'm like one of those betta fish, stuck in a tiny container, watching all the other fish across the aisle swimming in a big aquarium. An outsider with a bad reputation. A fish, but not *one* of the fish.

What I want more than anything right now is just to feel like I have somewhere to *be*.

So when I check the schedule and see that Vivien is in the rehearsal tent, an overpowering amount of relief floods through me. I know we're not best friends or anything, but Vivien and Dexi are the only people who make me feel like there's still a chance things might change. Like there's still a chance I might one day join the other fish.

Vivien is in the middle of her act, smiling to an imaginary crowd with a blindfold over her eyes. Her dark braids are tied back with a thin scarf, and she's wearing a purple tank top and black leggings. The glint of a silver blade peeks through between each of her fingers like she's a menacing, clawed creature out of a horror movie. She throws one, two, three knives at her target board, hitting a trio of colorful balloons that pop beneath each blade. Then four, five, six, *pop, pop, pop*.

It's enthralling to watch her, the way her body moves like a cat prowling through the grass. She's strong, and subtle, and so very deadly. She's juggling a new set of knives a moment later, the board of balloons now spinning. It's hypnotic. *She's* hypnotic. She turns and throws, turns and throws, turns and throws—everything is moving faster and faster, like a chase scene nearing its end. My breath is caught in my throat, but I'm too afraid to take in more air—too nervous to let anything out. Only one balloon remains, bright and red in the very center. Vivien picks up a bow with her feet, does a handstand, and curls her legs over her head, pointing an arrow directly at the balloon. Drawing the string with her toes, I can see the flash of her teeth.

She loves this, the way I love the trapeze.

The arrow releases, sailing across the ring.

Pop.

Vivien is standing, the blindfold in her right hand, waving at the empty spaces around her and taking a low bow. When she lifts herself back up, she spots me at the edge of the mat and grins.

"That was incredible," I gush, taking a few steps toward her.

Three fire-jugglers are standing at the back, going over their routine with practice pins. They look at me for only a split second before turning back to their equipment.

I try to ignore the sinking feeling trying to pull my entire body down with it.

Vivien smiles with her whole face. "Are you going to stick around and watch? I still have another half hour left before the contortionists take over. It would be so much easier if they could just practice in the yard, but Simon has a strict no-performing-for-free policy. Guess there's too big a risk of people pulling up outside to watch us through the fence like we're part of a big zoo."

I open my mouth to tell her I'd love to stay, but the words come to a halt on the tip of my tongue. I feel the fire-jugglers staring hard.

Maybe they want privacy, or maybe they just don't like me. But either way, it's obvious they don't want me here.

It was easy to make friends at Teatro della Notte. Everyone was nice. Welcoming. And they always made me feel like I fit in.

I guess I thought every circus would be the same.

But maybe it was only easy for me because my parents were the owners. Maybe everyone *had* to like me, by default of who my mom and dad are.

The possibility that Mom wasn't the only person who lied to me makes me queasy. Teatro della Notte was my family—I don't know how I'm supposed to feel knowing it might've all been an illusion.

Am I a difficult person to like?

And if so, what am I doing wrong?

Vivien turns around, and it only takes her a second to put all the pieces together. She looks back at me apologetically and rolls her eyes. "Maggie told everyone you were after her job."

"What?" My heart sinks. So *that's* why everyone is pretending I don't exist. They don't just think I screwed over a stranger—they think I screwed over one of their own.

Of course they hate me.

She clicks her tongue against the roof of her mouth and shakes her head. "They think they're doing her a favor by giving you the cold shoulder or something. But don't worry—Dexi and I told everyone she's lying. It will all blow over in a few days, you'll see."

A few days. Okay. I can handle a few days.

Right?

I force a smile. "Thanks—for sticking up for me, and for the invite to watch the rehearsal. But I'm actually pretty tired, so I'll probably head back to the trailer for a while." *Tired of feeling like what I want will always be just outside my reach.* I bite down on my thoughts and shrug like it's not a big deal. "I'm supposed to be shadowing Maggie in a couple hours anyway."

Vivien smiles and skips back to her target board, retrieving the knives, arrow, and scraps of ravaged balloon.

I sulk out of the tent and chew my bottom lip. I feel like I'm losing control.

I think about what Mom and Dad would say if they were here. Probably something along the lines of *I told you so.* Popo might be a bit more forgiving. She'd scold me for breaking my parents' trust, but I think she'd understand, too.

And Chloe, who seemed so mad at me earlier—what would she say?

I think there'd be sympathy, but then she'd tell me to come home. She wouldn't remind me that I came here knowing it would be hard, and that encountering a few roadblocks just means I have to try harder. She wouldn't tell me I joined Maison du Mystère for a reason, and I can't leave until I've trained with Maggie and accomplished what I set out to do.

I think I'm the only person in the world I can trust right now.

I just wish it weren't so hard to remember why.

Maggie's feet balance carefully on the metal bar, the static trapeze lifted high above the room like a grand chandelier at the heart of the big top. Except instead of crystal shards or an abundance of candles, there's a woman with lavender hair and a smile that explodes across the room with all the brilliance of a fireworks display.

I can only imagine what she'll look like in full costume. She's wearing pink yoga pants and a black sports bra, and she still looks like magic incarnate.

Dexi told me the flyers and aerialists are the only ones who rehearse in the big top because of the way the equipment is set up. But a few months ago, Simon lost his flying trapeze act to another troupe. Since then, it's just Maggie who trains in here, four days a week with two spotters, like she's circus royalty.

Gripping the ropes, Maggie pulls herself off the bar and does a backward roll. She slows into an upside-down pose, the muscles in her arms sharp and lean. With incredible control, she holds herself for five counts, before lowering herself back onto the bar. In one fluid movement she pulls her entire body upward again, this time pointing her toes and stretching her legs into an over-split, her teeth flashing like every movement is effortless.

I stay close to the back of the ring, trying not to draw her attention while she's performing, but when the bar lowers and her toes graze the floor, her large eyes snap toward me like a rubber band.

"This is a closed rehearsal," she says. "You shouldn't be in here."

I try not to let her see me flinch as I walk toward the center of the ring, not wanting to shout my thoughts from the stands. I'm not sure my voice would even carry that far—not when I feel flimsy and nervous and desperate for her to train me.

"Simon says I'm allowed to shadow you. I thought maybe—" I start.

"The thing about shadows is that you don't notice they're there." She circles her finger toward me like she's motioning to every inch of me.

I bite my lip, reminding myself this is *not* the time to start blurting out whatever pops into my head first. She clearly doesn't like me. I need to neutralize that somehow.

I could even forgive her for all the rumors she's spread, if she's willing to give me a clean slate.

"I don't want to get in the way," I say firmly. "I just want to learn."

Maggie stares at me for a long moment, and hope starts to brew in my chest. I imagine her eyes softening, her shoulders sinking into a sigh when she tells me to come closer so she can teach me about technique and style.

But I guess my imagination has always been too big for this world, because none of that happens. Instead, she points behind me and purses her lips. "Take a seat at the back, where you won't be a distraction. You can watch the routine—be a shadow, if that's what you want. But I don't have time to help you, or answer your questions, or do anything other than what I always do, which is *rehearse*. Do you understand?"

I clench my teeth and nod.

She fluffs her hair. "I know you think I'm being a bitch, but this is my career. I work hard—too hard to have Simon play his silly mind games, and for entitled, starry-eyed strangers to think I'm supposed to drop everything to teach for free."

The bright lights send my brain spiraling into a panic, but I try to speak anyway—to tell her she's wrong. "This isn't a mind game, and I'm not starry-eyed. I've wanted this my whole life. I just—"

She tuts. "You don't honestly think Simon would've taken you on if he weren't trying to get to me? He calls me his Sapphire Peacock. And do you know the thing about birds? They fly away, eventually. Not because they have to, but because they want to. And it doesn't matter how many jewels you decorate their cage with—a bird will always be a bird." She shrugs. "He's trying to get under my skin—and you're getting in my way. But when I'm ready to leave this cage for something bigger, neither of you is going to be able to do a thing about it."

I take a seat at the back and spend the next hour watching Maggie rehearse, wondering if maybe she's right—maybe I do have a sense of entitlement.

Tatya had offered to train me, but she was a friend of the family. A friend to *me*.

Why did I think it would always be that easy?

I chew on my thoughts like they taste stale and wrong until I convince myself that they are.

Maggie leaves without even a glance my way, and when her spotters leave too, I find myself transfixed by the static trapeze still hanging in the air.

Empty. Solemn. Waiting to come back to life.

And before I know it, I've lowered the bar and pulled myself to a standing position, feeling the grip of rope between my fingers. Remembering what it felt like to come to life in the air.

I pull myself up, imitating Maggie's split. I know my legs aren't as straight, and my core isn't as strong. I can feel my arms trembling slightly when I shift from one position to the next. But I can do what she did.

I can be a trapeze artist.

And with the right training, I think I could be a *great* one.

Maybe that isn't Maggie's problem, or her responsibility, and deep down I know I can't be mad at her for that. She doesn't owe me anything, and maybe it wasn't fair that Simon and I made a deal that involved her without even *involving* her.

It was bad form. I didn't know it before, but I know it now.

But maybe I don't need Maggie's help. Because here, where it's quiet and I'm alone with my thoughts and everything I've learned over the years, I can train by myself.

I could keep practicing, the way I've *been* practicing, but I'll work harder than I ever have. I'll put in as many hours as it takes, and I'll prove myself without Maggie's mentorship.

And maybe one day it will be enough to prove myself to my parents, too.

I won't give up now. Not when there are still options left.

I place my feet back on the bar, considering where to move my legs, when Sasha's accented voice makes me jump. I grip the ropes tighter, finding him in the doorway with his eyebrows raised.

"You can't be in here alone," he says. "Aerialists have to have a spotter at all times. Even the non-flyers."

"I'll keep the bar low," I say. "I just wanted to practice."

He twists his mouth. "I'm sorry, but rules are rules."

I let myself down from the bar, my face burning fiercely.

"If you ask someone to spot you, you can train as much as you like," he offers.

I nod a few times as I walk past him, and I feel my mind imploding with so much frustration.

Because where would I find a spotter? Most of the people here have already decided to ignore me, and if I ask Vivien or Dexi, I risk making them feel the same way about me that Maggie does. Like I'm entitled and I expect help and free labor.

I can't ruin what little trust I've built with them. And I won't be someone who spends her time here begging for scraps.

I'll just have to find another way.

CHAPTER FIFTEEN

I'm almost asleep when I hear my phone vibrate. It's an email from Mom.

To: FlightOfTheRedPanda@gmail.com
From: Delilah.Milano@teatrodellanotte.com
Subject: The time you lost your tooth

   Do you remember that day at Disneyland? You lost your tooth eating a churro. You were so worried the tooth fairy wasn't going to visit you in California that you asked me to look up her email address on the internet. I always thought that was funny–how you'd see a problem, and immediately start coming up with solutions. You never believed something just couldn't be done.

   You carried that tooth around the entire day but lost it sometime between Pirates of the Caribbean and meeting Mary Poppins. Your dad and I were worried you'd be upset, but you started laughing and couldn't stop. You said most people lose a tooth, but you *really* lost one. It made us laugh too.

You were happy when you were little. It seemed like you'd always be happy.

Is it my fault that changed?

Please call me.

Love, Mom

I'm happy right now, I want to write back.

But I don't. Because I'm not sure I can handle any more lies.

CHAPTER SIXTEEN

*J*he next day and a half drag on and on and on. But when I step out of my trailer on Thursday evening, my heart pings up into the air like a balloon filled with helium. It's a nice surprise—I've spent the last few days feeling so heavy and sluggish, I thought I was slowly sinking into the Upside Down.

But tonight, Maison du Mystère is *alive*.

Lights spiral up every tent, twinkling with energy. The smell of perfectly buttered popcorn weaves through the crowd. Music blares from the overhead speakers. It doesn't sound haunted like Teatro della Notte's infamous tune—it's more like a whimsical puppet show, full of trills and lazy cascades and clever oboe riffs.

It's still an hour before the curtains to the big top open, but the eager crowd is already beginning to grow, their faces beaming with euphoric joy. And how could anyone blame them? They drove through the Phoenix desert, stepped through an archway covered in lights, and crossed over into another world.

The outer ring is a city of smaller purple and red tents in varying shades, most of them big enough to fit ten people or so. Inside are magicians, illusionists, fortune-tellers, and even a ventrilo-quist. Guests disappear inside with mild curiosity, and when they emerge, they're full of giddy excitement.

It's an excitement I share with the rest of the spectators, because I've never experienced Maison du Mystère before; I don't know the show intimately the way I know Teatro della Notte. I don't know its secrets—the little enchantments that all combine to form the magic of the circus.

But knowing seems like a good first step to belonging.

A clown on a unicycle rolls past me, his brightly colored suit three sizes too big for him, and his makeup painted to make him look wildly happy. I see children giggling nearby, and a young couple twisting their fingers together and sharing a box of fresh popcorn.

I weave through the crowd like I'm invisible. Nobody suspects I live in a trailer a hundred yards away. I'm dressed in ripped black jeans and a baggy shirt that hangs off my right shoulder.

I look ordinary. And ordinary has no place in a circus.

A family emerges from one of the small tents, laughing together with wide eyes, like they've seen something they'll never be able to comprehend.

I want to see it too.

As soon as my fingers graze the fabric opening, a hand clamps down on my shoulder.

Sasha's brows are furrowed, and his white shirt is unbuttoned all the way down his chest. "What are you doing? Cast and crew are supposed to meet behind the big top," he says.

"I—I didn't know I was supposed to be anywhere," I stammer, frowning. "I thought it would be good to get to know the circus."

Sasha motions for me to follow him, seemingly concerned that someone might recognize him as a performer and ruin the illusion of the circus. Maybe that's why he seems to be missing half his costume.

"Archie didn't give you my message?" he asks again, trying to make sense of it. I don't even know who he's talking about, so I shake my head. He lets out a sigh. "Never mind, it doesn't matter. From now on, you meet with the rest of us half an hour before the gates open, got it?"

I try to hide my grin. Because if I'm meeting with everyone, it means they think I'm part of the troupe. It means they think I'm one of them—that I might even have a place here.

That I might have a place as a *performer* one day.

We step through the side entrance to the big top that leads into the covered foyer. The smell of corn dogs is overpowering, and I can practically feel the quake of the cotton candy machine against the dirt floor.

The last time I was in here, everything looked skeletal. Now every counter is stocked with pretzels, chips, and confectionary. The sound of the soda machine is constant. There's even a glass case full of T-shirts, key chains, stuffed animals, and sparkly magic wands with stars on the ends that twinkle in neon colors.

"Here, put this on," Sasha says, handing me a bright purple apron covered in yellow spots, and a jester hat complete with jingling gold bells. He nods to the oversized glass box next to me, perched on a red counter. "You're on popcorn duty. Pia will show you how to put the new kernels in, but otherwise it's pretty self-explanatory."

Popcorn duty. Simon put me on popcorn duty.

Because the people here don't look at me like someone worth taking seriously. They look at me like someone who needed an after-school job.

Do not cry, I order myself. *Not now. Not when everyone is watching.*

I know I wanted something to do—something that made me a part of the circus in some small way. But this? This doesn't feel like inclusion. It feels like someone slamming a door in my face.

I slide the apron over my head and tie it quickly, facing away from Sasha so he can't see that my heart has just splintered for the hundredth time and there are so many tiny cracks and splits that it's only a matter of time before it explodes.

What am I going to do if my heart breaks during my first week?

I shut my eyes and wish with everything inside me that I can find a way to get through tonight without breaking down in tears.

It's strange how one moment I'm in the middle of a traveling town of light and wonder, surrounded by strange faces and a never-ending chorus of laughter and applause, and the next moment I'm alone, the tents empty and the lights dimmed and the parking lot void of a single car.

My apron is folded in my lap, and I'm sitting on an empty bench behind the big top, the stars flickering above me and the night sky velvety black.

The crew has already been inside to sweep popcorn off the floor and collect empty bottles and candy wrappers from the stands. Now it's just me and the echo of my empty chest.

I think about Maggie, dangling from the bar. I think of Dexi dancing across the high wire. I think of Vivien earning gasps and cheers from the entire room with each pop of a balloon. And I think of me, refilling cartons of popcorn and forcing smiles at strangers who feel more a part of the circus than I do.

I hate that I'm so bitter, but I don't know how else to feel.

What else do I *do*?

I wipe my fingers across my cheeks, not even realizing the tears have started to fall. Something pings inside my chest. A fragment of stubbornness, maybe. And I decide right this very moment that I don't want to waste any more time crying.

I came here to train, so that's exactly what I'm going to do.

Even if it can't be on the static trapeze.

I slip into the big top from the hidden back entrance. It's eerily quiet and a bit unnerving, with all the empty chairs, the dim lighting, and the flicker of metal from the equipment hidden at the height of the tent.

Nobody trains here but Maggie—Maggie, and now me. Because nobody will bother me here, and I won't be taking up anybody's time. I'll come here every night if I have to, when everyone else is at the Lunch Box or in their rooms or out drinking in the local town.

I'll be here, practicing handstands and leaps and splits and bends. I'll make myself stronger, and more flexible, and more accurate. I'll make sure I'm in the best shape I can be in, so that the next time I'm on that bar, it won't feel like I've gone backward.

I step into the center of the ring, turning in slow circles as I imagine the crowd around me. I can almost picture them—smiling, pointing, waving like I'm a princess in some mystical city. I don't love the circus because of the admiration, but the magic in their eyes? The glow that emits from their hearts when they watch a performance they're utterly captivated by?

It's like breathing clean air for the first time. I will always want it. I will always need it.

And I picture my parents, too, sitting in the stands, looking at me like they're finally proud of me. Mom's bright smile. Dad's stern brow softening.

At least it's something I can daydream about. If I don't think too hard, I can almost pretend it's a real memory.

"I don't mean to be rude, but are you going to be here long?"

His voice makes me leap out of my skin, and when I spin around, I clamp my mouth shut, very aware that Vas has seen me smiling at an imaginary crowd like a total dork.

He's holding his violin in one hand, his bow in the other. "It's just that I always come here after the show, to practice." He looks up at the ceiling, his expression blank. "I like the acoustics."

"I didn't see you," I mumble awkwardly. "I . . . thought I could practice in here so I wouldn't be bothering anyone. But it's fine—I'll try the rehearsal tent." I start to turn.

His voice comes out gruff. "You'll be waiting a while to get a spot. Rehearsals go until eleven, even on show nights."

I hesitate, not knowing what to say, and not wanting him to think I'm as weak as I feel.

He casts his eyes around the room, assessing. "Look, I don't need the whole ring to rehearse. I can stay on one side, and you can practice on the other."

Thump goes my heart. "You wouldn't mind me being here?"

He shrugs, like it might only be a mild inconvenience, but one he can put up with. "I'm not generally good at small talk, so as long as that isn't a problem . . ."

No interacting. Just practicing.

I'll freaking take it.

"It won't be a problem," I blurt out quickly. I think it startles him, because his eyes widen. "From now on, I'm basically the flying carpet out of *Aladdin*. I won't make a sound."

His expression is still tense, like there's something he's trying to figure out. But whatever it is must not be very important, because he pulls his eyes away from me and presses his violin to his chin. A moment passes, and he's sliding his bow along the strings, lost in his own world.

I stretch across the floor and disappear into my own world too.

CHAPTER SEVENTEEN

*C*hloe texts me in the morning: I don't want us to be fighting. Can we please not be fighting?

I stare at the screen for a beat too long because it takes me a while to realize why she thinks we're not talking. And then I remember we haven't spoken since Monday, and we hung up on less than happy terms.

Avoiding Chloe wasn't intentional; I just forgot the conversation even happened.

Maybe Chloe doesn't need to know that part.

I don't want to fight either, I write back.

She starts typing right away. Oh thank God. I felt like we were going to break up or something. It was the literal worst. More typing. And I'm sorry if it seemed like I was yelling at you before. I was just surprised. I thought you'd tell me something as major as running away with a circus. You know, before your parents did.

I chew my lip. Okay, well I'm sorry too. But I swear it wasn't on purpose. And we're DEFINITELY not going to break up. I'm like the Hulk to your Bruce Banner. You're stuck with me!

Chloe: Haha. Okay. So we're good?

Me: Resuming Best Friend Mode in 3 . . . 2 . . . 1 . . .

Chloe: You're SUCH a nerd.

Me: We literally became friends over Pokémon cards. Nerd culture is our legacy.

Chloe: True. I miss you. It's not the same here without you. But hey, maybe you'll be back in Vegas at some point and I can watch you perform!

I decide not to tell her about the popcorn. That would be uh-mazing.

The three little dots appear, then vanish. It takes almost two minutes for her to start typing again. I'm happy you're happy.

I don't want to lie, so I send a thumbs-up emoji and hope it's enough.

She doesn't write back, so I guess it is.

CHAPTER EIGHTEEN

$\mathcal{L}$ oad-out begins as soon as Sunday's matinee performance ends. The small tents come down first, and when the Lucky Thirteen begin dismantling the big top, the motor homes start to pull away, one at a time.

"They're like a house of cards," Dexi says from the driver's seat. Our trailer is already hooked up to the back of the truck, and we're waiting on our cue that it's our turn to go. "There's an order to how everything fits—if you start moving stuff around too early, the entire system collapses."

Vivien yawns from the passenger seat, stretching her arms behind her head until I hear a crack in her shoulder. "Was that as loud to you as it was to me?"

Dexi snorts, and I try to feign laughter. My heart feels tired. I wish there were an easier way to explain that—an easier way to fix it. But I feel like I'm wading through peanut butter. Everything I do feels like a struggle.

I want to work hard. I want to do *more*. More than serving

popcorn and lurking in the back of Maggie's rehearsals and doing handstands in the big top late at night.

I need to massively readjust my expectations. I know that. But sometimes it's difficult when my heart still feels so set on an idea. I guess it's hard for me to wrap my head around a change of plans.

One of the crew members waves us forward, and then we're on the road, headed to our next tour stop with our home trailing behind us.

It feels like it's been *months* since I first got into the truck with Simon, but it's only been six days.

Six days doesn't seem like enough time to make such a big change. I once spent six days building the perfect house on *The Sims*, which seems excessive in hindsight, but at the time it only felt like a few hours.

Time is funny like that. When you're content, it goes by in a blink. But when you're unsettled? In those moments, time feels eternal.

I settle into the back seat, watching the scenery shift and wondering how many more car rides it will be before I can say I've been on a static trapeze again.

I know my need to feel joy doesn't always make sense to other people. Happiness is common. It's a feeling most people don't think twice about, because they feel it so often, they take it for granted.

I'm different. Sometimes it feels like I'm forever chasing a high. It feels like I'm trying to replicate a feeling of bliss—a feeling that's hard for me to hold on to.

I know I'm sad more often than not. I know maybe that's part of who I am.

But the other part of me? The part that doesn't accept that that's *all* I am? It feels like I'm constantly running in the opposite direction. The opposite of sad. And all the while, sad is trying to pull me back down.

I feel the darkness creeping through me, so I quickly wave away the clouds in my head, making space for something else. *Anything* else.

And I guess it works, because my ears start to perk up every time a motorbike passes us on the freeway, my eyes peering through the window to see if it's Vas. It's a bit like when you're waiting for a package, and every time a car drives by, you're hoping it's the delivery person.

Not that I'm hoping to see Vas, exactly. But he's watched me train alone for the last few nights, and as far as I know, he hasn't told anybody how sad and pathetic I am. In some obscure way, it's almost like we're sharing a secret.

I'm sure Vas doesn't see it that way, but then again, who's asking him? Definitely not me. I am as silent as a clam when we're around each other, just like I promised.

We reach a new city around midnight, and even though I'm exhausted and ready to collapse into bed, I can't help but picture the big top in my head. I think of all the hours I've missed out on, unable to train because the Lucky Thirteen won't start putting the tent together until tomorrow morning.

I fall asleep dreaming of me in the big top, balancing on the static trapeze to the sound of Vas's violin.

Albuquerque, New Mexico

August—Week 2

CHAPTER NINETEEN

I'm alone in the trailer, doing planks and push-ups to pass the time until Vivien and Dexi come to get me for dinner, when I notice all the photographs tucked beneath the top bunk where I sleep. They're stuck between the metal bars, facing down toward Vivien's mattress. Pictures of her family and her friends, and one of her with her parents.

Vivien's mom looks almost identical to her—just a little older, and a little darker. But they have the same nose, a heart-shaped face, and eyebrows even a movie star would envy.

Her dad looks like Chris Hemsworth. Like, *exactly*. He's basically Thor with short hair.

And when I look at their smiling faces, it makes me want to smile too. But the pang in my chest holds me back.

I wonder if my parents and I will ever smile like that again.

When my phone buzzes, I'm convinced some otherworldly force has sent me a message from Mom and it's a sign everything is going to be okay between us.

But it's a text from Chloe.

I have a best friend emergency and I need your help!

I text back: Please tell me you didn't try to bleach your own hair again. I can still taste the fumes in the back of my mouth from last time.

Chloe: Haha, funny. NO. I met a boy!

Me: And the emergency is he has a girlfriend/he's in prison but innocent/you met him on the internet and he says you've inherited a million dollars from a long-lost relative?

Chloe: STOP MAKING JOKES THIS IS SERIOUS.

Me: Okay, sorry, I'm listening.

Chloe: His name is Jack, and he goes to A-TECH. You know, the computer geek school? Anyway, we've hung out a few times with friends, and the other day he asked me to come to this play he's in—he does theater too—but his entire family is going to be there, and it seems kind of soon to be meeting the whole family, and at first I thought that seemed weird, but then I wondered if maybe he . . .

Her texts come in fragments, parts of the story at a time, like she's giving me a chance to soak in the information, but I'm distracted by the voices outside my window.

I push myself off the floor, leaving my phone behind, and I do my best to be inconspicuous when I peer through the glass.

Vivien looks like she was on her way to our trailer when a conversation stopped her. I think it's something Maggie said, who's standing a few feet away. Dexi is beside her, with Vas,

Jin, and a few other people too. It's hard to make out everything they're saying, but Maggie is waving her hands in the air like she's refusing to do something, and Dexi seems to be pleading with her.

Vivien looks annoyed, turning like she's trying to get closer to the trailer, when Maggie's voice booms through the window.

"If you invite her, then the three of you can go find a different restaurant to eat at. She's not part of our group, and if you don't like that, then you don't have to be in it either."

I see Vivien roll her eyes, and Dexi drops her shoulders. She says something else—something that seems to irritate Maggie even more—but then they're all walking away from the trailer toward the parking lot.

They don't come back.

I know I shouldn't take it to heart. I'm new—it takes time to make friends when you're new.

But the rejection feels like a sucker punch to the gut.

I'm wallowing in loneliness and self-pity for at least thirty minutes before I remember I was in the middle of a conversation with Chloe.

I pick up my phone and look at the most recent messages.

Chloe: Are you there?

Chloe: HARLEY.

Chloe: Okay, well I guess you're busy.

And even though I know I've let her down by not replying, I'm relieved I don't have to pretend to be excited when I feel like a ghost with no friends, haunting a house that nobody wants to live in.

Another day passes, and there's another email from Mom.

To: FlightOfTheRedPanda@gmail.com
From: Delilah.Milano@teatrodellanotte.com
Subject: The time you decided to start a business

I remember the flyers you made: Harley's Pet-Sitting Service. And you drew a different pet on every single one. I think the one with the guinea pig was my favorite.

You were so focused on the details. You were focused on everything, really. Because whenever you'd get an idea in your head, it would take over your world. It was like nothing else mattered except your new business. It never occurred to you that it might fail—all you saw was a new adventure and the world at your fingertips.

And then your dad said he'd walk you around the neighborhood so you could tape flyers to the mailboxes. I told him not to—I'd heard it was illegal to advertise things on mailboxes. I think it gave you a complex, because suddenly you didn't want to hand out flyers anymore. You were always so serious about rules. I think you got that from me. And that was all it took—I said one thing, and it was like all the lights went out, and your dream died.

I wish I hadn't said anything. I should've just let you put your flyers up. I took the fun out of something when I didn't mean to. You've said I do that a lot, but I never used to understand what you meant until today.

But it's not on purpose. I don't mean to. It's just that sometimes you don't look at the details. You don't think about the potential risks. You don't think about what could go wrong.

I look at the details because I don't want you to get hurt. I don't want anything to go wrong. And because it's my job to think about these things, when I know you don't.

I regret telling you about those flyers. But I don't regret telling you to go to school. I wish you could see the difference.

And despite what you think, I do want you to have fun. I just wish you didn't have to run so far away from your parents to feel like you could.

I miss you, Harley.

Love, Mom

I didn't have to run away, I want to reply. *But you tried to take the trapeze away from me. I had no choice.*

Except I know, deep down, there's *always* a choice.

And talking to Mom might make me feel like I made the wrong one.

My parents aren't bad parents. Maybe, with another daughter, they might have been happier. She might have listened to them, and trusted them, and been okay with venturing down the path Mom and Dad had set out for her.

But I don't want to follow anybody's path. I want to make my own—through the woods and beyond the mountains and into the stars. I want the circus, with all its ups and downs. With all its *uncertainty.*

Because even with everything going wrong, I still know I'm more content here than I'd ever be at school.

Mom won't see that. She'll only see how I'm wrong, and how I've been a bad daughter, and how I'm not mature or responsible enough to take charge of my own life.

She didn't even trust me enough to tell me the truth about *her* life.

But . . . still.

I know I was wrong to hurt them.

What I did to Dad can't be justified with my dreams, no matter how big they are.

And since I can't defend myself, I shove my phone under my pillow and pretend I didn't see the email at all.

CHAPTER TWENTY

I don't know why tonight is different.

I shouldn't look. I should stay by the popcorn machine, in the empty foyer, listening to the hum of the soda machine and Pia giggling with her boyfriend who's busy showing off his juggling skills next to the corn dog stand.

What's going on inside the big top has nothing to do with me, and no amount of audience cheers should tempt me to leave this spot.

But I've always been terrible at standing still, and worse at listening to my own advice.

I move across the room, half expecting one of the other crew members to warn me away from the curtains, but they don't. I think they've forgotten I exist at all.

Pulling back the dark fabric with my hand, I peer inside and see Maggie, legs stretched into an oversplit, her weight held up by her arms. She moves like a feather dancing in the wind—a delicate creature covered in turquoise and gold jewels, with a headpiece around her forehead and a bundle of lilac curls. When she stands on the bar, I see the feather-and-sequin skirt, and the way she lifts her chin like a dancer, graceful and proud and strong.

A cascade of blue silk ribbons hangs from the sky, and lights flutter around the room in time to piccolo arpeggios. Maggie wraps herself in the ropes, hitting pose after pose effortlessly. And then she's hanging from the bar with one hand, feet moving in slow motion through the air like she's underwater. She pulls herself back up, resting her body against the bar, and stretches her arms out like she's spreading her wings.

Up in the air, covered in sparkles and light, she looks like a princess from another world.

And in that moment, the fragmented shell of my heart shatters, and emotion floods out of me in one powerful wave. There isn't a thing I can do to stop it.

I'm kidding myself, thinking I have any chance of ever getting to where Maggie is. I've been naive, and horrible, and I can't make myself belong in a place that doesn't want me.

I don't even remember leaving the foyer or making my way back to my trailer, but the next thing I know, I'm slamming the door and sobbing big, hot tears into my hands, grasping at my skin and hair like I wish I could take everything back.

What would I have done differently if I could go back in time?

Maybe train with Tatya anyway. Because at least Tatya saw something in me—even if it was something small.

And then I remember how she hates me too. Because I ruin things. Because for some reason my brain won't stop shooting words out of my mouth like we're Commander Shepard under a Reaper attack.

I have nothing left to go back to.

I should call Mom. She's good at fixing things—she *likes* fixing things—and maybe she could fix this.

I call Popo instead.

"Hello?" She sounds alarmed, maybe because she wasn't expecting to see my name on her caller ID.

"Hi. It's me."

Popo must know I'm crying, because she makes a noise like she understands everything. "Ah. Have you called your mother yet?"

I shut my eyes tight and try to get all the words out. "I can't. I don't want her to know she was right, and that Dad was right— that I'm not good enough to do this, and it was a terrible idea. Because everyone here hates me, Popo. They won't even give me a chance—they won't let me anywhere near the trapeze to train, and they have me selling popcorn like this is some crappy summer job and I'm nobody worth paying attention to. And I know I sound like a brat, but I didn't come here to sell popcorn—I came here because I wanted to become a better aerialist. And it's not going to happen, and I know I have to come home, but I feel like I've messed things up so badly. With Mom and Dad, and Tatya, too, who will probably never agree to train me again. I feel like such a total and complete failure. I don't know what to do. Tell me what to do?"

It's quiet for a moment. "So you're at a circus. Where?"

I let myself fall into a chair. I forgot they still don't know where I am. I guess Chloe kept her promise after all.

"Maison du Mystère," I say, my voice sinking.

Another pause. "At least you're safe."

I don't know what to make of her response. I know there must be disappointment somewhere, but I can't hear it. Or maybe I just don't *want* to hear it.

"I saw the photo of Mom on the trapeze," I say, like this is supposed to explain everything.

"Your running away was my fault," Popo replies, and she doesn't say it like a question—more like an acknowledgment. Something she plans to file away for later.

"It wasn't your fault. Mom shouldn't have kept such a big secret from me. Especially when she got to experience all the things I was asking to experience." I flick a piece of lint from my apron.

"Your mom has her reasons." Popo sighs into the phone. Reasons nobody wants to explain to me. "It was very wrong of you to frighten your parents the way you did."

I swallow. "I know." This is it—the part where she tells me to come home. The part where I give in, because my heart can't take it anymore.

"And you need to apologize to them. They were so worried—so was I. And they didn't deserve that kind of worry," she adds.

"I know," I say again, the tears soaking my cheeks.

"But I don't think you should come home," she says.

My heart thuds. "What?"

"I don't like the way you left, but you left for a reason. And I'm not saying it's okay to disrespect your parents' wishes, but sometimes following your own path isn't disrespecting them. Parents feel like it is sometimes, but it isn't. Because you have your own life to live, and your own path to follow. It's never easy when you're trying to prove yourself, and it shouldn't be. Success is the end of a very long and bumpy road. Do you understand?"

"I thought you were going to tell me to come home," I say softly. At least I think I thought that. Maybe deep down I knew Popo would tell me I have to stay. Maybe that's why I called her and not Mom.

"I want you to be happy. But I think sometimes you try too hard to be happy—and when it doesn't happen, you feel like your world is collapsing. But emotions aren't black-and-white—you don't have to be either happy or sad. There can be an in-between, you know." The rasp in Popo's voice is so familiar and soothing. I miss her. I miss being home.

But maybe missing home isn't the same as wanting to be there. Because I don't want to go home—I want to stay here and train.

"I don't know what it feels like to be in the in-between," I admit. Everything is always extreme for me, like when I'm happy, I need to be ultraviolet-elated, and when I'm sad, it's like a vacuum is sucking away all the colors in the world and I'm drowning in black.

Maybe that's not normal, but it's *my* normal.

But it does make living hard sometimes, because I'm always chasing extreme joy rather than just "happy enough." Crawling out of the darkness always feels like it takes so very long, and falling back into it can happen in a second.

"It's good to stay motivated, but if you're putting so much

pressure on yourself that you're making yourself unhappy, that's not good. Try not to be so hard on yourself, okay? Set a pace you're comfortable with. Enjoy the journey." Popo hums into the phone, like she's said something even *she's* proud of.

"I don't know what to do," I say.

"You work hard. You don't give up. You keep trying. And you sell popcorn in the circus that agreed to give you a chance," Popo says. "Because it is a chance, Harley Yoshi. A chance not everyone gets. Don't let it go to waste because the reality of your dreams isn't as pretty as you'd imagined."

I wipe my cheeks one more time, even though they're mostly dry. "Look, I won't ask you not to tell Mom and Dad where I am because I know you won't agree to it, but will you at least not tell them I was upset?" I chew my lip. "I don't want them to know I almost quit."

Popo chuckles into the phone. "I think I can work with that."

"Thanks, Popo," I say. "I love you."

"I love you too. Now go and chase your dreams."

CHAPTER TWENTY-ONE

I mostly keep to myself. I show up to Maggie's rehearsals, sitting in the back like a ghost. I don't ask questions, or interfere, or try to change her mind about training me. I accept her decision, like I've accepted my place here. I serve popcorn to guests during shows. I smile, and I never complain, and I don't cause any trouble at all. I send Popo emails to let her know how things are going, because it helps to feel connected to family again.

And at night I train in the big top, while Vas practices his violin.

We don't say a word to each other.

Not even when he's caught me looking at him.

Not even when I've caught him looking at me.

El Paso, Texas

September—Week 3

Amarillo, Texas

September—Week 4

Oklahoma City, Oklahoma

September—Week 5

I text Chloe to ask how she's been. It takes her hours to reply, but when she does, she tells me about her classes and a teacher she hates and the boy she's now officially dating.

And it usually takes me hours to write back too because I'm training or watching Maggie or at the Lunch Box trying to seem engaged with the people I desperately want to like me.

Even though they don't seem concerned about engaging with me.

And we go back and forth like that for a while, until one of us forgets to respond at all.

It should upset me more than it does, but I'm so busy *trying* to be busy that I mostly don't even notice.

After Thursday night's show, I make my way to the big top. It still smells like buttered popcorn, and some of the floor is still sticky from where someone must've spilled their drink.

I don't know why it takes me so long to register what I'm looking at in the center of the ring, but when I finally do, I feel my chest tighten. The static trapeze has been lowered, the ropes barely swaying in the silent room.

And I know the room is still lit up by a handful of spotlights from above, but for a moment the only light in the room is the one shining on the trapeze.

It's a flame in the darkness.

A flame inside of *me*.

Vas appears, and my world changes color once again. I wonder if he sees how ripped apart I feel when I think about not being able to train the way I want to. I wonder if he knows how much it hurts me to be so close to those ropes, only to know they're still out of my reach.

I wonder if he feels sorry for me.

And I'm embarrassed to admit that for a fleeting second, I hope he does, because it might actually make me feel better to think that I'm not the only one who sees how sad this entire situation is.

And just as quickly, I take the thought back and bury it with all the other emotions I'm trying to ignore.

Because the truth is, I'd rather have Vas's admiration. And people never admire someone they pity.

"I can be your spotter," he says, and his words throw me up into the air and around the room, disorienting me.

Did I hear him right? Did he say . . . ?

He motions his hand to the equipment, his violin tucked beneath his arm. "I'm not going to coddle you or anything, but you can use the bar while I practice. I can vouch for you if anyone gives you a hard time about it."

I can barely find my words. "I don't know what to say."

"You don't need to make a big deal out of it." He pauses, assessing me with his hardened green eyes. "Just . . . don't break any bones. Especially in your neck. It would be terribly inconvenient to have your death weighing on my conscience."

"Thank you," I blurt out, not wanting to give him the chance to take it back.

I spend the rest of the evening practicing on the bar, and for the first time in weeks I feel my heart illuminate.

CHAPTER TWENTY-THREE

*E*very night I step into the big top wondering if I'll get another chance to practice on the static trapeze, or if Vas will be too busy to show up and I'll spend another day with a desperate ache in my chest.

But every night he's there, standing at the back with his violin and his sad songs and his hair pushed angrily to the side like he's fighting the world behind his eyes.

I wonder what he's battling.

I wonder what makes him so sad.

And I wonder why he hasn't skipped practice for a single night since he said he'd help me.

Little Rock, Arkansas

September—Week 6

CHAPTER TWENTY-FOUR

Maggie's rehearsal doesn't start for another ten minutes, but I like being early. It makes it easier to find a seat in the back and pretend I'm not there, which is how Maggie prefers it.

So seeing her in the center of the ring arguing with Simon Tarbottle catches me off guard.

I freeze midstep, wondering if I've somehow mixed up the time. Maggie is pointing angrily behind her, and I only catch the end of her sentence.

" . . . it's unfair to the other aerialists, and it's unfair to me." She crosses her arms and leans into her hip.

Simon presses his hands together like he's begging her to see reason. "Yes, it will be work. But this act—your act—it needs to be bigger for the new season. The new song I have—"

"I don't care if *Beyoncé* personally wrote you a song. I am not turning my solo into some over-the-top performance piece," Maggie practically barks.

"I'm not asking for your permission," Simon says thinly. He

lets his hands fall back to his sides, but I can see the tension in his balled-up fists. "This is not your circus, Maggie."

She lowers her chin. "Last I checked, people weren't lining up to see *you* perform."

"I'm not fighting about this with you." He lifts his hands. "What is the big deal? Is your ego so tender that you can't handle a few sideline aerialists to add a bit of excitement? You'll still be the star. Everyone will still be watching you."

"You don't get it." Maggie tuts. "This isn't about me being the center of attention. It's about throwing together another stolen idea with performers you keep poaching from other troupes. Do you know how hard it is for anyone to move on from this place? How much you're hurting our reputations?"

Simon scoffs. "Apologies that my practices have been making it so difficult for you to find a new job." His voice drips with sarcasm.

Maggie rolls her eyes. "I'm not talking about me. I'm talking about people like Wendy and Marco. The people who haven't quite built a name for themselves yet. The ones who'll rely on their résumés to find work. People like *her*."

It takes me a second to realize Maggie is pointing at me, and when I do, I feel my legs turn to jelly. Even though it wasn't my intention, it looks very much like I've been eavesdropping.

"I—I was just here for rehearsal," I stammer sheepishly.

Simon lets out a heavy sigh, his mismatched eyes pinned to me for only a brief moment. And then a twinkle of mischief appears. "Harley, how are you with the silk ropes?"

Maggie looks like she wants to set him on fire.

My entire body goes stiff. "Well, um, okay, I guess?"

"He's toying with you," Maggie snaps, and her words pinch me.

Simon's laugh tumbles out of him as carelessly as his words. He wags a finger at Maggie. "I'm going to talk to Sasha about what it will cost to hire a few more aerialists. If I can cut a deal, then this is happening whether you like it or not." He winks his amber eye at me as he passes. "Maybe next time, kid."

When he's gone, I swallow the lump in my throat and let my shoulders relax.

"Don't look so disheartened," Maggie says pointedly. "It wasn't like he was really offering you a job."

"If I'd been better at the silk ropes . . . ," I start. *If I'd been better, he might've let me perform.*

"Silk ropes or not, if Simon were genuinely considering putting you in an act, he wouldn't have you serving popcorn," she retorts. "Besides, as soon as Sasha tells him what it will cost to hire what he needs"—she shakes her head, her purple curls swaying back and forth—"he would've only disappointed you. Trust me."

I nod, biting down at the edge of my lip. Maybe she's right. I *hope* she's right.

Otherwise I've just missed my first real opportunity at being a part of Maison du Mystère.

Maggie stalks toward the stands, pressing her foot against the edge of one of the chairs to adjust her leather leg warmer. When she catches me staring at her, she twists her face and drops her foot to the floor. "What?"

I shift my weight. "That was nice, that's all. What you said about Wendy and Marco. And me." I shrug. "I didn't expect you to care that much." *Or at all*, I think, but I keep that part to myself.

She lets out an irritated huff. "I only said that to make him listen."

"Oh." I don't know whether she's telling the truth, or whether she'd rather keep pretending she has a heart made of stone.

Maggie lifts up her other foot to adjust the next leg warmer. "Simon has this ridiculous idea of having six more aerialists performing on silk ropes during my solo. It's something he ripped off from a troupe in California."

"Sounds like it could be cool," I offer.

She blinks slowly. "He wants everyone to dress up like an animal. Like we're all part of a menagerie."

"Well, at least you've got the peacock covered. You're one-seventh of the way there," I say.

She straightens herself and tilts her head. "You think this is funny."

"No," I say seriously. "I actually like the idea. I mean, it's a little busy maybe, but it would be cool to watch. It feels kind of like royalty, in a way, with you in the center and a bunch of other aerialists all around you."

Maggie rolls her eyes. "Well, it's not going to happen. Simon can't afford that much new talent. Not to mention I refuse to do it. It's too distracting." She puts a hand on her hip. "It's *tacky*."

I say the words we're both thinking. "And it's stolen."

"Exactly." She looks up, her eyes following the smooth stretch of fabric above our heads. "I didn't know about his reputation when I first took this job. I was just excited to leave London and come to America." Her gaze falls back to me. "You still believe the illusion that this place is somehow full of magic. That it's going to solve all your problems. But that's just because the circus hasn't disappointed you yet."

I flatten my mouth. "You don't know anything about me."

She tilts her head again. "You didn't come here to escape your homelife? To run away from people who don't understand you? You didn't show up here hoping to be a star—to be admired by strangers and finally feel like your life has meaning?" Her smile is equal parts poisonous and beautiful. "Your heart didn't leap at the thought of performing on those silk ropes? To be a bird in a menagerie, like me?"

My tone turns icy. "I don't want to be a bird. Or you."

Her laugh makes me flinch. "All wannabe trapeze artists liken themselves to a bird. You want to fly away, right? Isn't that the dream?"

"No," I insist. Because that's not my dream at all. When she starts to turn away from me, my words tumble out all at once. "I'd rather be a red panda than a bird."

She pauses, her gray eyes snapping back to mine. "A red panda?"

I nod. "Yeah. Because they don't fit in a box, and they're okay with it. Scientists came up with a totally new name just for them. Because they aren't a bear or a raccoon or a cat or a weasel. They're just themselves. A mix of everything and nothing. And they didn't let anyone tell them what they could or couldn't be—they made the world change for *them*." I dig my heels into the ground. "I know you don't like me. I know *why* you don't like me. And I'm not going to try to change your mind. But I'm not who you think I am. So if you're going to hate me, at least make sure you know who you're hating first. Because I'm not going anywhere."

It's quiet for a moment, but Maggie doesn't pull her gaze away.

Eventually she shrugs. "I don't hate you. Hating means I'd have to care."

Even though her words are sharp, there's a twitch in the corner of her mouth. It might even be a smile.

I don't know what to make of it.

So I cross my arms and say the next best thing I can think of. "And I can't believe you'd actually turn down Beyoncé. Even hypothetically."

Maggie raises a brow. "I told you—I'd have said anything to make Simon listen."

And then she turns away, and I retreat back to the shadows of the big top, watching her train and imagining what it could've been like if we'd started out as friends instead of enemies.

CHAPTER TWENTY-FIVE

*D*exi moves across the high wire like she's under a spell. Her dark eyes never lose their focus, even when she's halfway across the tightrope and she sinks slowly into a split.

Everything is slow and calculated at first, her solo almost as captivating as Maggie's.

And then Zhìháo and Guānyǔ—cousins from Taiwan and two-thirds of the high-wire act—appear on opposite ends of the tightrope. They step closer to Dexi before crouching low, and then Dexi leapfrogs over the tops of them like it takes no effort at all.

The act moves quickly after that. Zhìháo rides a unicycle across the wire, a long pole firmly wedged in his hands, and when he comes back for round two, Guānyǔ is upside down on his shoulders.

Then Dexi is across the rope again like a spider, her feet moving so quickly, it hardly looks like she's walking at all. And then she's jumping rope—on a *tightrope*—and my mouth feels permanently ajar.

She's amazing. They're all amazing.

When the three of them stand on one another's shoulders like a human tower and Zhìháo takes the first step onto the wire, I cover my mouth with my hand like I'm too afraid to breathe.

And then I feel my phone buzz from within my pocket.

I hurry out of the rehearsal tent before anyone notices the distraction, and when I look down at the screen, I see Chloe's name and the photo of the two of us.

"Hello?" I answer.

"Hey," she says hesitantly. "It's me."

I grin, realizing for the first time how much I've missed her voice. "I'm glad you called. I feel like we haven't talked in forever."

"Yeah, well, one of us has to make an effort to stay friends." There's an edge to her voice that makes my shoulders stiffen, and I get the feeling she isn't just calling to catch up.

My smile fades. "What's that supposed to mean?"

"You're really bad at this whole 'keeping in touch' thing, you know. I feel like I'm losing my best friend," she says.

"Oh God, I know, and I'm so sorry. Things are just so hectic here, and I don't always remember to check my messages." I pause, feeling like I'm bracing for a lecture. "But we're still best friends. That hasn't changed."

Chloe hums like she's tired. "So I guess this means you've officially gone into hyperdrive?"

"I appreciate the *Star Wars* reference, but what do you mean?"

"When you get in one of your moods and get so wrapped up in whatever it is you're doing that you forget about everything else going on in the world."

My stomach tightens. "I don't do that."

She laughs into the phone, but she sounds more irritated than happy. "Yes, you do. You even forget about me. You know—the person you used to talk to every single day and now text maximum once a week?"

She's angry. Why is she so angry? "I swear, I'm just busy. I don't have a hyperdrive that makes me forget about you."

It's quiet for three long seconds.

"You don't see it. You never do," she says finally.

"Where is this coming from? I said I was sorry. What do you want me to do?" I ask, and my voice is beginning to match her irritation.

"It sucks, okay? It sucks being the only person in this friendship that tries to stay in touch."

"I know I haven't been the greatest friend lately, but I feel like you could cut me a little slack. If you were the one who had just moved away and were starting out at your dream job and things got a little busy, I think I'd be more understanding."

"But this isn't even the first time you've done this!" Chloe snaps. "This is your 'thing.' You get excited about something and it takes over your whole life. You start ignoring me. It feels like you want a *new* life—like you're trying to move on or something."

I step farther away from the rehearsal tent and find a quiet place near the empty parking lot. "That's ridiculous. I mean, yeah, I get excited about stuff, but you know that about me. We've been friends for years, and you've *known* that about me. But you're acting like ditching you is a pattern when it's absolutely not."

"But it *is*. Like when you first switched schools and you spent all semester hanging out with those two girls you said you were going to start a band with, and then basically forgot I even existed," Chloe says.

I fling my hand up in the air like she's making zero sense at all. "I was trying to make friends. That's what people do at new schools."

"By trying to start a band when you don't even play an instrument?"

"I was trying new things!"

"It felt like I was being replaced."

I kick at the scattered pebbles on the ground and watch them scurry in the opposite direction. "I know I'm not texting super often, but you're acting like I'm the worst friend in the history of the world."

Chloe sighs. "I'm not saying that. But okay, what about the time my parents asked you to house-sit, and you ditched school for an entire week and barely said a word to me the whole time I was gone because you were scrapbooking or whatever?"

"Seriously, since when did you start keeping a list of all the times you were mad at me and never bothered to tell me?" I ask angrily. "And I was not *scrapbooking*. I was writing a comic."

"Minor detail. My point is that you let things take over your life sometimes, and you don't think about who it affects. You don't even think about how it affects *you*."

"Oh my God, you sound like my mom. What the hell, Chloe? I don't understand why you're mad at me." I clench my teeth and stare angrily in the opposite direction of the circus.

"It's not easy telling someone you feel ignored, you know. But I hate when this happens. I hate being the half of our friendship that is always forgotten about."

"I'm not ignoring you on purpose! I don't know how many times I have to say it."

It's quiet for so long that I look at my phone to make sure she's still there.

Chloe's breath catches, like what she's about to say keeps getting stuck in the back of her throat. "It's not just that I feel ignored," she continues cautiously. "I'm concerned, too. You do things without thinking. Sometimes you put yourself in dangerous situations, because you get so excited about whatever it is you're doing. I know it sounds like I'm lecturing you, but I honestly don't know how else to say this to you. Because to you, it's just excitement. But to me—your *friend*—it's a warning sign."

"This is one thousand percent a lecture. And how is writing comics or starting a band dangerous?"

Chloe doesn't miss a beat. "Inviting a random stranger over to my house, when my parents gave you the keys to house-sit and your parents thought you were in school, was dangerous."

I blink.

She doesn't wait for a response. She just keeps talking, like she's trying to drill her point into my brain, and I guess I must be able to feel it because my skull is throbbing. "You knew him for less than an hour, and you invited him to a house where you were alone and nobody in town even knew you were there," she says matter-of-factly. "And you didn't even tell me until, like, a month later, when you let it slip by accident. It felt like you had some secret double life you didn't want me to be a part of."

"Seriously? I didn't tell you about it because it wasn't a big deal. He said he wanted to look at my comic, and I thought he seemed nice, so I said yes. But it ended up being super awkward, and he left twenty minutes later. It was nothing. I literally barely remember it even happened."

"That doesn't matter—what matters is that it was dangerous, and you don't see it. I mean, you didn't know anything about him. You met him in a Target *parking lot*. He could've been lying about the comics. He could've been a freaking serial killer!" Chloe says exasperatedly.

"I was fine." I chew the inside of my cheek.

"You were lucky. Just like how you were lucky nothing happened when you got into a car with a total stranger and drove across a state border." Her words pierce my chest.

It feels like there's an iceberg between us, even though we're both on fire. How is that possible? What is happening to our friendship?

I'm trying hard not to cry. "I can't believe you're acting like this right now. What the crap, Chloe?"

"I care about you."

"You're guilt-tripping me."

"I just want you to be safe."

"You want to yell at me."

"I'm not yelling!" Chloe shouts at full volume, and then she takes a breath. "You don't see the signs, but I do. I've been your best friend for years. Ignoring me? Being impulsive? Throwing all your attention into one new interest? These are signs."

"Signs of what?" I ask testily.

"The high before the crash."

Out of all the words she's spoken, these are the ones that hurt the most.

Because I thought Chloe knew me better than this. I thought she *trusted* me more than this.

But here she is, trying to psychoanalyze me. She thinks she knows what I'm feeling better than I do because of what happened in November.

Just because I needed a little extra help once doesn't mean I'll need help forever.

And why do people keep *assuming* I need their help rather than asking if I even *want* it?

"I'm done talking about this," I say, the flames heavy in my voice.

Flames she's too afraid to touch.

"Okay," she says softly, her own fire withdrawing. "Can you at least try not to be mad at me? Friends are supposed to tell each other the truth."

I dig my fingernails into my palm. "The truth is, you're making me feel bad about the first thing that's made me happy in a really long time."

"I don't want you to feel bad."

"You just want me to be safe," I say dryly.

"I know you're being sarcastic, but it's true."

I shake my head. "I have to go."

"Okay," she says.

I tap the screen, and the second her name disappears, something changes. By the time I reach my trailer, most of the heat has left my face.

I want to be angry at her. Because she's wrong, and I don't deserve the way she's treating me. Like *I've* done something wrong. Like what I'm doing is wrong.

But in the quiet, when I can't hear the hurt in her voice, my anger feels like a kindling burdened by rain, too damp to catch fire.

Burdened by the things Chloe said—the parts that might even be true.

Because I *do* forget about her when I'm busy. Not on purpose, but it happens. I get so caught up in the frenzy of whatever I'm focused on that texting my best friend just takes a back seat.

The worst thing about people being a little bit right is that sometimes when you tug that one tiny thread, what starts to unravel looks a whole lot like more truths.

But right now, there's too much going on. I don't have the emotional resilience to unpack whatever it is Chloe is trying to tell me.

Some truths are better left tangled and distorted.

Because if I can't see them clearly, I can pretend that none of them really exist at all.

CHAPTER TWENTY-SIX

ivien's shriek sends an ache through my ears. When I spin around, I see her and Dexi in the doorway, clouded in smoke.

I wave the dishcloth at the air frantically, trying to push some of the clouds from the room. "I'm sorry—it was an accident."

"What is that smell?" Dexi presses the back of her hand to her mouth and coughs, waving her other hand in the air and running to the back of the trailer to throw open the rest of the windows.

Vivien peers into the kitchen sink, where a tray of burnt food sits abandoned, too ambiguously charred for her to make out. "Is it dead?" she asks with widened eyes and a goofy smile on her face.

I'm still waving smoke through the open doorway. "I was trying to make you guys brownies." Embarrassment washes over me.

Dexi appears with a towel and tries to coax the smoke toward the windows. "Are you sure? Because it kind of looks like you were trying to burn the trailer down."

Vivien glances nervously at the microwave. "Did you remember to turn it off grill mode?"

"What the heck is grill mode?" I ask like I'm in pain.

Dexi shakes her head. Vivien stifles a giggle.

"Come on," Vivien says. "We'll leave the door open and wait for the smoke to clear."

The three of us plant ourselves in the grass out front. Every single person who walks past us freezes in concern when they see our trailer, which makes sense, being as it looks like a giant fog machine on wheels. But then they spot me, wedged between Dexi and Vivien, a look of deep remorse plastered on my face. It's enough to make their concern fade.

"You know they make brownies at the Lunch Box, right?" Dexi eyes me suspiciously.

"I know," I say. "But I wanted to make them myself. It was supposed to be like a thank-you present. You know—for being so nice to me."

I was trying to make an effort. I wanted to prove I wasn't a terrible friend.

Vivien wraps her arm around my shoulder and squeezes. "Aww, Harley!" She pauses. "Maybe just a good old-fashioned card next time, though, huh?"

Dexi snorts. "Or some new batteries for the smoke detector."

Vivien nods. "Yeah. We really need to get that fixed."

I fold my arms over my knees and hide my face. I feel like I'm ruining everything. I'm a bad friend when I don't make an effort, and I make things worse when I try too hard.

How do people find a balance?

Is it this hard for other people to maintain basic friendships?

"We were only kidding," Vivien says gently. "It's really not that big of a deal."

Dexi nudges me with her shoulder. "Yeah. I like you even better now that I know you're a low-key pyromaniac."

I lift my head and scrunch my face at the sunlight. I start to speak, but my eyes snap toward the nearby crew members pointing and whispering like we're exotic fish in an aquarium.

"Move along," Dexi barks protectively.

"What happened?" one of them calls back anyway.

"We're steam-cleaning, obviously!" Vivien shouts.

The crew members look at each other and shrug before walking away.

Vivien rolls her eyes. "So nosy." She looks at me and grins. "You were saying?"

My smile feels heavy. "I wanted a fresh start because I felt like my parents weren't being supportive, but now that I'm here—I don't know. It feels like I can't start over, because everyone else is still holding on to the past. And I just want to move on and be happy." I shake my head. "I don't know why that's so hard for everyone else to see."

Vivien and Dexi exchange glances.

"This is about more than friendship brownies, isn't it?" Vivien asks.

I laugh. "I guess I'm tired. I feel like whenever I'm trying really hard at something, nobody ever notices. They just point out all the things they think I'm not trying hard *enough* at. It makes me feel like I can never do enough to make everyone happy." I tap my fingers against my knee. "Also, I think sometimes I can be a really crappy friend when I don't mean to be."

Vivien shrugs, tucking her dark curls behind her ear. "Maybe what you think is being a crappy friend is just you outgrowing a friendship. Sometimes that happens, and it's nobody's fault."

I think about Chloe. It's always been the two of us, for as long as I can remember. I never imagined a day when we'd stop being friends. I didn't think we'd ever grow apart.

"Is it still outgrowing each other if neither of us wants to stop being friends?" I ask.

"All relationships take work—even the non-romantic ones," Vivien offers.

Dexi flicks the grass with a slender finger, her nails painted the color of black cherries. "But at the same time, if someone is making you feel bad about yourself . . . Well, there's a difference between a friend who is just being honest with you and one that's negatively affecting you. If you're spending more time arguing than just being friends, then I think that's usually a pretty good sign that a relationship is less than healthy."

"Unless you both *like* arguing," Vivien notes. And when Dexi makes a face at her, she adds, "What? Everyone is different, right? You just have to make sure you're both on the same page. That you're both okay with the terms of the friendship."

I nod. "That makes sense."

"If it makes you feel better, lots of people notice how hard you try," Vivien says with a smile.

I sigh, letting my knees drop to the grass. "It still doesn't make anybody want to be my friend."

"Oh, come on," Dexi says. "Even you must've noticed it's not as bad as it was when you first got here."

I'm trying to think of the last time someone ignored me, or pretended they couldn't see me, or ran in the opposite direction when they saw me approaching.

And the truth is, I can't remember when it was.

I've been so busy training and worrying about my parents and Chloe that I hadn't noticed there was a change.

Slowly, without even realizing it, I stopped being the new girl.

I notice his leather boots first, and when I look up at Vas—dressed in gray and black even though it's September in Arkansas—he's peering down at us like we're the neighborhood kids who've egged his car.

"Is everyone okay?" His voice scratches like sandpaper.

Vivien flashes her teeth and points her thumb in the air. "All good here. Harley was trying to cremate some brownies, that's all."

Vas's green eyes fall on me. "Was there a fire?"

It takes me a second to remember myself. "No," I say finally, shaking my head to be clear. "Just a lot of smoke."

"I didn't hear the alarm go off," he says, and I realize that what sounds like stiffness is actually concern.

"The batteries died in our smoke detector," Vivien says with a sigh.

Vas frowns. "Do you have any spares?"

"Nope," Dexi says, squinting from the sunlight. "They've been dead since the last time we almost had a fire and you lectured us about the importance of fire safety."

"So you haven't had batteries for seven months?" he asks, lifting his brow.

Dexi clicks her tongue. "Correct."

Vas shakes his head and walks back to his trailer without another word, returning with a box of AA batteries and a scowl on his face. He disappears into our trailer, and a few minutes later the alarm sounds for a brief second. When he steps back onto the grass, he's holding an empty box.

"Thanks, Vas. You're the best," Vivien says in a singsong voice.

"The best," Dexi repeats.

Vas clenches his jaw, shakes his head, and wanders off without a word.

Vivien and Dexi laugh beside me, but all I can think is how even if the rest of the circus has started to look at me differently, there's one person who has been the exact same since day one.

And even though I shouldn't care what a boy thinks—especially when I have a trillion other things going on—the thought of Vas truly seeing me sends sparks through my bloodstream.

Shreveport, Louisiana

October—Week 7

CHAPTER TWENTY-SEVEN

I have vegetable korma, rice, and peshwari naan for lunch, along with an enormous glass of water. People always talk about drinking eight glasses a day, but I think I'm the only person I know who actually does it. Because if I don't hydrate, I'll wake up in the middle of the night with the most painful leg cramps in the history of the universe. Seriously, Wolverine probably went through less pain when they bonded his bones with adamantium.

Dexi told me bananas help too, so now I eat one first thing every morning. The Lunch Box has a whole crate of them that never seems to run out.

Vivien plucks at her own meal—boiled rice with grilled chicken, steamed spinach, and carrots. "I think my favorite things in the South are deep-fried Oreos."

Dexi pretends to gag, and I scrunch my nose.

"Gross," we both say.

Vivien narrows her eyes at us. "I bet neither of you have even tried it."

"I don't need to, the same way I have no interest in tasting cyanide." Dexi blows gently at her ginger tea, scattering the rising heat. "You don't have to try something to know you don't like it."

"I thoroughly disagree," Jin scoffs, falling into the empty space beside Dexi. His bowl of curry lands with a thud on the table. "I try everything once. Some things twice. And some things I know I don't like, but I try them again anyway because who says you can't change your mind?"

"I swear to God, if you're talking about sex—" Vivien is already rolling her eyes and she hasn't even finished her sentence.

"I'm talking about food, you perv," Jin corrects. "Though, to be clear, it works in any scenario."

I laugh before realizing how strange it is for Jin to be sitting here of his own accord. Normally I'm like a social land mine—wherever I am, nobody will be.

"What, did your latest hookup end in disaster, or is there a *more* garbage reason as to why you're sitting with us again?" Dexi challenges. I guess I'm not the only one who thinks it's weird.

"Yeah, traitor," Vivien barks. "Doesn't Maggie have you under strict orders not to associate with us as long as we're friends with Harley?"

My skin prickles. It's the first time any of them have said out loud what I've known all this time. That Maggie wasn't just trying to turn people against me—she was straight up telling people they weren't allowed to talk to me.

Because she wanted me to feel isolated.

Jin laughs easily, like he's incapable of feeling cornered. "Maggie's had her fun for long enough. Besides, I don't take orders from her." He looks at me seriously. "It wasn't personal. Some of us just don't like to get too attached to the feeder fish."

I frown, but Vivien leans in with an explanation. "He's talking about the people who turn up thinking the circus is going to be some kind of magical party, and then get eaten alive by reality a few weeks later."

"In other words, he's being rude." Dexi scowls.

"No," Jin says. "I'm being honest. Are you two seriously going to tell me Harley didn't scream of wide-eyed naivete when she first turned up?" He flattens a hand on the table. "But everyone gets things wrong sometimes, and in this case, I was very wrong. I'm sorry for assuming you didn't have it in you." His words morph into laughter. "I hear you've been training every night in the big top. Sometimes until almost midnight. You're a fighter, which is a good thing to be around here."

My stomach twists up and over and under, like taffy being pulled apart and pushed together again. "Did Vas tell you that?" For weeks it's felt like our untouchable secret. I'm not sure I like our late-night rehearsals being common knowledge.

"Vas? Not a chance. I've known that guy for years, and believe me when I say he has as many secrets as a cat has lives." Jin shovels a bite of food into his mouth.

"So he has nine secrets? That's . . . oddly specific," Dexi says blankly. When Jin looks confused, she sighs. "Never mind."

Jin shakes his head while he chews, looking at me. "No, I heard it from the many little birds who've seen you walking from the big top to your trailer at all hours of the night."

"Wait"—Vivien stiffens, hazel eyes pinned to mine—"are you and Vas hooking up?"

My cheeks blossom carnation-pink at the suggestion, words wanting to come out in rapid fire but getting all mixed up on the tip of my tongue.

It's not true. Of course it's not true.

So why is it so hard for me to say the words?

Jin's laugh breaks apart my tangled thoughts like a sword slashing through a web of vines. "The only thing he's in love with is his violin." He leans into Dexi. "And I know you're about to make a joke about him not being interested in me, and me being bitter, but I'm telling you—he spends all of his time with his music. And I've seen plenty of girls try to flirt with him over the years, and they don't have any more luck than I do."

"He's right," I say, the words almost tart. "There's nothing going on between me and Vas. We spend the entire time practicing, separately. We don't say a word to each other." When everyone makes a face like they don't believe me, I add, "I'm serious. He says he doesn't like small talk."

Dexi laughs in disbelief. Jin looks sideways, like he's saying, *I told you so.*

Vivien frowns, leaning her brown cheek onto her palm the way Popo always urged me not to. Not that Vivien needs to worry. Her complexion is *flawless*. It's kind of unfair. "If you needed someone to train with, why didn't you ask one of us?" She motions between her and Dexi.

I shrug. "I didn't want to bother you. I mean, you were the only two people who would talk to me. The last thing I wanted to do was make you feel like I was using you for something."

"That's very noble," Jin says, swallowing another mouthful of curry.

"It's the Hufflepuff," Vivien whispers, winking at me.

Dexi raises a brow, her lip quirking up like she's almost smiling. "You keep doing what you're doing, and the rest of the troupe will come around. You'll see."

Vivien nods enthusiastically.

And I want to believe them, because belonging is so very important to me, but I also know they're wrong. Because "the rest of the troupe" means everyone. Even Maggie.

I'm not sure there's anything I can do to make Maggie like me. And after the welcome she gave me over the last few weeks, I'm not sure I want her to, anyway.

But everyone else?

Maybe there's something there worth hoping for.

To: FlightOfTheRedPanda@gmail.com
From: Delilah.Milano@teatrodellanotte.com
Subject: The time you spent a night away

    You were seven. Your dad and I were so busy with the company that we were worried you'd start to feel neglected. We thought you were old enough to spend a weekend at Popo's house without us. We thought it might feel like an adventure. But you cried from the moment we put our shoes on and stepped out the door, and you didn't stop for hours. I think that was frustrating for Popo—not being able to calm you down. Having to admit defeat.

We picked you up the next morning and brought you to work with us. And that's when I realized you weren't upset about being away from your dad and me—you were upset that you were missing rehearsals. You spent the whole day in the skyrise, watching the flyers and the aerialists, and you had this look on your face that I'll never forget. It was like you were glowing.

I knew then how much you loved the circus. I've always known. And I'm not trying to dim your glow, Harley. In my own way, I'm trying to protect it.

I know you don't always trust me. And I know I don't always do the right thing. But to me, you're still that seven-year-old girl in the skyrise. A little light so desperate to shine.

But I know you better than you think I do. You burn fast and bright, and then you burn out.

And the last thing I want is for you to burn out. Not again.

I hope you're taking care of yourself. I hope you'd call me if you weren't.

Love, Mom

Not again.

Why can't anyone see this is nothing like November?

I'm happy. I'm trying to be happy.

Maybe Chloe is only *half* right about me ignoring the people I care about when I get busy. Maybe I just don't want to keep in touch with people who don't understand what I'm trying to do.

Because *I'm trying*. Here, at Maison du Mystère.

If they don't want to understand that, then maybe it's not that I'm burning out—maybe I'm burning fast and bright and *away*.

Maybe the dark space they think is me is the dark space I left behind.

Someday I'll prove it to them. I'll show them they're wrong about what this is—that the circus isn't a phase I'm going to tire of eventually. That I'm not here because I can't control my excitement.

I'm not in any danger.

And if Mom would only listen, she'd understand that the more she pushes—the more everyone pushes—the more it makes me certain that I can never go home again.

CHAPTER TWENTY-EIGHT

I'm more nervous than I want to be, and it feels ridiculous. I've been training in the same room as Vas for weeks. What makes tonight any different?

I wonder if it's because of what Jin said earlier—about Vas not loving anyone but his violin. And I'm not silly enough to think Vas loves me, but sometimes he looks at me when he's between songs, and it feels . . . like there might be something there other than indifference.

The problem is that I can't tell if the *something* is good or bad. He could be starting to like me, or he could equally loathe me. Maybe he shows up every night because he wants to, or maybe it's because he thinks I'm a sad stray puppy he's throwing a bone to but also secretly wishes would get picked up by animal control so it could be someone else's problem.

Tonight, I'll pay more attention. I'll look for signs—even the ones he thinks he's good at hiding. Because the last thing I want is to assume we're friends only to get rejected. I'm barely holding my heart together as it is.

But when I see the twinkling lights scaling down the big top and step through the parted curtains, I hear nothing but my padded footsteps on the carpet, and my breathing echoing into the open chamber.

Vas isn't here.

He might be late, or sick, or tired, but my mind immediately thinks the worst.

I worry he's not here because he finally got tired of *me*.

I spend the next hour doing floor exercises and core work, trying not to think about Vas's reason for not being here, or how bummed I am that I'm not on the trapeze, or how maybe Vas found out everyone knew about our rehearsals and now he's embarrassed people might assume we're friends. Or *hooking up*, as Vivien put it.

It's the last thought that mortifies me.

On my way back to the trailer, I see him walking toward me with a heaviness creased between his brows.

"Hey," he says carefully, his green eyes darkened to gray.

"Hey." I try to match his tone, but my nerves cause my voice to crack.

Great. This is going super well already.

"I was on my way to find you. Thought you might still be practicing," Vas says, shifting his weight from one leg to the other. I notice the absence of a violin case in his hands. "I'm sorry I wasn't there tonight, but something came up."

"It's fine," I say, trying to sound like I had never been disappointed to begin with.

He hesitates, and there's a hardness in his jaw that I'm sure is anger.

"Is everything okay?" I ask, not sure if we know each other well enough to talk about feelings.

He fiddles with the rolled-up material of his sleeves, pushing them back over his elbows, and crosses his bare forearms over his chest. "I had a meeting with Simon that didn't go very well." He inhales deeply, and I realize he's about to tell me more.

My stomach flutters. Maybe I'm *not* just a stranger who takes up half the room during his rehearsals. Maybe he sees me as a genuine friend. Someone he can talk to. Someone he *wants* to talk to.

"I asked Simon for another shot at composing a new set list for next season, and he promised he'd give it a listen. I was sure I'd done enough—sure that he'd prefer original music to the knock-off tracks he asked for." He shakes his head angrily, and I still my face to hide my emotions. "He called me in to tell me his decision. It seems he's going with the music he . . . acquired."

"I'm sorry." My voice is tiny. Minuscule.

He looks flustered, his eyes avoiding mine. "I have to rework everything, put together every new track. It's going to take me weeks." He pauses, his gaze finally finding mine. I can't look away. There's Vas and nothing else, like he's a single lantern in the dark.

Does he know what I did? Does he blame me?

I feel so horribly guilty, and it bubbles up inside me and makes my stomach churn. I know how badly I've betrayed my parents, but I haven't had to see their faces yet. Seeing how hurt Vas is and knowing it's my fault?

I wish I were the kind of person who didn't care, who could convince myself my ambition was worth any casualties, accidental or otherwise.

But I'm not that person. I do care. More than I want to admit.

I open my mouth to apologize, to tell Vas I didn't mean to keep him from composing, but he's talking before I can find the words.

"I won't have time to be your spotter anymore." His voice is final. Hollow. An echo bouncing through a rocky canyon.

"Oh."

What else is there to say?

He runs a hand through his hair, shoving it to the side roughly the way he does in between every piece he plays on the violin. It makes me follow his fingers, and the way they glide through his honey-colored hair. I picture them dancing across the strings, clinging to his bow as it flies up and down like a boat being rocked by mountainous waves.

And in that moment, I'm not thinking about how hard it will be to train without him. I'm thinking about how much I'll miss his music.

"Maybe you could write something else? Ask him for one more chance?" I offer.

He pulls his face back barely an inch, his eyes flitting back and forth like I've caught him off guard. And then they harden.

"Simon only makes offers once. He doesn't give second chances. Anyone who joins Maison du Mystère learns that pretty quickly."

My mind flashes to the deal I made with Simon. There was no room for interpretation, no second chance, no time to even think.

But Vas's expression is so severe, I don't think empathy is what he's mulling over.

I think it's judgment.

Because it was me who stole Dad's set list. It was me who made it so Vas couldn't compose his own music. And it's me who is getting in the way of Vas's dreams, the way Mom and Dad always got in the way of mine.

And I can see it in his eyes—he knows all of this too.

"I know it's an inconvenience, but you really don't need to look so worried. I'm sure you can ask someone else to spot you in the evenings." Vas kicks his foot at the dirt. "It's the circus, after all. We're all easily replaced."

He turns, marching back to his trailer, and I'm desperately trying to connect dots I don't fully understand. He thinks I'm disappointed that he won't be there to help me. And I know maybe sometimes I'm selfish, but I'm not heartless.

But how do I correct him? How do I fix something I helped break?

I'm not Mom. I don't know how to make things better.

I only know how to make them worse.

CHAPTER TWENTY-NINE

It's only been two days since Vas told me we wouldn't be practicing in the big top anymore, but it feels like it's been weeks. I find myself distracted by shadows and anyone with a leather jacket, wondering when I'll see him again, and if I'll know the right thing to say to explain that I felt bad about what *he* lost that night, not what I lost.

I know he's around because his bike is still parked alongside his trailer, but he's either purposely avoiding me or too busy computerizing Dad's set list to make an appearance.

I hate that I have to add his name to the list of people I've wronged. It was never my intention to hurt anyone—but then Tatya happened, and ever since then it's felt like a ping-pong game of hurt, back and forth and back and forth, between me and the rest of the world.

Mom and Dad. Chloe. Maggie, in her own way. Vas.

I still feel hurt too, though the more days that pass, the less I'm sure I have as much right to be hurt as I did when I first saw the photo of Mom.

Things are . . . fuzzy. My feelings are fuzzy.

And since I can't understand them, I'm choosing to ignore them.

Vivien and Dexi went for an early breakfast in town with some of the other performers. It's normal for everyone to spend at least one day a week seeing a bit of the local area.

It's also normal for nobody to invite me. I'm sure there are probably a few reasons, all ranging from "she stole a set list from another circus" to "we just don't like her," but the most obvious is that Maggie is a permanent fixture in their group. Even if Vivien and Dexi *wanted* to invite me, I have no doubt Maggie would veto the crap out of even the suggestion. And everyone else would probably let her.

Jin might be talking to me, but to the rest of the circus, I still have a long way to go before I'm accepted.

I head to the big top after breakfast. It's the only window of opportunity I have to train on Sundays because there's a matinee performance shortly after lunch, followed by load-out. And I don't want to miss even a day of training, especially now that I'm back to doing floor exercises. I know I could ask Vivien or Dexi to help, but I can't bring myself to cash in a favor—especially when neither of them technically *offered*. They just asked why *I* hadn't asked, which is not the same thing.

I'm surprised to find the Terzi Brothers when I venture inside, standing across from each other and juggling so many colorful pins between them, it's hard to count them all. Galip is older than Emin, but only by a year. Dexi mentioned it weeks ago when I asked if they were twins. Their faces are so similar, with thin, dark eyebrows and chiseled noses. But while Galip sports a mustache and short hair, Emin is clean-shaven with his hair in boyish curls.

Galip sees me first, and he makes a guttural noise to his brother. Within a few seconds, they catch pin after pin until every object is locked in their fingers like claws.

"Can I help you?" Emin asks with a thick accent, his bare arms glistening with sweat.

"I didn't realize anyone was in here," I say quickly, taking a step back toward the door.

Galip holds up a fistful of pins. "Want to join us?"

My feet lock into place. I blame the shock of actually being invited to something that doesn't involve scraping gum off the stands. "I don't know how to juggle," I admit.

Emin flashes a wide smile, eyes creasing. "We can help with that."

I make a move toward the center of the ring, my heart doing tiny little flips like a nervous tadpole.

"It's good to pick up an extra skill or two in the circus. You never know when someone might need you to stand in, you know?" Galip nods toward his brother. "When we were younger, we used to help our parents take care of the elephants at one of the old forgotten circuses. And we picked up juggling in our free time, usually in the evenings when everyone else was busy performing. One day there was an accident, and one of the jugglers was injured. They asked us to step in while he recovered, and we've been working in circuses ever since."

He passes me two of the pins, motioning for me to copy his movements.

I can't stop my eyes from drifting up toward the static trapeze high above us. "It's different for me. I came here because I already have a dream of being a trapeze artist. The two of you are incredible at what you do, but juggling isn't my dream."

Emin nods, the pins twirling and spinning like he's created a Ferris wheel from his own hands. "You want a place on the trapeze, but someone is sitting there already. It won't do you any good to stand around waiting for your moment. Carve a new place for yourself—make a name for yourself, so the circus will know you're worthy. Otherwise all you are is someone watching from the sidelines."

I spin one of the pins, and it topples from my hands to the floor.

Galip laughs and pats my shoulder. "I'm sure you don't need to worry about anyone forcing you to be a juggler if you don't want to be one. But, maybe if you practice, you might get a chance at performing sometime. It's better than watching, isn't it?"

I nod, scooping the pin back up and trying again. They slip in my hands, unable to go in the directions I want them to, but I keep trying, again and again.

Maybe that's the lesson I need to learn. Not to give up, but not to be too set on my dream, either.

Maybe I need to be flexible, so that I can find a detour that will lead to the trapeze, despite the many roadblocks that stand in my way.

The Terzi Brothers teach me their tricks until just before lunch when our stomachs start to grumble. I'm able to juggle three pins without a single one of them hitting the floor, and it feels like such a massive accomplishment, I can hardly stop smiling.

CHAPTER THIRTY

We're in the truck driving toward the Louisiana state border when Vivien looks over her shoulder. "I hear the Terzi Brothers were keeping you busy today."

I lean my head back, thinking of how nice it was to feel like someone actually wanted to teach me something for a change. "It was fun. And they were really patient with me, even though I clearly sucked at juggling."

Dexi taps her finger against the wheel. "Must be a drastic difference to being around Vas, who looks like he's in physical pain when he has to talk to anyone."

I look out the window and try to focus on something that won't make me emotional.

Vivien laughs, not noticing I've gone quiet. "I once drove all the way from Napa to San Diego with Vas—back when we were both pretty new—and he didn't say a word. Not *one word*. It was so painfully uncomfortable, but when I asked him later why he was so quiet, he said he didn't even realize it. He was just lost in the music."

"Basically what she's saying is don't take it personally if he's quiet. He's quiet with everyone," Dexi says, her eyes glancing at me in the rearview mirror before pinning back onto the road.

I twist my mouth and bite down on the urge to point out that Vas isn't quiet with me—he actively dislikes me. Maybe even hates me, after what stealing my dad's music cost him.

Vivien tells another story about Vas, and mostly I'm trying not to listen because even the sound of his name causes a burn inside my sternum. But then Dexi says something that I can't tune out.

"Simon can be such a jerk. It's so shitty what he did to Vas. And you, too," she says.

"What do you mean?" My voice is metallic, sharp, and defensive.

Vivien turns around, frowning. "You do know nothing stays a secret in the circus, right?"

I cross my arms irritably. "I mean, I knew Vas was mad that Simon is going with the other set list, but I didn't think he'd tell everyone it was my fault. I get that he blames me, but it's not like I meant to hurt him."

"Who said it was your fault?" Vivien's face is scrunched up like she's confused.

"Dexi just said I did something shitty," I point out. "And okay, maybe I did because it was my fault Simon had the other set list in the first place, but I didn't know about the music Vas had written. I didn't even know who Vas *was*."

"No, that's not what I said." Dexi tuts in the mirror. "I meant what *Simon* did was shitty to *you*."

I feel my blood simmering because everything about the situation with Vas is still too raw. "Simon didn't do anything to me. Not directly. He hurt Vas when he turned down his music. And for the record, I really hate that everyone keeps assuming I care more about training than Vas's music. Because it's not true. I don't care that I have to train alone again—I care that I'm responsible for ruining Vas's life."

Vivien holds up her hands, her hazel eyes wide in alarm. "Okay, I think we are all getting our wires crossed here. First of all, nobody said you ruined Vas's life."

Dexi raises a finger from the wheel. "I definitely did not say that."

"And secondly," Vivien continues, "Simon never turned Vas's music down. Quite the opposite, in fact. He told Vas he could write new music for the entire next season."

Confusion swarms me, pulling my thoughts in conflicting directions.

"Vas turned down the offer," Dexi adds, like this is supposed to clarify things. Except it only makes it worse.

My head feels like it's spinning. "That's not true. Vas told me—" I start, but I can't find the words. Because maybe it is true. Maybe Vas lied to me. "I don't understand. Why would Vas turn down his own music?"

They look at each other for a brief moment, and the realization that there is so much more to this story makes me feel microscopic.

"Simon said if they used Vas's music, then there'd be no reason to keep you here." Vivien looks at me, her face full of warmth even though her words are cold. "Vas didn't want to be the reason you got sent home, so he agreed to set his music aside."

Vas helped me?

I blink. "I . . . didn't know that."

I also didn't know Simon had considered sending me home—or that it was even an option. I guess I was so sure I was here for the long term that it never occurred to me that our arrangement could be broken. I mean, it *should've* occurred to me. Nothing lasts forever.

Besides, it's not like we signed a contract.

The coil of embarrassment wraps itself around me. And guilt, too, that Vas gave up something so important to keep me around. Because I'm suddenly very aware there's a countdown on my time here. How long will it be before the next time Simon thinks of a loophole to get rid of me? He might not even *need* a loophole. It's not like we talked about the broader terms of our arrangement—specifically, how long I get to stay.

Vas will have thrown away his chance for nothing. Wasted on a girl naive enough to believe a handshake was going to bind an agreement built on deceit.

He shouldn't have done it. Not for me.

I don't deserve his kindness, and I don't think I can repay it.

I might not be here long enough to even try.

New Orleans, Louisiana
October—Week 8

CHAPTER THIRTY-ONE

*L*oad-in finishes on Monday evening. I pull a thin sweater over my head because it's a touch chilly, when someone knocks on the door.

I can't explain why I think it might be Vas, or the disappointment that follows when I realize it's not.

Vivien's smile is wild. "Want to come into town with us? We're grabbing dinner at the Fire House."

"Dinner?" I look toward the people gathering in the open space behind her, all dressed for going out. I see Dexi, the Terzi Brothers, Jin, Sasha, and the contortionist sisters from Zimbabwe, Danai and Aneni.

Vas isn't there, but I'm not surprised. He might be the reason I'm still here, but that doesn't mean he's happy about it. Guilt can do funny things to a person, like when you feel obligated to offer the last piece of cake to someone and then they accept it and you spend the rest of the day quietly irritated because deep down you didn't want to share in the first place.

And Vas often looks irritated.

When Maggie turns up in her white shorts and red leather jacket, I'm sure I'm not understanding correctly. Maybe this is less a group thing, and more of a roommate one.

"Dinner with who?" I ask carefully.

Vivien motions all around her like it encompasses everyone. "With all of us, of course."

"You say that like Maggie isn't standing right behind you," I hiss. "Are you sure that's okay?"

Dexi pushes past both of us, reaches inside the room, and grabs my bag from the hook. "It's a troupe outing, and you're part of the troupe," she says, thrusting it toward my chest.

I feel the flutter of a thousand hummingbirds inside me.

We pile into two cars, with me, Dexi, and Jin in one of the back seats, all cramped together without any elbow room.

I don't stop smiling for the entire twenty-two minutes it takes to drive into the city.

We park the car in one of the multistory garages and set off on foot through the French Quarter. I don't think I've ever been to a city with so many distinct smells—smells that change in a matter of footsteps, depending on what restaurants or street corners you're closest to. It's a mixture of sautéed vegetables, dark coffee beans, fried shrimp, fragrant jasmine—at one point I can even smell fresh bread. There's also the smell of cigarettes, cheap booze, and urine, which seems to grow stronger near Bourbon Street.

I'm enamored by the street art and brass bands and hidden

courtyards, and when we get to the restaurant, I feel like we've barely seen a fraction of the city's rich culture.

The Fire House turns out to be an actual firehouse—or at least it was, at some point in time. It's clear there used to be three garage doors, but the two on the sides have been replaced with big glass windows, and the one in the center is now a metal door with the words THE FIRE HOUSE spray-painted on the front in white. The rest of the building is faded red brick, wedged between a bar and a small café that resembles a dollhouse.

When we get inside, a doorman asks to see our IDs. Everyone who is twenty-one or over gets a stamp on the back of their hand—which basically only leaves me, Dexi, Vivien, and Maggie.

"Aw, you guys are such babies," Jin mocks, flicking Vivien's ear. She turns around and pretends to upward-jab him in the stomach, and then he blocks her, thrusts both his wrists forward, and says, "Hadouken!"

I'm laughing so hard, my sides hurt.

Dexi shakes her head. "And *we're* the babies?"

When I look over at Maggie, I realize there's an actual smile twitching at the corner of her mouth. And not a condescending one—a *real* one.

But then she turns, following after Sasha and the others toward the stage at the back of the building, and maybe that's all I'll ever get from Maggie. Glimpses of who she is that are never meant for me.

After everything, I think I'm okay with that.

The host seats us in one of the large private booths in the

corner, and the way Sasha is talking to him makes me think they've been here before.

I look through the menu, my skin buzzing as I listen to everyone talk about their lives and inside jokes and behind-the-scenes stories. Hearing them describe the world of the circus captivates me.

When Mom and Dad discuss Teatro della Notte, it's always about numbers and contracts and policies. To them, the circus is a machine with pieces that need to be perfectly right. And I'm sure that part is important, but it's not how I look at the circus. It's not how the people *here* are describing the circus.

I think the circus is less a machine and more like those hypnotic YouTube videos of people mixing paint together. It's never exactly the same as the time before, and the possibilities are quite literally infinite.

It's a world of color and emotion and constant change.

Being here with them makes me feel like I'm a small part of that world. Like maybe the colors I am—the ones that never fit anywhere else—aren't so unusual here.

At some point a woman makes her way to our table and gives Sasha a warm hug, and I find out she used to be one of the acrobats at Maison du Mystère before she decided to retire at the ripe old age of thirty-two.

And when I look around at the restaurant, at the pianist onstage playing earthy jazz and singing with a gravelly voice, I think about what Mom and Dad once told me—about needing a backup plan.

And the more I think about it, the more frustrated I get by the entire concept of a backup plan. Because it only ever seems to pertain to people who are interested in art, music, theater—and yes, the circus. Nobody would ever *dream* of going up to someone in medical school and telling them, "Gee, I really think you should have a backup plan. You know, *just in case this doesn't work out for you.*"

I realize the end payoff of becoming a doctor might be more financially viable than an aerialist, but money isn't everything. Not to me, at least. Besides, formulating a backup plan takes time, energy, and money—all of which could be used on the *original* plan.

I think telling someone to have a backup plan is just an attempt at shaming someone for their life choices while also trying to appear well-meaning.

I don't want a backup plan.

I want *this*.

When our food arrives, the musician trades places with someone else. It takes me a moment to recognize him—maybe because I've spent so long looking for his face in the crowd that seeing it here doesn't make sense—but when I see his thick hair pushed to the side and the dip of his eyebrows as he rolls up his shirtsleeves, I feel my heart pound.

Vivien cups her hands around her mouth and lets out a cheer. When the others turn, they all clap and call his name.

And even though it's impossible that Vas doesn't hear them, his face doesn't change even a little bit. He sits down at the piano, brings his fingers to the keys, and starts to play the opening to "Goodbye Yellow Brick Road." Except Vas doesn't play it the way it's written—there's a haunted quality to it, like he's rewritten it in his own style.

It's the same way he plays the violin.

When his voice croons through the microphone, every inch of me comes to life.

I can't take my eyes off him.

I almost forget where I am completely, until Dexi bumps her shoulder against mine and motions to the bread basket, implying she wants to know if I want the last piece.

I shake my head quickly. "You can have it," I say breathily.

She makes a face and a small grin builds in the corner of her dimpled cheek, but she doesn't say a word.

Vas plays cover after cover, all of them so beautifully morphed with his own personality. Mysterious, atmospheric, and full of longing.

It's hard to remember to eat, but I try anyway.

Jin offers to buy everyone a round of drinks, and when he does, I realize half our table is now dotted around the bar socializing with strangers. Even Maggie is up there, cradling a glass of water in her hand and chatting with Sasha.

When the song ends, Vas seems to look out at the audience for the first time. His gaze is aimless, like fingers brushing over grass. But then our eyes meet, and his entire body stiffens.

Heat rises through me, building in my chest and shooting out in every direction.

I tell myself to look away—order myself to stop staring—but I can't. I'm transfixed.

And despite everything that's happened in the last few weeks, I see his green eyes soften.

I'm afraid to wonder what it means.

The next notes make everything in the room disappear except Vas and the piano. I'm no longer in a restaurant—I'm somewhere in a distant galaxy, floating to the sound of his soul.

A dark, raspy version of "Lucy in the Sky with Diamonds."

And when he hits the high notes of the melody—when his voice fills the room like the aurora borealis in the night sky—I burst into stardust.

CHAPTER THIRTY-TWO

*V*as spends the entire night with Maggie and Sasha at the bar. He doesn't know what his voice did to me, and *good*, because I never want him to find out.

But staying near Maggie—that part feels intentional. Because wherever Maggie is, I know I'm not supposed to be.

After an hour of watching them deep in conversation, boxed in by Jin and Galip flirting hard with a couple strangers, I feel silly for even imagining he might've been singing to me.

At some point the venue seems to transform from restaurant into nightclub, and the line at the bar becomes a full-blown crowd. Galip's new friendship has already fizzled out, but Jin has his arm wrapped around a woman with ridiculously long legs and perfect makeup. Dexi's been bored for at least the last hour, and eventually everyone is rounded up together and in agreement to head back to the campsite.

Outside, everyone starts to pile back into the cars until I'm all that's left on the sidewalk, staring awkwardly as Jin, in his half-drunken stupor, realizes his date has taken my seat.

He starts to get back out of the car. "My bad, Harley. We can call a cab."

"No," I say, desperate not to screw up my first night out with the troupe. "I don't mind waiting for a taxi."

Jin's waving his hand furiously, his feet clumsily hitting the sidewalk. "There's no way I'm letting you wait here all alone. Me and Charley will be right behind you." Charley smiles behind him, unable to get out of the car because Jin is still blocking the way.

"That's not necessary," Vas's voice sounds from behind me. When I turn around, I see he's thrown his black leather jacket over his dress shirt. There's a helmet under his arm, and another smaller one held out toward me.

My stomach flutters.

He's offering me a ride. On the back of his bike.

My brain is malfunctioning, like someone on *Mario Kart* has set off too many green shells and banana peels and I'm struggling to make sense of what's happening.

I glance at the car and see Vivien practically beaming from the driver's seat. "Jin, get back in the car," she orders.

"But I really don't mind—" Jin slurs.

"Now," Vivien barks, and I see Dexi reach across Charley's lap and yank Jin backward until he topples onto them both. "See you back at the trailer," Vivien sings, and the car peels away in the direction Sasha and the others already left in.

I turn back to Vas, the helmet still in his outstretched hand.

"Is it safe?" I ask.

215

His frown deepens. "I wouldn't offer you a ride home if I wasn't absolutely positive I could get you there safely."

"Sorry. I wasn't trying to offend you."

"You didn't."

"I really don't mind taking a taxi."

"Would you prefer a taxi?"

"No, I just don't want to bother you."

"The only thing that's bothering me is that my arm is getting tired."

My face flushes.

He hesitates. "That was . . . supposed to be a joke."

I laugh, like I'm not sure *that* was the joke. "Sorry, I couldn't tell. Most people smile when they're joking."

"I—I know. I forget to do that sometimes."

I raise a brow. "You forget to smile?"

Vas shrugs, letting his arm drop to his side. "I get nervous. You didn't smile, so I didn't smile."

"Nervous," I repeat in disbelief.

He nods. "I don't always know what the right thing to say is. I find socializing with strangers difficult sometimes, that's all."

"We're not exactly strangers," I point out quietly.

His green eyes soften, and this time I *do* wonder what it means.

I don't know if it's the aftershocks of hearing him sing, or the buzz of fresh air after being in a dark room for hours, but something makes me less afraid to speak my mind.

Or at least, less afraid to face the consequences of what I'm about to say.

"Vivien told me what you did for me." I ball my fists together and try not to lose my nerve. "Thank you. I know what your music means to you, because I think it's what being an aerialist means to me. But I want you to know I never meant to hurt you, or get in the way of your dreams. I know it seems like I don't care about anything but getting what I want, but it's not true. I wouldn't have made a deal with Simon if I knew it would hurt you."

Vas taps his thumb against the helmet. I think maybe he doesn't believe me.

Maybe because it's a very blurry truth, with too much gray area and uncertainty.

Because hurting someone you don't know—someone without a face or a name or a history—is different from hurting someone you've spent hours with, listening to the cry of their violin and the way their breath catches at the end of a song.

If I could go back in time, I want to believe I'd do things differently. That I wouldn't hurt Vas, or Tatya, or my parents. That I'd find another way.

But then I wouldn't be here.

So how honest am I really being with myself by apologizing in hindsight for a reality I'm probably grateful for?

"I'm sorry," I say, and that part is honest.

Vas's expression remains unchanged as he fiddles with the helmet strap. Finally, he holds it out again. "Can I take you somewhere? It's not far."

Even though there're a million more words I should probably say, I take the helmet because sometimes words just get in the way.

CHAPTER THIRTY-THREE

My arms are wrapped around Vas's chest as he rides along the road, away from the city, the chill of the wind blowing against us. At first, I try to keep my body a polite distance away from his, but every turn and brake forces me closer toward him.

Eventually I stop trying to inch away and relax against his back, hoping he can't feel how fast my heart is racing.

If he asks, I'll blame it on the motorbike.

Every now and then I pick up a scent from his neck—like trees and chocolate, woodsy and warm.

It sets my skin alive like I'm a sparkler on New Year's Eve.

The moment before the fireworks.

Vas maneuvers across the road, turning down a narrow path. The trees zip past us like we're fast-forwarding through time. I'm barely conscious of how dark the sky has gotten, or how the bike's headlights make the road look like a tunnel.

When we reach a small dirt patch at the side of the road, Vas pulls in and kicks the bike stand down. He helps me slide off first, holding my fingers through his gloved hand, and then we dangle our helmets over the handlebars.

Vas's hair is wild, and it makes me laugh thinking that even a helmet couldn't tame the mess on his head. "Was that okay?" he asks, tucking his keys into his jacket pocket.

I nod, fighting the flush I'm sure is all over my body. "Still in one piece, so you're clearly a man of your word."

Unsmiling, he points toward the trees. "It's just a few minutes' walk through there."

The thinning woodland lets a considerable amount of light through the branches, but the path is overgrown with marsh grass and reeds. There are mushrooms tucked away near some of the trees, and a symphony of crickets and wildlife is scattered around us. I try not to think about all the snakes that are probably nearby.

And then we step into a clearing, where the grass fades to dirt and rock and there's an old lighthouse a few feet away, looking worn and forgotten.

"Are we allowed to be here?" I whisper nervously.

Vas pulls the door open, the creak sending an echo through the hollow space. "Probably not, but I didn't see a sign. Besides, it will only take a second."

I'm about to argue that I'm almost positive there's a sign somewhere, and that we probably just didn't notice it because it's dark and everything is overgrown. But Vas seems so determined, that I don't want to be the one to kill the mood.

So I follow him up the stairs until we're both standing at the railing, shadows rippling across the wide body of water below us.

Vas sets his hands on the metal bar, soaking in the glow of the faraway town on the other side of the water. I'm standing beside him, hypersensitive to the curves of his neck and the way his ears are just a little pointy at the tips. And then I see why he brought me here.

The town in the distance isn't a town at all. It's Maison du Mystère, the twinkling lights wound up every tent and the spotlights waving at the entrance sign. And beside it is our campsite, the collection of trailers and motor homes in shades of white, gray, and brown, the massive trucks at the back, the bunkhouses, and even the Lunch Box in all its colorful double-decker glory.

It's a view of the world I love so much, with the clusters of smoky starlight above it. It's a view of the place I so desperately want to feel like home.

I lean forward over the railing, taking in a breath of swampy air, and imagine there's no ground below me. I imagine I'm floating high above Maison du Mystère, like I'm hanging from a static trapeze with silk ropes stretching all the way to the moon and beyond. I imagine I exist among the clouds and stars.

I imagine I live in a world where *I* belong.

Vas's feet shifting on the floor bring me back, reminding me I'm not alone. I turn my head, my face undoubtedly brighter than any of the lights in the distance, and smile.

"This is amazing," I say. "It feels like we're a million miles up in the sky, doesn't it?" I take in the night, enveloping around us like everything above the earth is melting together.

Vas lets his hands drop to his sides, shifting his body toward me so we're facing each other. He studies his feet, and then he lifts his chin up so we're looking into each other's eyes.

His are such a soft green. Too gentle for those harsh eyebrows. But too wild for that warm, chocolaty smell.

Pieces that don't go together.

Like me.

I feel my lips part, wanting words to exist between us. Wanting *something* to exist between us.

Vas's fingers twitch at his hip, longing for something the way he longs for the touch of his violin.

I want to capture that longing, bottle it up, and press it close to my heart.

"I see the way you look at the circus. The way you look when you're rehearsing, and you think nobody is watching. Like this is your only chance, and you're so scared of it slipping through your fingers." He tilts his head, hair falling across his eyes. "I want you to know that you don't owe me an apology. I made a choice because I wanted to. Because I didn't want to be the person who got in your way."

My heart sinks into my stomach like it's a black lagoon. Once again, my ambition is showing.

Vas isn't trying to be cruel—he's stating a fact. But knowing people can see me for what I am—a desperate person who wants to chase her dreams so badly, she isn't even looking ahead to see who's in her way—makes me feel so horribly guilty.

Ashamed, too, because I know what I did to my parents.

That wasn't just ambition. That was betrayal.

Would Vas look at me the same way if he knew I didn't just steal a set list, but I hurt my parents?

I'm too afraid to know the answer. Too ashamed that if I let Vas really see me, I won't be able to pretend that what I did wasn't so bad.

His eyes darken, sensing something has changed between us.

Or maybe I'm being silly to think anything's changed, since that would imply there was something there to begin with.

"Thanks for showing me the view, but if it's okay with you, I'd like to go home," I say.

Home. A word that tastes so much like a lie.

Mobile, Alabama

October—Week 9

CHAPTER THIRTY-FOUR

*M*e: Hey, long time no talk.

Me: Sorry it took me forever to write back. I've been mega busy.

Me: Are you still dating what's-his-face?

Me: Hellooooo are you alive?

Chloe: His name is Jack.

Me: You're there! Success!

Chloe: I've got a lot of homework right now.

Me: Okay, no problem. Talk to you later?

Chloe: Sure.

Maybe I should've just told her I miss my best friend, but I couldn't figure out what words to use.

Our friendship doesn't feel the same way it used to. I'm worried it's my fault.

I guess I can add this to my list of things I keep screwing up.

CHAPTER THIRTY-FIVE

On Wednesday night I head to the big top to train. The Terzi Brothers wave from the Lunch Box as I walk past them. One of the clowns, too. Even Simon gives me a nod from nearby.

Everyone knows where I go at night. And it might not be written on a schedule, but it's still my time. I've spent so many weeks hoping people would carve out a place for me, and it turns out I did it all on my own.

Well, mostly on my own.

Vas's not being here still feels like there's a missing piece—most noticeably because I can't use the static trapeze to practice. But I have other things to work on now too.

The Terzi Brothers gifted me a set of juggling balls to practice with. Dexi has shown me a few new ways to stretch that have already made me feel more limber. And one of the clowns has been giving me lots of advice on stage presence and how to interact with the audience.

I no longer feel like a stranger here. I feel like I'm falling into place.

When I hear movement near the curtain, I look up from my handstand, certain the upside-down figure is going to be Vas with his violin.

Maggie's purple curls make my brain do loop-the-loops, and then I'm right-side up with a look of pure confusion overtaking my face.

She makes her way to the center of the ring, her gait like she's on a catwalk. "Not in the air today?"

I fight a scowl. "You know I'm not allowed to train without a spotter."

She folds her graceful arms across her chest. "It's not like you aren't a fan of breaking rules."

"Did you come in here just to give me a hard time about the set list? Everyone already knows, and they don't care. So whatever attempts you had to poison everyone against me failed." I shake my head irritably. "I don't bother you during your rehearsals—don't bother me during mine."

Her lips curl into a smile. "I suppose everyone knows your parents own Teatro della Notte too?"

The world slows to a stop. If I were able to breathe, I'm sure I would see the cloud of air still in front of me like I'm trapped in a photograph.

"Who told you that?" My voice is hollow.

Maggie shrugs. "The circus is a small world. We trade gossip as often as we trade performers. And my boss going to Las Vegas to poach a performer he intends to replace me with is most *definitely* gossip." She lets out a sigh. "Look, I'm not here to reveal you or anything like that."

"Then why are you here?" I ask angrily.

"To tell you I get it now. I understand you." She shrugs.

Is that . . . resignation on her face?

I don't believe it. I can't.

"I thought you were just a girl with a circus fetish who desperately needed a rude awakening, but now I realize you're just like me." Maggie blinks, her gray eyes as bright as glass. "You're ready to put your ambition in front of everything—even your relationships." She pauses. "Even your family."

"That's not—" But I can't finish my sentence.

Because she's right, and we both know it.

Feeling remorse or wishing things could be different doesn't change the fact that I came here because I cared more about myself than about anyone else.

Not wanting to hurt people doesn't change the fact that I did.

Maggie steps closer, her pink heels leaving temporary dents on the padded floor. "People automatically call me a bitch because I'm driven and I don't waste my time on distractions. But if I were a man, do you think for a moment they'd associate those qualities as negative? No. They'd praise me as a hard worker. They'd find my initiative and determination impressive. But women are snobs and brats and whatever else. Because I don't smile and take people's shit, or accept less than what I deserve."

She circles around me, her voice growing less patient. But she's not being aggressive—she wants to be understood.

"I don't doubt any of that's true, but you tried to get everyone to ignore me. You tried to *alienate* me. And I know assuming you'd teach me anything wasn't right, but you didn't have to make it so difficult for me. I just wanted to belong." It feels good to let my thoughts out.

"Like I said, I didn't understand you at the start. But that's also why I'm telling you this now." She stops in front of me, eyes calculating. "You can't get through life always being the good guy. At some point, someone is going to take advantage. And the nicer you are, the more often it will happen. People call me a snob and a bitch, but so what? I'll embrace it if it means my voice will actually be heard. Ambition doesn't always work well with nice."

I bite my lip. "I . . . don't know if I agree with that."

"You don't *want* to agree with it, because you don't like the idea of people hating you. But the higher you climb, the greater you might fall—every trapeze artist knows that. So toughen up your heart, because ambition is more than a sword—it's armor, too. Wear it well on your way up the ladder, and fight off the people who want to drag you back down." Maggie shrugs. "Consider that the most important lesson you'll ever learn from me."

I pause. "Why are you helping me all of a sudden?"

Maggie laughs. "Because if someone early in my career had told me this, it would've saved me a lot of time holding myself back over some ridiculous feeling of belonging."

"Sounds kind of lonely," I argue.

"It's lonely at the top because the truth is, nobody wants to see you up there," she warns.

Her words swirl around my mind like they're trying to find a place to fit. And I so desperately want to reject her advice, but parts of it make more sense than I want to admit.

Silence consumes the room for a long, long time.

I look back at her not as someone who did something unforgivable, but as someone who might be a little closer to a reflection than I let myself realize. "Have you changed your mind about training me?"

Maggie's laugh fills the room. Dazzling, cruel, and so unbelievably beautiful. "No. I think you're doing just fine on your own."

She leaves the tent, her soft lavender hair hanging near her shoulders, and I wonder whether I've underestimated her just as much as she's underestimated me.

CHAPTER THIRTY-SIX

*J*he news spreads like wildfire before anyone's even made it to breakfast: Maggie quit last night, got on a plane to London, and is the new lead in a world-class circus show that is no doubt going to skyrocket her to superstardom.

It's a huge deal. Even I'm impressed on her behalf.

Simon, however, has been in a rage since he woke up and read her resignation letter.

I hear him inside his trailer, objects clattering and animal-like roars escaping through the thin metal walls.

Jin falls into an empty chair next to where Vivien, Dexi, and I are sitting beneath the awning outside the Lunch Box, where Sasha has called an emergency meeting.

"He's taking it well," Jin says.

Vivien whistles dramatically.

"It's not like she hasn't been dropping hints for the last year," Dexi mutters, scooping up a bite of fruit muesli.

"I didn't think she'd quit. I mean, not this soon," I say,

thinking about our conversation last night and searching for a telltale sign.

I guess that was her way of saying goodbye.

Sasha appears near the table, his eyes a bit worn out. He glances around the grassy area, counting heads, and claps his hands together. "All right, everyone. As you know, Maggie left us last night and has taken a job with another troupe. We all wish her the best, and her presence here will certainly be missed." In the background, Simon throws something so hard that one of the windowpanes rattles. Jin covers a hand over his mouth to hide his laughter, and some of the other performers flatten their lips and stare intensely at the ground.

I think I'm the only one who *doesn't* find the whole thing wildly amusing.

Maggie's gone, which means Simon doesn't have a trapeze artist.

As of this moment, I'm the only person in Maison du Mystère with a chance of taking her place.

This isn't amusing—this is an opportunity.

Sasha crosses his thick arms, sending warnings like laser beams from his eyes. "But we now have the problem of replacing our closing act." The pounding in my chest feels limitless. "The plan is to rework the lineup a little bit and have the Terzi Brothers close. Our thought process is that as long as the audience leaves laughing, they won't miss out on the magic Maggie's act brought to the show. Galip and Emin, does that sound okay to you?"

The brothers both nod in agreement, and I feel like I'm watching a sandcastle crumble within my fingers.

After the meeting, I stay beneath the awning. Everyone is

running around frantically making decisions to draw out acts in places, and add more comedy in others, all to cover up the gaping hole Maggie has left in the show.

I wait until the late afternoon, watching the door to Simon's trailer, anxious for even a hint of movement.

Finally, he shows his face.

Dressed in black—his everyday uniform—he has a cell phone in one hand and a notebook and pen in the other. He's already typing hurriedly on the screen of his phone, and I know if I don't say something now, he might bury himself in another phone call and disappear somewhere I can't reach him.

"Simon? Do you have a minute?" I ask.

He doesn't hear me, so when he almost runs into me, his face crumples in confusion. "Whatever it is, take it up with Sasha. I'm a little busy at the moment."

I think about what Maggie told me, about being assertive and taking charge of the moment.

I clear my throat. "This will only take a second, I promise."

He raises a brow, his thumb clicking the end of the pen in a mechanical pattern. "Well, then a second is what you'll get."

"I want to replace Maggie as the new trapeze act." The words don't tumble out of me—they burst.

Simon doesn't bother looking amused. "Kid, don't waste my time." He starts to move around me, but I cut in front of him. It's what Maggie said I should do, right?

I won't let Simon stand in my way—I'll get in front of his.

He sighs and holds up the paper in his hand. "You see this?

This is a list of some of the best trapeze artists in the country, all who've been interested in Maggie's job in the past." He pauses for effect. "Your name isn't on it."

"But none of them know the routine like I do. You'd have to train them—spend time that you don't have. But I know Maggie's routine perfectly. I've even practiced it. And I know how everyone else works, and what would be expected of me here. It would be an easy swap," I say. "It's good business."

"There is no way on earth that I'm going to let an untrained, unseasoned aerialist try to replicate my best act. It would be a disaster," Simon says. "You don't hire a child to stand in for a lead in a Broadway show. Because it doesn't matter how talented the kid is—they're still a kid. And you, kid, are not ready for the spotlight."

My face gets hot. "I'm not a kid. I will work harder for you than any act you've ever had. I will be *better* than Maggie. I just need you to give me a chance."

Simon shakes his head.

"Just one night to show you what I can do. Please. I can do this," I say.

"I told you a long time ago, I'm not in the business of doing charity." Simon waves me aside.

"I'll train her."

Simon stops, his eyes widening.

I turn around and see Vas walking toward us, hands stuffed in his pockets like he's been there awhile.

I don't understand. Vas is a musician, and learning the violin isn't going to get me a place on the static trapeze.

I also don't understand why Simon looks so intrigued.

"I've been spotting her in the evenings. She's really good—she could be great, even," Vas says, and I realize there might be a hint of admiration in his tone. "I'll train her every night, make sure she's at the level she needs to be at. We both know how hard it would be to get a replacement trapeze artist here at the end of the season without paying a fortune anyway. It wouldn't hurt anybody to give her a chance. If anything, it works in your favor."

"You really think she can handle it," Simon confirms slowly.

"I do," Vas says. "She's talented. She just needs to be trained."

Blood is rushing through my body. Since when does Vas know anything about the trapeze?

He's talking about it like he knows more than I do.

"I don't want Maggie's act replicated," Simon says finally. "It wouldn't work. Nobody in the world could do it exactly like she did, and I'm not settling for a half-baked version of the best act we had." He looks between Vas and me, the spark in his gemlike eyes growing with every second. "But a new act? Well, that I could get behind."

Vas's jaw shifts like he knows what's coming.

I'm staring wide-eyed between them like a lost animal.

"A double static trapeze act, the way you and Maggie used to perform all those months ago," Simon says. He wags his finger at the two of us. "You give me that—get something ready in the next three weeks—and I'll consider using it for the new season in January."

The entire world spins.

Vas is an *aerialist*?

An aerialist who used to perform with Maggie?

Vas still hasn't looked at me. His eyes are locked on Simon's the way someone would watch a poisonous snake in the grass. "I'll agree to perform again, but only if I can compose an original song for our act."

Simon opens his mouth to argue, but Vas is in no hurry to let him derail his plans.

"I'm not asking for the entire set list. Just one act," Vas says firmly. "You let me have a song, and I'll give you your double act back."

Simon stares at him for a long time before relaxing into a smile. He holds up three fingers. "You have three weeks. If it's not performance-ready by then, I'm hiring a new trapeze artist." And then he pushes past us, patting Vas on the shoulder once before heading off toward the rehearsal tent.

For the first time since the bike ride, Vas looks me in the eyes.

"I'm sorry if I've overstepped," he says stiffly. "I . . . wanted to help."

I feel torn between throwing my arms around him and yelling at him for casually forgetting to mention that he was *a professional freaking trapeze artist*.

I try to find something earnest in his eyes, but I can't read him. All I see is the heaviness in his brow, and those green eyes that drink the world in but hesitate to give anything back.

"Thank you for your help. I have a million things I want to say right now, but 'thank you' is probably the most important," I say, my words clipped because I'm too worried my brain will betray me and I'll word-vomit all over him.

I need time to think. Time to process. Time to cradle my words carefully before setting them free.

He nods.

Okay, maybe a *few* more words won't do any harm. "I don't know whether you did all this because it was the only way you could compose a song, or because you genuinely meant all that stuff you said about thinking I could be great, but it doesn't matter. Because I'm honestly just grateful for the opportunity."

A chance to learn. It's all I've wanted since I got here.

Vas opens his mouth like he's about to say something else, but instead his eyes snap toward the Lunch Box. When I look up, I realize there are a whole lot of people staring at us.

Maggie wasn't lying about the circus loving gossip.

"Meet me in the big top in an hour?" Vas says, and I think he's embarrassed of the attention. He starts to turn away but pauses. When he looks at me, there's an actual gleam in his eyes. "And wear gym clothes. We've got a lot of work to do."

CHAPTER THIRTY-SEVEN

*V*as is sitting in the center of the ring, his body folded in half and his hands wrapped around his ankles. He's wearing a sleeveless shirt that shows off the curved lines of his lean muscles. It's low enough at the sides that I can see the start of a tattoo on his left ribs.

God, I hope it isn't a bunch of Chinese characters that are supposed to translate into "Live long and prosper," or whatever tattoos people get when they think they're being "exotic."

My cheeks burn when I realize how long I've been standing here staring at his bare skin, wondering if Vas Lukov, Serious McSerious, has turned himself into a culturally appropriative human fortune cookie.

I gulp away the jitters in the pit of my stomach, clearing my throat to get his attention.

He lifts his head, slowly rolling back into a seated position. His stretches are so deliberate and careful.

Clearly this is not the first time he's done a warm-up.

I feel silly for not realizing his secret sooner.

"Why didn't you tell me that you were a trapeze artist?" I ask, my volume way too loud.

He pushes himself up, pausing to study me. "It never came up."

"And you didn't think it should've? I mean, we could've used something to—well, bond over." I twist my face, certain I'm not explaining my thoughts right.

Vas raises a brow.

I sigh. "I know you didn't want to talk to me, but this just seems too big to *not* mention. Even in passing. You know—so I knew we had a common interest." And also, I want to add, so I could've paid more attention to whether or not I was embarrassing myself.

I thought I was practicing in front of a musician—not someone who knew the difference between a bird's nest and a mermaid on the bar.

Now I can't stop thinking about all the times I fumbled, or messed up a pose, or let my foot slip.

But then again, he did tell Simon I could be "great," so I guess there's that. . . .

"The trapeze isn't an interest of mine," he says simply. "And I never said I didn't want to talk to you."

"Oh, you definitely did. You said . . ." I clamp my mouth shut, thinking.

"That I wasn't good at small talk," he finishes slowly. "Which is true. I tend to close up around people I don't know, and people some-times mistake it as me being rude. I was . . . trying to be helpful."

I'm thinking about all our interactions. Even the nonverbal ones. "So you get anxious around people." That makes an obscene amount of sense, in hindsight.

He shrugs. "I mean, I don't know what it's called, exactly. Or if I'm allowed to call it anything at all. It's just something I live with. Something I don't feel like I need a name for to understand." He clenches his jaw like he's not sure if he's said too much. "I don't know if that makes any sense."

"It does," I say quickly, and he looks surprised. "I—I have these shifts in mood sometimes. Like, I'll feel really positive and motivated and whatever else, and then I'll just plummet. Sometimes there's a reason, but sometimes there's not. And I've spent enough hours on Google that I know what it *probably* is, but my parents aren't very good about taking mental health stuff seriously. They think 'everyone has *something*,' which is sort of code for 'I don't believe any of this is real.' They also are really against having anything on a permanent record, which means talking to a professional about any of this was never an option."

"Do you want to talk to a professional?" he asks seriously.

"Not really," I say. "I mean, I did for a little while. I had kind of a bad spell last November. Usually my lows only last a few weeks, but that time it lasted . . . well, a while. But I'm not sure if I wanted to talk to someone because I needed to, or because I just wanted someone to tell me that what I was feeling had a name and it was normal."

Vas tilts his head, taking all my words in. "Do you think having a name for it would make a difference?"

"I don't know. It kind of sucks not knowing for sure, because when I explain it to people, they just look at me like I'm making it up. But if someone has a diagnosis and medication? Then it's 'legitimate.' And don't get me wrong, those things are super important for a lot of people. But I feel like associating legitimacy with a formal diagnosis sometimes leaves people behind—people like me, whose families really frown on anything to do with therapy and meds, or people who have found their own ways of coping with it, or people who can't afford it. It doesn't mean they don't still feel what they feel—they just don't have the privilege of being told by someone with a degree what they're allowed to call it. Shouldn't the focus be on what we're feeling rather than what box we can neatly fit ourselves into?" My eyes widen. "Oh my God, I'm sorry—I'm totally rambling, aren't I? Not to mention we were talking about you, and I'm steamrolling the entire conversation."

Vas smiles—a real, actual smile. "You don't have to apologize. I like when you talk like this. It's how you look on the trapeze—like you forget you're being watched."

I really hope my face isn't as red as it feels.

I clear my throat awkwardly. "So . . . what made you become an aerialist?"

Vas leans back on his heels, trying to wrap his head around the change of topic I so expertly deployed. "I was trained in the circus at an early age; it was something my family expected me to excel in. And I did for a while. My mom and Maggie's mom were old friends, even though Maggie's parents lived in London. When I was eleven, I went to live with them. It was around the same time my brothers started getting into trouble. I think my mom wanted to get me away from it—give me a clean slate so I could focus everything on acrobatics. Maggie and I trained at the same school and eventually came to the States together as a duo."

Together. I hesitate. "Were you a couple?"

"No, never," Vas says. "I'll always care about her, but it's . . . complicated." He says it like there's history there—maybe even hurt—but I don't want to pry. "She's the kind of person I can only handle in small doses, which is why working together nearly ruined us. I quit when I realized continuing would permanently destroy our relationship. She's the closest person to family I have left." There's a flash of sorrow in his eyes. "I'm not saying Maggie's always a good person, but I do think there's good in her."

I can't help but remember her words. "Maggie said we were the same. That our ambition is what pushes people away."

Vas shakes his head. "I didn't quit because she was too ambitious. I quit because she didn't care who she trampled to get where she wanted to be. There has to be honor in success, otherwise it isn't earned—it's taken. And I'm not sure she understood the difference."

Part of me wants to know what happened, but the other part of me hopes he'll never say. Because what if it's along the same lines as what I did to my parents?

Or what if what I did was *worse*?

I chew my lip, hating what I'm about to say. "If you feel that way, I think you're going to regret working with me. Because I'm not sure I understand the difference either." I lift my shoulders.

"Look what I've done to get here—stealing a set list from another circus, begging for Maggie's spot less than twenty-four hours after she left. I think she might be right. I think I might be more like her than I want to admit." I think about what I did to Mom and Dad and feel a wave of shame.

Vas doesn't move. "I guess I'm willing to take the risk."

I frown. "But why?"

He sighs. "Because I don't think you're like Maggie. I think you feel like you have to be, but I think despite wanting success, you do actually care about who you kick down the ladder on your way up. And—I don't know—I guess I think about all the opportunities I had that I never really appreciated, and I see in you someone who would've killed for it. Maybe even literally." He pauses.

I narrow my eyes. "One of your jokes?"

He smirks with only the tiniest bit of his face. "I just think you deserve a chance. Like how I wish someone would give me a chance with music."

"Well, thank you," I say.

He moves toward the wall and pushes a button. The static trapeze lowers, and I feel like a magnet being pulled toward it.

We spend two hours training, with Vas cemented to the floor, circling below the metal bar and instructing me on so many aspects of my style and form that I almost feel like a beginner again.

He's firm, blunt, and as serious as ever.

But with every criticism—every suggestion on how to be better—I feel like I'm being pushed in the direction I've been so desperate to go in but didn't know where to start.

When we're finished for the day and I return to my room for a shower, my muscles are aching, there are fresh bruises on my thighs, and my legs feel like orange marmalade.

And I'm beaming from head to toe.

CHAPTER THIRTY-EIGHT

When I step into the big top the next morning, Vas is sitting on the bar. He asks if I've ever been lifted onto the trapeze before. I tell him I've never done any of this before.

He talks me through what we're going to do, and the next thing I know, he's hanging from his knees, his hands locked around my forearms. I do a backward roll and he swings me up until my legs are wrapped around his waist, before pushing upward against my feet until I'm high enough to pull myself onto the bar.

We practice the move, again and again, until our bodies move together like water.

Which isn't a surprise, because every time he touches my skin, I melt.

Tallahassee, Florida
October—Week 10

CHAPTER THIRTY-NINE

*V*ivien and Dexi invite me out to dinner with some of the other performers, but as much as I love being a part of their group, I decline.

"My body can't take it," I say. "I just want to lie on the bed and not move."

A few minutes after I close the door, a series of quick knocks sound. When I pull the door back, I see Vas's distorted image through the screen.

He's wearing jeans and a black shirt, with his silver dagger necklace hanging from his neck.

I push the screen open. "The rehearsal tent isn't even set up yet. You can't possibly be here to tell me we need to rehearse."

"It's a different kind of rehearsal," he says. "We need to talk about choreography, and style. It helps to know these things before I get too invested in a song." He nods toward his trailer. "Do you have a moment to chat?"

I follow him across the yard, acutely aware we're about to be alone together. Where he sleeps every night. Which feels very different from being alone in a circus tent.

Vas and Jin's trailer smells like soap and leather. It's meticulous in a way that reminds me of Dad's office. Everything has a home. An order. And even though there're only two of them in here, Vas has a keyboard and a bunch of recording equipment in the corner that take up a decent amount of floor space.

One of the beds is covered in satin gray sheets with purple and yellow throw pillows, fairy lights, and a smaller blanket with the famous neon Andy Warhol images of Marilyn Monroe.

The other bed is plain navy blue.

"Which one is yours?" I ask.

Vas looks at me for a moment, studying me to figure out if I'm being serious or not. Against everything his broody nature is probably telling him, he relaxes his face. "Very funny."

I smirk, watching him grab a notebook and pen out of a nearby drawer. We sit at the table, and Vas finds a fresh page and starts jotting down the beginnings of an outline.

"I was thinking we should do something that ties our act in with everyone else's, which means matching a similar sound to the—um—acquired set list." Vas pauses. "I'm assuming you've listened to it before?"

I close my fingers together under the table. "Not really, no."

Vas taps his pen against the table, thinking. "Okay. Well, to me it was kind of a darker version of 'It's a Small World.'"

I frown. "Like the Disney ride?"

"Yeah. All the songs have this quirky, marionette-puppet

vibe to them, but each one feels like it has its own culture. It felt like the composer was showing the differences of the world, and how we're all strung together, and part of something bigger." Vas runs his hands through his hair. "At least, that's the way I interpreted it."

My mind flashes to Dad in his office, always working. I think about all those times I felt so different and alone, like I was a puzzle piece in the wrong box.

Like I had a family that wanted me to fit in more than I did, but parents who were so used to *not* fitting in that they forgot how hard it was.

And to know Dad wrote music that represents some of the things I've always struggled with?

It feels like a message.

A message I wish he had tried to give me a long time ago, before I started to believe he had nothing to say.

"Do you want to hear some of it?" Vas asks, reaching for his laptop.

"No," I practically bark, which makes him recoil in alarm. "Sorry. I just . . . don't really need to hear it right now, that's all." Hearing what I've taken from Dad will only make things worse. I'd rather pretend for a little while longer that I won't have to one day face the consequences of doing something so unforgivable.

Vas straightens himself again, staring at the paper like he's willing his ideas to be realized right in front of him. "The reason Maggie is so good is because her passion comes through every performance." He looks up at me, his eyes locking onto mine.

"I know you have passion too, but I think whatever we come up with should speak to you the most. More than me. You want the audience to be drawn to you the way you are to the circus. We need to hone in on what that is. Give you a chance to perform from your heart."

My heart. Do I really know what's in there anymore?

Things are so messy now. I've destroyed relationships and broken trust and I still don't feel sorry enough to want to make it better.

Because deep down, I'm still angry Mom and Dad didn't care. About the circus, about my choices, about my hurt. They kept brushing me away, and if you neglect something long enough, eventually it's not going to come back.

I needed my parents, and they weren't there for me.

Apologizing now would feel like I'm saying what they did is okay, when it isn't.

"My heart is conflicted." I laugh. "I don't think that's going to make for a very good act."

Vas frowns. "Conflicted about the circus?"

"Oh my God, no!" I shake my head fervently. I might be stubborn and have too many regrets, but my love for this life hasn't changed even a little bit.

If anything, it's grown.

I try a different approach. "Conflicted about who I am, I guess. Am I good or bad? A part of something or a part of nothing? Ambitious or selfish?"

Vas is watching me so carefully. There's something about his stoic patience that makes me feel like I'm allowed to talk for hours if I want to.

"I guess I've always felt like there are parts of me that don't really make sense together. Like, I'm either extremely happy or extremely sad. I'm either super motivated, or I feel hopeless." I pinch the material of my leggings, organizing my words. "And sometimes I feel white or Asian, but never both at the same time. And I know I *am* both. But my family has always felt so separate. They look at one another like they know one thing is not like the other, which makes me feel like an oddity. Like a person who lost all her culture when her grandparents met. And I hate that, because I see how important culture is to my grandma. But it's like I don't have any right to it."

"Everyone has a right to their family," Vas says simply.

"I know it *should* be that way, but I don't know if it is." I pause. "Asian people call me 'too white' and laugh at me for not knowing enough about Chinese and Japanese culture. And white people only ever see me as Asian. They see me as exotic—someone too different to be their version of 'all-American.' Not to mention how broad the whole Asian category is. Do you know how many countries that covers? How many cultures? But 'Asian' is just lumped together, like people can't be bothered to learn the differences. Which is *also* frustrating because, like, people who identify as East Asian or Southeast Asian or South Asian want to be understood for their differences, but then when someone is biracial, it's suddenly like, 'No, you don't get to claim all the things that you are because you're not Asian enough.'

"Both my parents are biracial. I'm a product of two people who probably felt split between cultures themselves. But I feel like my heritage is even *less* mine because I'm only a quarter of everything. A quarter doesn't feel like enough to belong to something. But then that just means I don't belong to *anything*. Does that make sense?" I shake my head like my thoughts are too heavy.

Vas sets his pen down. "I'm sorry you feel like that. It must be difficult to feel like so many pieces that don't fit together."

"Yes!" I explode. "I just want to feel like a whole person, and not someone who is broken into fragments. And maybe that's why I love the idea of the circus. Because I could see that— all these different people from different cultures with different skills coming together to be a family and perform. I know it isn't real life, but it's still a family. A family I've always wanted to be a part of."

Vas lifts his shoulders. "Longing. Separation. Family. I think we could find something there to work with."

I raise my eyebrows, worried I'm being too intense or honest or *me*. "It isn't too much? I'm not too much?"

Vas looks at me like the thought had never even occurred to him. "I think it's perfect."

I bite the smile forming in the corner of my mouth.

We pass ideas back and forth like we're on a tennis court, but nothing sticks. Eventually my eyelids get heavy, and I'm struggling to concentrate on what we've said and haven't said, and I *must* be tired because I'm sure Vas has smiled at least five times in the past thirty minutes.

I ask him if we can talk more about it tomorrow, and when he says yes, it takes us both a long time to actually stand up.

Maybe I'm dreaming, but I feel like Vas doesn't want me to leave.

Maybe I don't want to leave either.

I float all the way to my trailer, and when my head hits the pillow, I let the dream consume me.

CHAPTER FORTY

*I*n my sleep, I am surrounded by smoke and mirrors.

I look from side to side, seeing my face over and over again, stretching into infinity. The clouds beneath my feet expand across the floor, consuming it. The smoke licks at the air like a flame, and I hear Popo's voice telling me a story from my childhood. A story about two stars who couldn't bear the sight of each other.

The same, but different.

A conflict between family.

Two parts existing at once, but never together.

Smoke fills the room, and the mirrors shatter.

And then I am floating through the sky, reaching for Mom, Dad, Popo, Grandpa Cillian, even the ghost of the grandmother I never met—each family member appearing one after another. But my fingers slip through them, like they are no more physical than a reflection. I can't hold on to them. I can't feel them.

I am not a part of them.

And then I see a version of myself, sleeping in the starlight, holding firmly to the ropes on a static trapeze.

A girl living among the planets.

I try to pull my reflection toward me, to make us the same, to make her dreams mine. But every time I move, she moves too. We are trapped in a dance, like magnets forcing each other away.

Because we exist in two different worlds.

CHAPTER FORTY-ONE

*V*as is in the Lunch Box eating breakfast when I collapse into the seat across from him, my breath ragged because I've been in a hurry to find him since the minute I woke up.

"What's wrong?" he asks, his voice layered with concern.

"I have an idea for our act," I say impatiently. He sets his fork down to signal that I have his full attention. "Have you ever heard of the Chinese folktale about the morning star and the evening star?"

He shakes his head.

"My popo used to tell it to me when I was a kid. It's about two stars who were brothers—sons of the Golden King of the Heavens. One day they got in such a huge fight that they could no longer stand the sight of each other. So they take turns being in the sky, one appearing in the evening and the other in the morning." I raise my shoulders. "It's kind of like how I've always felt about my heritage. Like I can only be one thing at a time, and never all at once."

Vas nods slowly. "Okay. So an act that represents two people wanting to be together again?"

"Maybe not *wanting* to be together, because that makes it sound like it's romantic." As soon as I say the word, my cheeks go pink because my blood is a total traitor. "It's more about the push and pull of being unable to belong, even when you should. Like two people who should fit together, but don't."

"Conflict," he says.

"Exactly," I say.

A genuine smile spreads across his face, and I feel my heart lift. "I like it," he says.

I smile back. "I take it we're still on for rehearsal tonight?"

"Tonight? Try this *morning*." He picks up his fork and motions to me. "You should probably eat something. You're going to need the energy."

I'm so excited about our new act that I hardly notice all the eyes staring at us, and how strange it must look to see me and Vas eating breakfast together and grinning like kids with a secret.

I can't help but feel like this is the start of something wonderful.

CHAPTER FORTY-TWO

*V*as says to imagine we're magnets. When our bodies are too far away, they're pulled back together. But when we get too close, the feeling reverses, and we push away again.

We practice on the floor at first, holding our hands inches apart, mirroring each other's movements.

I can't help that my heart refuses to stay still.

Or that Vas's woodsy scent is intoxicating.

Or that when we move the wrong way and our skin brushes against each other, I feel like I'm Tinker Bell exploding with pixie dust all over the room.

When we move to the bar, our hands grabbing arms and legs and bodies, we make sure our faces are always turned away.

When we practice, we are the evening and morning stars, refusing to look at each other for even a second.

But the rest of the time I can't take my eyes off him.

CHAPTER FORTY-THREE

To: FlightOfTheRedPanda@gmail.com
From: Delilah.Milano@teatrodellanotte.com
Subject: The time you brought me flowers

It wasn't just one time. It was so many times. Every time you went outside, you'd come back with daisies and dandelions and sweet peas and anything else you could find. Because you always wanted me to know you were thinking about me, even when you were out playing with your friends.

I wish I'd made a bigger deal out of those flowers. I wish I hadn't taken them for granted. I should've savored the moment—those moments when you were my little girl—because I don't get that time back anymore. You're grown up. You don't bring me flowers anymore.

And that's okay. I knew it wasn't going to last forever. But maybe it could've lasted a little longer, if I'd told you how much it meant to me.

I miss you. It's not fair that you won't talk to me. Just like it's not fair that time goes too quickly, and I can't go back to those days and scoop you up in my arms and tell you how much I love you. Back then, you'd have listened to me.

Please talk to me. You don't have to listen. But please talk to me.

Love, Mom

I feel brittle. Cold. *Guilty.*

I did a horrible thing to my parents, yet Mom is still here, trying to get me to talk to her. Trying to keep me in her life, in whatever small way she can.

She's making an *effort.*

And I know it doesn't mean she's changed her mind about everything. It's not like she sent an email telling me she doesn't care about school anymore, and that it's okay if I want to pursue a life in the circus. But she sends emails like she's trying to remind me she loves me, even when I've cut her so deeply out of my life.

It wasn't fair what I did.

It's not fair what I'm doing.

Mom is right, and I don't know what I could possibly say to make any of this better.

Because I've been ignoring the people in my life I love the most. I let *busy* take over everything. Maybe I wanted it to take over everything. Because when I was busy, I had an excuse not to think about what I did to my parents.

How my leaving so suddenly hurt the people I care about.

Is this what Chloe meant? That I don't think about who I'm affecting?

And Mom is still here, despite all of it, because I know she loves me as much as any mother in the world could love their child.

The tears well up quickly, pooling in the corners of my eyes until my cheeks are damp and my vision goes blurry.

And all I can think about is how I should've brought my mother more flowers.

I want to call her, but I don't know how.

Savannah, Georgia

October—Week 11

CHAPTER FORTY-FOUR

I have bruises in places I never realized could bruise. My body feels stronger. Rehearsals are getting easier.

I collapse into bed every night and don't stir until morning.

Vas is composing whenever he isn't with me. Sometimes he composes when he *is* with me. And I like those moments in his trailer almost as much as I like our time in the big top. I like watching the way he taps his pen to his lips when he's concentrating, and the way he writes in delicate, swooping cursive, like every single letter needs to be *exactly right*.

Sometimes he'll be so lost in his music that his voice disappears for long stretches of time. But when he realizes how long it's been—and he always does—he'll look up from what he's doing and ask me if I'm okay.

I like that part too.

We train every spare minute we can. Sometimes other

people come to watch us, like Vivien, Dexi, and Jin. They seem impressed, which feels like high praise.

I have never been more exhausted in my life.

But I've never been happier, either.

Charleston, South Carolina

November—Week 12

CHAPTER FORTY-FIVE

I'm not late, am I?" I look past Vas at the yard, which is empty because everyone is getting ready for tonight's performance in the big top. "I swear I just checked my phone—I thought I had another ten minutes." Maybe exhaustion is finally catching up to me.

Vas has a strange smile on his face. Or maybe it's just strange to me because he rarely uses it. "Congratulations—as of this moment, you're on an extended hiatus from selling popcorn."

I lean into the doorframe, considering his words. "Did you clear this with Simon?"

He nods. "I pointed out that you rehearse longer hours than all the other performers and still work in the concession stands four days a week. He didn't seem bothered until I mentioned there might be labor laws involved, considering you don't actually get paid."

I raise a brow. "What did he say?"

"He called me a few less-than-affectionate terms and told me he's getting sick of my demands. But you're also off popcorn duty," he says.

I laugh. "Well, thank you. You're a real knight in shining armor." My eyes narrow, recalling his choice of words. "Wait. Does this mean I'm considered a performer?" I'm buzzing at the thought.

He grins widely. "I think so. But not today—today, we're guests." When I frown, he takes two steps away from the door like he wants me to follow him.

We walk side by side toward the music and lights, finding ourselves in the midst of an excitable crowd flowing through the outer ring.

Vas leads me into one of the smaller purple tents, and I see an illusionist in the center of a small, round stage. She's dressed in a black gown, with items strewn all over the set—everything black, gray, and white, like all the color has been drained from the room. One by one she transforms the objects around her—a black rose into a red one, the gray velvet of a chaise longue into an elegant pink. All around the room she brings color to her little world, the audience soaking in every bit of it with wonder. And then she twirls, and her black dress is replaced with the most incredible gown I have ever seen. It's pink turning to blue turning to purple, with most of the fabric covered in glittery starbursts.

The audience is bewildered, cheering because they think this is the finale.

But the illusionist isn't finished yet.

She spreads her arms and starts spinning again, and when all the layers of her dress pick up speed, she tugs at her hem until she's hidden beneath the material and then—vanishes.

All that's left is her dress on the floor.

I realize my mouth is hanging open when I catch Vas grinning at me.

The crowd is still looking at one another like they can't figure out how she did it, when we slip back outside.

We wander into a tent with Archie and his ventriloquist dummy, who seems more human than he does, and another with a magician who spends half his act pretending he has no idea what he's doing, only to pull off the most incredible tricks, like cutting an entire orange in half to reveal a person's card.

And then we pay a visit to Gwen, the fortune-teller, and it's just the three of us in the room. She asks us a few questions, staying in character even though we all clearly know one another, and then she snaps her cards against her velvet-covered table.

She gets as far as "the musician" and "the lover" and suddenly Vas is pulling me by the arm to get us out of the room as quickly as possible, with Gwen's voice singing after us, "The cards never lie!"

And because I don't think either of us can recover from so much embarrassment, we decide to head straight into the big top.

It's strange seeing Pia at the popcorn machine after all the nights I spent doing the same job.

I wonder if that's what life feels like when you make a change—like you've jumped ahead in time. Like your entire life just feels *different*.

Vas and I sit in one of the back rows. I feel giddy watching all the people pour in, their faces twinkling with a nervous, excited energy. Kids are bright-eyed and curious, stuffing cotton candy and popcorn into their mouths, their parents struggling to hold on to all the balloons and flashing toys from the souvenir stand outside, all of them waiting in delight for the show that's about to start.

They don't know what to expect, and sometimes I think that's half the magic.

When the lights dim and the music begins, Simon's voice bellows over the loudspeaker.

"Welcome, welcome, one and all, to the most wondrous circus in the world . . . Maison du Mystère!"

When the crowd cheers, my skin sets on fire.

The lights flash every color of the rainbow, and the clowns bound in as the opening music plays. Some of them show off their acrobatics, others their comedic timing. One is on a unicycle throwing confetti into the crowd.

Simon enters next, his top hat and suit partially decorated in black and red crystals that command the attention of the room. His arms are spread wide, and the ends of his mustache are curled up like he's an unforgettable character from a cartoon.

Except I can't tell if he's a villain or a hero, and I wonder if maybe that's the point.

But I can't deny that he's captivating. He has the entire audience laughing until their sides are aching, and his stage presence, the way he moves around the room like he's half cat and half man, is truly impressive.

When he asks the audience if they're ready for a show, every person in the room goes wild. Even me, because I feel like I'm five years old again and the circus is full of magic.

I catch Vas smiling next to me.

"What?" I mouth.

He shakes his head, still smiling.

It only makes my stomach flutter more.

We watch the contortionists, the magician, and the high-wire act. Then the clowns come back in, and Simon infuses the show with sharp humor—some of it deceptively meant for the adults.

And then more acrobats come in, performing difficult routines and balancing on pieces of the set that make the audience wide-eyed with nerves. Vivien comes out next and performs her knife-throwing, arrow-shooting balloon act, which has the audience on their feet by the end.

There are more clowns, more magic, more jugglers. There's Dexi on the tightrope, with Zhìháo and Guānyǔ.

And then the Terzi Brothers perform, and there isn't a single person in the audience who isn't beaming from ear to ear.

Everyone takes a turn around the ring in the closing performance, to take a bow and blow kisses of gratitude toward the crowd. When the music finally ends and the ring is empty, my face muscles hurt from smiling so much.

We're the last ones in the stands, listening in silence as all the guests make their way back to their real lives.

Back home.

And I'm lucky enough that I get to stay.

"What is it?" Vas asks in the dimly lit room, the big top still filled with a slight haze from the smoke machines and littered with popcorn and confetti.

I turn to him and try to smile. Even though I miss my parents terribly, and I feel bad about what I did to get here, I love where I am. I love this place, and these people.

I love feeling like I'm a part of something that accepts me.

Somewhere I just fit.

"I feel like I'm home," I say.

We sit quietly, listening to the cars emptying out of the parking lot, and I know when his fingers brush against mine that it isn't an accident.

CHAPTER FORTY-SIX

I scroll through all of Mom's emails. The ones I never answered. The ones I've been too *ashamed* to answer.

I've been so desperate to feel like a part of the circus—a part of this new family—that it distracted me from my own.

But things are different now. I'm accepted here.

I'm a part of Maison du Mystère, just like it feels so deeply a part of me.

So why does it feel like there's suddenly a gaping hole in my chest?

I wonder if it's always been there. Maybe I've just become good at ignoring it.

And I know the circus isn't going to make me feel whole again. It isn't going to fix the damaged parts inside me that I've neglected for far too long.

No.

There's only one way to fix what's wrong with my heart.

And it starts with me.

CHAPTER FORTY-SEVEN

*I*t takes me forty-five minutes to finally hit the call button.

Mom's number and photo appear on my phone, and I wonder for the entire time it takes her to answer if I'm making a mistake.

"Hello?" She sounds calm. Too calm.

"Hi. It's me."

Three excruciatingly long seconds pass. "I was wondering when you'd call," she says finally. "How are you? Is everything okay?"

My eyes are already watering. "I'm fine. And—I'm sorry it took me so long to call." I pause. "I've been busy," I add, as if that's supposed to make everything okay.

"Yes, I know," Mom says, and I get the feeling there's nothing about where I am and what I'm doing that's a surprise to her.

"Did Popo tell you?" I ask quietly.

"Of course she did." Mom sighs. "She let me read your emails. I wish you would've called."

"I know."

"I hate that you ran away," Mom says, her voice picking up like her emotions are kicking in. I guess she could only contain them for so long. "It wasn't right, leaving without saying goodbye like that. You don't know what could've happened—what could've been the last thing you said to us."

"I wasn't in trouble," I say. "It wasn't like that."

"You don't have to be in trouble to get in a car accident," Mom argues. "Not to mention you ran off with a strange man who had no right luring you away like he did."

"He didn't lure me," I say, my voice picking up momentum. "I was the one who called him."

Mom goes quiet. I guess I forgot to tell Popo that part. All this time they thought Simon was the one who sought *me* out.

I wonder if it would've been easier to let them think that—for all of us.

"I know it wasn't right, but I didn't have a choice. You and Dad wouldn't listen to anything I said. And I couldn't go to school—it would've killed me." I shake my head despite the fact that she can't see me. "I told you all of this before I left, and you didn't care. I left because I couldn't live my life around you. Because I couldn't be *myself* around you."

"It breaks my heart that you feel like that," Mom says. "Because it's not true."

"It's true to me," I say. "That should matter."

Mom sighs. "And what did your truth cost?"

I blink.

"We know copies of the set list went missing. And we know Simon Tarbottle doesn't do favors unless he's getting something bigger in return," Mom says.

The tears burst out of me, and I'm engulfed in the shame I've spent weeks hiding from.

"Oh, Harley. How could you do that to your father? To me?" she asks, and it's too gentle for what I deserve.

"I don't expect you to ever forgive me," I say through heavy sobs. "But I want you to know that I never would have done it if there was another way. But it was either 'throw my life away and go to school' or 'join Maison du Mystère.' Those were the only choices I had."

"Nobody ever has only two choices," Mom says, and her disappointment is big enough to fill a whole room.

"Well, you and Dad seemed pretty determined to only give me *one*, so I disagree," I say sourly.

"I know how badly you wanted to train in the circus, but was it really worth it?" Mom asks.

And I hate how easy it is for my heart to scream, *"Yes!"*

"I love it here. I know you'll never understand, because even if you loved being a trapeze artist once, you still quit. But I would *never* quit. This is everything I wanted, and I'm good at it, and people treat me like I'm one of them. Maybe you don't understand how much I needed that, but I'm tired of trying to convince you." I wipe the tears away from my cheeks.

Mom is quiet for a long time, and it occurs to me that she might be crying too. "When are you coming home?"

"I don't know." I pause. "Is Dad really mad at me?"

"You really hurt him. *Really* hurt him." Mom keeps her voice steady. "But we both love you. That will never change."

I can't see through the blurry haze.

I manage to come up with an excuse as to why I need to hang up, and then I crumple into my open palms and cry until my face hurts.

CHAPTER FORTY-EIGHT

I step on Vas's feet more times than I can count. Our noses collide twice. I'm so distracted that during a move where Vas swings me from my toes and I reach up to grab his arms, my fingers slip and I end up falling ten feet onto the safety net below.

Which is frustrating, because it's the first time I've fallen since we've raised the bar high enough to *need* a safety net.

I'm better than this. I know I am.

"Are you okay?" Vas grabs the bar and lowers himself to the net, the impact making my body bounce back up. I take the opportunity to get back on my feet.

I rub my shoulder, steadying myself. "It was nothing. I'm fine."

Vas looks at me carefully. "I don't just mean about the fall. I mean are you okay, *generally*?" He crosses his arms. "You've been distracted all night."

"No, I'm not. I just want to train," I say stubbornly. Motioning to his hands, I say, "Can you give me a boost back up?"

He blinks, unmoving.

My frustration overpowers me. The conversation with Mom floods through my mind like a dam bursting, and hot tears spill down my cheeks. I throw my fingers against my face to shield myself from Vas, who's staring at me curiously.

"Do you want to talk about it?" he asks. When did the jagged edges of his voice become so soft?

I don't know if I'm ready to tell anyone the truth about my parents. But if there were ever a person I could trust to keep it a secret, it would be Vas.

But would he understand?

Would he forgive me for keeping it from him? He thought he was giving up his music for someone who needed a break, not a girl whose parents own a circus in Las Vegas.

Maybe he'll decide I wasn't worth the trouble.

But when I look at his dark lashes and parted mouth and the way he has too much hair on the right side of his head, I don't see someone I want to keep secrets from.

I see someone I want to share the whole world with.

"I did something really horrible," I say, tasting salt on my tongue. "And I don't know how to make it better. I don't think there *is* a way to make it better."

Vas tilts his head. "Is this about stealing the set list?"

I look up at his eyes, deep and green like a galaxy of trees, and nod. "But it's more than that. It's about where it came from. *Who* I stole it from."

He stills, and I wonder if maybe he preferred never knowing. Maybe it was easier to tweak music he just ignorantly assumed

Simon acquired less than legally. But to know the name behind the writer? I think it makes things more real.

But he waits anyway, willing to listen because I so desperately need to speak.

"It came from Teatro della Notte," I say.

Vas's eyes don't change. He knows this much. But the rest . . .

I look away. "My dad . . . My dad is the composer. Actually, he and my mom kind of own the circus. That's why it was so easy for me to get the set list."

Vas shifts his weight. Takes a step back on the net. Turns to the side.

All of his movements are jerky, like I've disrupted his thought process, or distorted his understanding of what's happening.

Of who I am.

"I know you're probably mad because you thought this was my last chance, and you're probably thinking having parents who run a circus would mean I had a *million* chances, but I didn't. I came here because my parents wouldn't let me train, and I couldn't give up the circus. This isn't just my last chance—it's my *only* chance." When I used to say the words in my head, and even to Popo and Mom, they felt like the entire truth.

But telling these things to Vas? The words are sticky. Tart. *Foul.*

I think my truth is rotten at its core.

"I understand if you regret giving up your music for me—" I start.

Vas spins around, eyebrows furrowed deeply. "I don't care about the music!"

There's broken glass in my chest, and every heartbeat hurts. "Then why are you so mad?"

"You shouldn't hurt people you love. You shouldn't hurt people who love *you*. There has to be rules for how we treat the people we care about. You're acting like—" He stops himself. But he didn't have to—I know what he was going to say.

He thinks I'm like Maggie.

I feel like everything that's been building between us shatters.

And then I get angry back. "You don't know everything. You're making assumptions about me based on one bad thing I did— which I already admitted I know was bad! Whatever Maggie did to you isn't the same as what I did. It doesn't make us the *same*."

"I don't think you're the same," he says without hesitating, and I guess it's a small relief. "But I also don't think it's okay to take whatever you want out of this world without thinking about how it might affect other people. How it might hurt them."

I know if I sat and broke apart this conversation, I might be able to see that Vas is being triggered by something else. Something other than me. Maybe understanding that could've given me more patience.

But I don't break apart the conversation. I don't try to see where he's coming from.

I mentally shove him toward Mom, Dad, Chloe, and everyone else who doesn't agree with me and build up a wall to protect myself.

"My parents were making choices that were hurting *me*." I cross my arms. "I'm not going to defend myself to you, and I don't care what you think." More lies. "I told you the truth because I thought you were my friend. Clearly, we don't know each other as well as I thought we did. So forget it—let's just go back to not talking. I'd rather not be friends at all than listen to you judging me like you know anything about my life."

We go back to rehearsing, and the tension between us is so thick, it's almost easy to not look at each other.

CHAPTER FORTY-NINE

*V*as finds me at breakfast and tells me he has to work on the new composition, so we'll have to skip the morning rehearsal.

To anyone else it probably looks like Vas is being his serious self, passing on information that doesn't mean anything at all.

But they don't know about our fight last night.

They don't know that Vas used to look at me differently than he looked at everyone else, until I told him the truth about my parents and saw the version of myself in his eyes warp until I became unrecognizable.

To him, I didn't just tell a lie. I *am* a lie.

"Lovers' quarrel?" Vivien asks with a grin.

I snap back so quickly that even Dexi looks startled. "It's not like that. We're barely even friends."

Vivien holds up her hands. "Sorry. It was just a joke."

Dexi narrows her eyes at me, ready to defend Vivien. "You've been in a bad mood since last night."

Oh my God, what am I doing? Am I going to set *every* relationship I have on fire?

I press my face into my bunched sleeves and sigh with regret. "I know, and I'm sorry. I'm tired, and stressed out, and I'm being rude."

"Why don't you take the night off?" Vivien offers, trying to smooth things over. "Your body could probably use a break."

"I can't." I shake my head. "Simon wants to see our act next week. If it isn't perfect, he's going to hire someone else. I can't afford a night off."

Dexi leans in, head tilted to the side. "If it's any consolation, you're an incredible performer."

I look up, surprised, and find Vivien nodding.

"It's true. Everyone talks about it. They say it's too bad Maggie left when she did, because she would've had to eat her words about calling you a starry-eyed newbie. You're *really* good," Vivien says.

"Thanks," I reply meekly, with a combination of embarrassment and appreciation. "That means a lot."

We finish our breakfast, and it occurs to me that maybe I won't find my family just by proving myself as an aerialist—but also as a friend.

As a daughter.

I might be succeeding in my dreams, but I am failing abominably when it comes to my family.

But maybe there's still time to make things right.

CHAPTER FIFTY

I text Chloe when I'm back in my trailer.

I'm sorry for being a horrible friend. I know I've neglected you, and I haven't been around much. I guess I'm not really good at balancing the circus with everything else. Maybe I've never been good at that. I mean, you always did say I could only focus on one thing at a time, right? (Please be laughing. I don't want you to hate me.) Anyway, I've been a garbage friend and I'm sorry. So if you want to talk about school or Jack or literally whatever you want . . . I'm here. Always. Even if I'm a thousand miles away. Kind of like Obi-Wan Kenobi's voice inside Luke's head.

She reads the message a few minutes after I send it.

But she doesn't write back.

CHAPTER FIFTY-ONE

*V*as is in the big top, standing over an iPod dock he's perched on the wall surrounding the inner ring. I expect to feel the air turn to peanut butter when he looks at me, and I dread the thought.

I don't like fighting with Vas. I hate that I might have ruined what little we had. And I especially regret that he might hate *me*.

But when he turns, he doesn't look angry. He looks . . . tired.

Maybe we don't have to fight forever.

"Hey," I say, stopping at the bottom step.

He looks at the iPod dock, the muscle in his jaw twitching. "I finished the song."

My heart pings, and I take a few steps forward, unsure of how excited I'm allowed to be. "That was fast."

He shrugs. "I had a lot of inspiration."

I nod like I get it. "Conflict. Right." I force an awkward laugh and regret it immediately.

I really need to stop trying to be funny when people are mad at me.

Vas turns, his arms hanging at his sides like he isn't ready for combat. "I'm sorry about before." He lifts his shoulders. "It's a character flaw—forgetting to give people space to not be perfect." He pauses. "I shouldn't have reacted the way I did."

All the walls crumble to pieces like they're made of sand. "I'm sorry too, for getting so defensive, and for saying a bunch of crap I didn't mean. Because you weren't wrong—I am very aware I did something unforgivable. That's why I was so upset. I've made a mess I don't know how to clean up."

Vas looks down at the floor, rolling back on his heels. "And you needed a friend to talk to, and I massively blew it. Next time I promise to be better at listening."

I smile with the side of my mouth. "You were still being a friend. Maybe a more honest one than I was hoping for in that moment, but still a friend. Everyone needs to be called out on their bullshit now and then, right?"

He looks up, relieved. "So we're okay?"

"We're okay," I say. I nod toward the iPod dock. "All right, do I get to hear your masterpiece now or what? The anticipation is killing me."

Vas pushes a hand through his hair, grinning. "I was thinking maybe we could run through our routine while it plays in the background? The whole sitting-around thing feels really forced. And I'll just get nervous the whole time, wondering what you think. At least if we're moving around, I'll be distracted."

"I didn't think you got nervous." I laugh.

He frowns. "Why is that?"

I shrug. "You rarely show emotion on your face besides frustration. You know half the people here think you are part Vulcan, right?"

"I mean, I prefer Cylon. . . ."

We're both smiling at each other, sharing a joke I didn't realize we had.

And then he hits play on the iPod, and we're up on the static trapeze, our bodies moving like mirror images of each other, the tension and heart and passion of the music breathing life into every pose.

It's poetic and beautiful and *Vas* in so many ways.

And it's me, too, sewn into every line. Instruments that aren't supposed to go together but do. Melodies that move up instead of down. A tempo that plays on the longing of the audience, the hunger for more, and the devastation in knowing something will always be held back.

And that's how we move too, like we're both longing for something we can't have.

Something we'll never have.

When the song ends, our bodies are pressed close, our arms tangled up together, but our faces pulling away from each other.

I feel his chest rise and fall against mine, our breathing synchronized and heavy.

Normally one of us lets go by now. But in the quiet—in the aftermath of Vas's beautiful song—neither of us dares to move.

And for a second, I wonder if time has really stopped.

Vas turns his face. I do the same.

We are inches apart—centimeters, if you consider how subjective the way we talk about distance is.

A person could be a moment away, or a lifetime away. Hours, or days. They could be miles, or yards, or inches—it all depends on how you look at it.

On how close you want to feel.

And next to Vas, I feel . . .

When the next song starts with a violin, it catches me by surprise. I'm so used to hearing Vas play live that hearing him through a speaker is almost disorienting.

And then those familiar notes from the night I saw him sing.

It's utterly haunting.

I find my voice in a quiet corner of the world where I've forgotten how to breathe. "I know this song. 'Lucy in the—'"

Something about his smile stops me.

Vas's face softens into something so beautifully pure. "This one is different. This one is 'Harley in the Sky.'" His eyes hold on to mine. "This one is just for you."

I breathe in the scent of him, and my head swirls with need. I tilt my face toward him, his green eyes crackling with lightning, and I know he feels the same.

When he presses his soft lips against mine, I feel like we've been catapulted into the Milky Way, and every star in the universe explodes into a trillion more stars.

CHAPTER FIFTY-TWO

A long time ago, a teacher of mine suggested I keep a mood journal. She said it might help me express how I was feeling, and maybe find connections that would help me sense when my mood was about to change.

She suggested something visual, like colors. Something easy to track. Easy to remember.

I kept up with it for a whole year, until my worst spell in November when I kind of stopped doing anything at all.

When I was feeling better, I went through every page, trying to see if my teacher was right about a pattern. I couldn't find one—not in the way she meant. But I did realize that I never once used the color yellow. No daffodil, canary, lemon, or goldenrod anything.

I avoided yellow like it didn't exist at all.

And I think I finally know why.

I was saving yellow—the happiest color I can think of—for the most perfect day I've ever had.

Today I woke up in a trailer with two incredible roommates. I'm an aerialist in a beloved traveling circus. I have an audition next week for a lead role in the show. And the memory of Vas's mouth on mine still lingers in my bloodstream.

Today my world is shining the color of the sun.

Charlotte, North Carolina

November—Week 13

CHAPTER FIFTY-THREE

O kay, I think you were right. The combination of burger and orange Creamsicle float was not the best decision." I make a face when I step onto the sidewalk, shoving my hands quickly into my pockets to hide from the early evening chill.

Vas tugs at the collar of his leather jacket and grins. "You've been living on a circus diet. Your body doesn't know what to do with all that grease and sugar."

I try to feign queasiness—or at least exaggerate what I'm feeling—but it's too hard to stop smiling for longer than ten seconds these days. I'm too happy. I'm too *excited*.

And I'm wandering around the North Carolina suburbs with Vas on the most perfectly beautiful evening in history. There is no way I'm going to let a tiny bit of nausea ruin the day. Newfound sugar intolerance be damned.

"So"—I motion ahead with my lifted chin—"we've been to the Soda Shop. What about the Book Shop? Or wait, what's that one? Ah, the Village Store. Hang on, so is this a village? Are we in a real village?" I pause. "Do you think they have a town crier?"

Vas shakes his head, his grin overtaking his face. "You are a long, long way from Las Vegas, aren't you?"

I match his pace, feeling a sudden urge to rest my head on his shoulder just to feel closer to him. "I really want to hold your hand right now, but I also don't want to get frostbite and have my fingers fall off."

"Would it make you feel better if I told you nobody has ever gotten frostbite in fifty-degree weather before?" Vas asks.

"I'm not taking any chances. But just know that if it was safe, I'd hold your hand," I say with a shrug.

Vas rolls his eyes, takes my hand in his, and tucks our hands into his jacket pocket. "Better?" His green eyes twinkle. A twinkle meant only for me.

I'm practically beaming. "Yes. Much."

We continue down the main street, crossing a small park with a white gazebo decorated in lights and surrounded in bright pink hydrangeas. Bells and chimes sing each time a door is opened, and people trickle out into the street with their eco-friendly cotton shopping bags. Up ahead I can see the bell tower, the sky behind it a pale violet.

"This place looks like a postcard," I say, almost impatient with the way time stills here. Isn't anyone in a hurry? Doesn't the quiet make them anxious?

Right now, it's making me jittery.

Vas starts to reply, but I don't hear him because I've spotted something across the street—a brick building with a long white sign, and etched in bold letters: THE TATTOO PARLOR.

I must've stopped walking, because suddenly Vas is tugging at my hand, his brow raised quizzically.

"What is it?" he asks, following my gaze across the road. "Wow. They really don't like to leave anything up to interpretation with these names, do they?"

"It's a village thing, probably," I say, pulling him across the road in a hurry.

The window display is full of framed pieces of artwork—art that I imagine has been inked onto someone's body at some point in time. They range from cartoonish vampires to elaborate stories woven together with various symbols. Behind the art display is a scarlet red curtain, concealing the rest of the shop like it's a circus tent.

And my heart is thundering with so much intense, raw happiness that I don't think. I just let my feelings speak for me.

"I should get a tattoo," I say brightly.

Vas laughs. "Well, a place called The Tattoo Parlor can surely help you with that."

"I'm serious." I hold my arm out, motioning to the skin near my wrist. "I could get something here. Or maybe on my forearm. Something I could look at easily, when I want to be reminded."

"Reminded of what?" Vas tilts his head, the curiosity going serious behind his eyes.

I lift my shoulders like the answer is simple. "That I'm happy."

I can see Vas trying to speak again, but I'm already reaching for the doorknob.

"What are you doing?" his voice clips from behind me, making me jump.

"Getting a tattoo?" I frown.

Vas's face shifts into all the many shades of confusion. Startled. Amused. Concerned. He's looking at me like I've said something that makes no sense at all. "Wait, you mean right *now*?"

I look back at him like he's the one who makes no sense. "Yeah?" I pause, trying to understand why he looks so bewildered. "I mean, we're right here." I point at the sign. "At a literal tattoo parlor."

"But"—he hesitates, drumming his fingers against his leg methodically—"are you sure? Do you not want to think about it? I'm not trying to tell you what to do by any means. It's just . . . Well, does this not feel a bit sudden to you?"

What he means is "impulsive."

Sometimes impulsive is like a bright red warning sign that I'm afraid to go near. But other times it's bubblegum pink and cotton candy blue and bursting with confetti and fireworks and the nostalgic music they play when you step foot into Disneyland.

Sometimes *impulsive* feels like *magic*.

It feels good.

"You have a tattoo," I say, as if this small fact should explain everything I'm thinking. Like having a tattoo himself should mean that he knows precisely what I'm feeling.

"I know, but it's something I thought about. It's something I knew I wanted. And you have a right to make your own decisions, but maybe sleeping on a decision like this could be good? You know—give the idea time to marinate?" Vas lifts his shoulders.

"Tattoos are kind of a forever decision. Are you sure you want to make a forever decision in all of seven point five seconds?"

"I've thought about a tattoo before," I argue. "Besides, spontaneity is a good thing." Doesn't he see how excited I am? Doesn't he see the fun in this moment?

His face softens, but his eyes are fixed on mine, like he's deciphering something only he can see.

"What?" I twist my face.

"You're not usually this . . . jumpy."

"Jumpy?"

"Yeah. Like a puppy when they're let off the leash."

I snort.

Vas scratches the back of his neck. "Okay, that wasn't the best analogy. I just mean that you seem kind of hyper. Not *you*, exactly—but something in your eyes."

"I told you. I'm happy." I shrug like it's simple, even though happy is one of the most complicated things in the world.

He nods. "Happy. Okay."

I sigh, feeling the balloon in my chest start to deflate. The slightest hint of irritation prickles my skin. "You don't think I should get the tattoo."

"I don't think you should do anything you might regret in the morning." He pauses. "But also, tattoos can be quite sensitive for a while after you get them. And I've heard from a few very reliable sources that you have a big audition tomorrow."

The pressure in my chest eases. "That's a good point," I say thoughtfully. It doesn't matter how good of an idea a tattoo seems in this moment—nothing is worth jeopardizing our audition for a place in the show.

I need to be in the healthiest place I can possibly be. Physically and mentally.

I let out a sigh and take a step away from the door, and the buzzing feeling shooting through my entire body begins to dull. Still there, but a little more silent.

"I'm sorry if I ruined your fun," he says guiltily.

"It's okay," I say, fighting the sting I feel in my chest. I can't help it—when I'm really excited and plans suddenly change, it feels like someone has thrown me from a building. It's hard to find my footing again. It's hard not to feel like someone personally attacked me.

But I know Vas, and I know he isn't trying to be controlling. He's trying to be helpful.

The problem is that my brain doesn't want help—it wants to be enabled.

It's not an easy thing to explain to people. It's not an easy thing for people to understand.

Our footsteps fall into a similar pattern, and before long we're walking through a quiet courtyard with old-fashioned lampposts and a cobblestone path.

Vas's brows are pinched together like there's more he wants to say. And since his hands are still buried in his leather pockets and there's a whiff of tension in the air, the only way for me to find my way back to him seems to be with words.

"What are you thinking?" I ask. It's a polarizing question

depending on whether the person thinks it means nothing or realizes it means *everything*.

Vas lifts his chin back to the world in front of him. "I was thinking about what you said. About wanting a reminder to be happy." He looks at me gently. "What did you mean by that?"

My feet close together, and suddenly I'm thinking too fast to remember how to walk. "Sometimes—" I hesitate, and then my words start flying out of me like horses at the start of a race. Like each one is in more of a hurry than the one before. "Sometimes the world feels dark and cloudy and *heavy*, like no matter how many times I take a breath, it will never be enough to fill my lungs. It feels like all the color has been sucked out of the world. But other times I feel happy—really, really happy. Like everything makes sense again and I know where I'm supposed to be going. Where I'm supposed to *be*. I have to do whatever I can to get there, as fast as possible, because it's only a matter of time before the dark clouds come back. And I feel like I'm being thrown from one feeling to the other and back again. But sometimes when it's dark, it's like there's a monster telling me it's going to be dark forever. And right now, when I'm happy, I know that's not true. I know it's never forever. But when I'm there? When I'm *low*? It feels like I'll never be happy again."

"Does that happen a lot?" Vas's eyes flit between my own.

I shrug like it isn't a big deal. "I don't know. I guess. It's not really like clockwork, you know? It sort of just . . . shifts."

"When you don't see it coming?" he asks, trying to understand.

I pause. "It's kind of like being in this constant state of worry that something is going to go wrong. Something is going to trigger the figurative trapdoor beneath my feet, and I'm going to plummet. I don't always know what it is, or when it will happen, but I know it *will* happen. I know the darkness is nearby, waiting for a reason to ruin everything."

"But knowing that . . ." He twists his jaw. "Can't you make it stop? Can't you just—I don't know—stay happy?"

I laugh despite the concern in his gaze. "If I could do that, of course I would. But it's not like that. I mean, I can talk about it now. I can explain to you what it feels like. But when I'm feeling it? I can't reason with the monster." And then I'm tugging on his arm like I'm pleading with him to see that everything is fine. "You don't have to worry. I'm maybe oversharing—I do that sometimes—but I'm definitely not telling you this because you need to worry. But you asked, so I explained."

He nods slowly. "And you're happy now?"

I nod what feels like a thousand times. "Enormously. Like, volcanic levels of happiness. I'm so happy, I could punch a unicorn."

Vas locks his fingers around mine. "Well, if you're that happy . . ." He leans in and kisses my forehead. "I'll save all my worries for the unicorns."

I make a face. "I doubt this village has them. They don't even have a town crier."

I feel his laughter against my hair, and then we're walking again, through the park and back down the main street, like we're the only two people who exist in the world.

And my smile grows and grows until it's so wide, I'm worried it might shatter.

Smiles are like happiness—eventually, they break.

CHAPTER FIFTY-FOUR

To: FlightOfTheRedPanda@gmail.com
From: Delilah.Milano@teatrodellanotte.com
Subject: The time you ate too much ice cream

You wanted to go to that buffet for your birthday—the one at Green Valley Ranch. They had that soft-serve ice cream machine, and you insisted that was all you wanted to eat for your birthday dinner.

You kept going back, again and again. I told you to stop—I said you were going to make yourself sick. Your dad said to let you be, and that if you got sick, you'd learn your lesson for next time. So I left you alone to keep eating ice cream, because I didn't want to be the bad guy. I didn't want to be the person that ruined your birthday.

And then you got sick. You cried on the drive home because your stomach hurt. You threw up when we got home, and cried some more.

It felt like my fault. It was my fault. Because I should've stopped you. I should've been your parent and said, "No, that's enough ice cream." I should've protected you when you were too young to see when you were making a mistake.

After that, I didn't care about being the bad guy. I was the bad guy if it meant keeping you safe.

You aren't young anymore. In some ways you always will be, to me, but you aren't. Not really. And I don't know how to stop trying to protect you. I don't know how to be when I see you doing something dangerous or reckless. I don't know how to sit back and watch you do something I know in my heart you'll regret.

It's always been my job to protect you, since the very beginning.

And maybe you don't think it's my job anymore, but that doesn't mean I can suddenly just stop.

And it's not fair, you know. It's not fair that I'm the bad guy just because I care.

I don't want to be the bad guy. I just want to be your mom.

Love, Mom

The phone rings three times before Mom answers.

"Hello?" She sounds suspicious, like she's not sure if it's my voice she'll hear next.

"Hi, Mom," I say.

"Are you okay?" she asks.

"Yeah, I'm fine."

I hear the relief in her voice immediately. "Ah. That's good."

"I got your email," I add.

Mom stays quiet, and the sound of the surviving katydids chirping in the nearby bushes becomes overpowering.

I take a breath, focusing on my words. "You're not a bad guy, okay? I just . . . I wanted something different from what you wanted for me."

"Okay," she says.

"I'm not trying to hurt you," I continue. "Or punish you. Or negatively affect you in any way at all. But you can still be my parent and also let me make my own choices. Because maybe what worked for you isn't going to work for me. And what you think is a mistake, I see as an opportunity to learn." I pause. "You won't be any less of a mother if I live my life differently from what you had planned."

"Sometimes we hurt people even when we're not trying to." Mom's voice wilts at the end, like a flower too tired to hold up its petals.

Thinking of how I inadvertently injured my parents makes me wince.

Is it my fault for accidentally hurting them? Or their fault for being unintentionally hurt?

Sometimes it feels like a never-ending cycle of who-hurt-who. It's like a carousel with no start or end, and the more I try to make sense of it, the faster it goes. The dizzier I get.

I hurt my parents by taking the set list and leaving. They hurt me by not letting me live my own life. I hurt them by not being an obedient daughter. They hurt me by not recognizing I was a different daughter from the one they wanted.

Sometimes I think there's so much blame to share, but other times I think there's very little blame at all.

Maybe we can be right and wrong at the same time.

Maybe they cancel each other out.

And then, like an island appearing on the horizon, impossible to avoid, I picture Dad. Dad, whose heart and soul was in the music I stole. Dad, who I still haven't spoken to. Dad, who I hurt probably most of all.

My hurt doesn't cancel out what I did. It can't.

Because what I did feels unforgivable.

"I don't want to fight," I blurt out, like I'm in such a hurry to erase the darkness coiling around my thoughts. I also don't want Dad to hate me, even though he probably does.

"I don't want to fight either," Mom says with a sigh. "I miss you, Harley. And I wish you'd call me once in a while, or send me an email. I feel like we're becoming strangers, and I hate it."

I think about what Chloe said—about ignoring my friends when I get busy. Is that what I've been doing to Mom, too?

She doesn't wait for a reply. "I'm worried about you. I'm worried this is going to be like what happened last year."

My defenses go up like hackles on a werewolf because talking about November is too personal. And when people use it like a weapon against me? *It will always feel too personal.* "Why? Because I'm *happy*? Because I'm not calling you a million times a day, or asking for help, or complaining that things are going wrong and you were right all along?"

"It's just—with you—these things can be a warning sign. And I missed them last time. I didn't know what was coming." Mom clears her throat, and I think she's trying not to cry. "I don't want to miss anything this time."

I fight the burn in my face. "Happiness is not a warning sign. It doesn't have to be. It doesn't get to be something only other people have."

"Of course not," Mom says. "But sometimes you spend so much time chasing this idea of happy that you crash at the first sign of disappointment. It's like your expectations are never realistic. You want everything to go exactly the way you've mapped out in your head, and when they don't, you spiral."

"You don't know what you're talking about," I argue. "You haven't been here. You haven't seen how hard I've worked. Because things *haven't* been going the way I planned—not at first. I spent weeks making popcorn, for crying out loud. The lead trapeze artist refused to train me. I stayed up until midnight almost every single night just to practice on my own where I wouldn't get yelled at. And I didn't give up like you and Dad said I would. I kept working, and trying, and sticking with it. And now I've got an audition for a chance to be in the show and—" I stop myself. I didn't mean to tell Mom so much. I didn't want her to know there was still a chance everything could go wrong.

I bite my lip, salt stinging my eyes.

"Just because I have mood swings doesn't mean I can't still live a fulfilling life," I say.

Mom's voice cracks. "A year ago, you told me you wanted to die. So forgive me if I'm less worried about you feeling fulfilled than you being around to live a life at all."

Everything inside me constricts, and the pieces of my heart I thought had healed a long time ago begin to tremble.

I remember that day. It felt like I was living outside my own body, watching everything go on below me and being unable to stop it.

I don't think I meant it. I thought I did at the time. But I think what I really wanted was to stop feeling so trapped.

Because sometimes darkness is crushing. Sometimes it's hard to breathe, or think, or live.

I wanted the darkness to stop more than I wanted to die.

But I guess those are the only words I knew how to use. And now they're haunting me because they're the only words Mom remembers.

"That's not something you need to worry about," I say quietly. "Feeling like you want to die isn't the same thing as planning to die. I was depressed—and I'm not anymore."

"But I *do* worry. And I don't think it's that simple. Right before November, you were all over the place. You were barely sleeping. You were making all these big plans—plans to travel, and start a blog, and learn how to cook—it was like you were living in this bubble of chaos that only you could understand. And then it felt like the next day you were barely eating. You lived in your bed. You wouldn't hang out with Chloe. Your room was a mess. You were angry all the time." I can practically feel Mom shaking her head through the phone. "It's like you were just giving up. It was like one day you had a million reasons to live, and the next day you couldn't even think of one. So yes, I'm worried. I'm worried you're going to crash again and I won't be there to make sure you're okay."

"I *am* okay," I say. "You're not listening to me. Being depressed is just something I deal with from time to time. And okay, maybe it's not normal for some people, but it's normal for me. And I have it under control. I'm coping."

"But it shouldn't be normal—" Mom starts to say.

"It's normal for you," I bite back too quickly.

"What are you talking about?" Mom's voice recoils.

"You're just like me. You have highs and lows and nothing in between. I mean, how many times have Dad and I found you obsessively cleaning the house, or redecorating on a whim? I remember when I was little, you'd have these phases where you'd get into baking. And you wouldn't just bake a cake, or a tray of cookies—you'd bake *everything*, all at once. You'd use up every single dish in the house, and Dad would come home, and you'd just laugh like you got carried away. And you'd have sad days, too. Days where you wouldn't come out of your room. Days where you were too tired to hold a conversation. Even days when you told Dad you wanted to die." I wait, because I know I've brought up something Mom doesn't think I even remember.

Everything goes hollow between us. Sometimes silence really is louder than words.

"I never said that." She sounds uncertain, either because she doesn't trust my memory or she's not sure if she can trust her own.

"You did," I say. "You told Dad you wanted to die. You were in your room, crying, and you thought I was in the living room watching a movie. You didn't think I heard you, but I did. And I worried about you too—worried that my mom was too sad, and that you would never stop being sad. But you did, eventually. And then you'd bake cakes and laugh and make big plans just the same way I do. And I realized that was just your normal, the way it's mine."

Even though Mom and I have a million differences, some parts of us are the same. I wish she could see that.

If she could relate to me, she might actually understand me.

"I—I don't even remember saying that. I really don't." I hear Mom shuffle, and a long pause follows. "I'm sorry if I scared you when you were little. I didn't mean to. I guess sometimes I get so caught up in what I'm feeling that I forget who else is watching. Who else might be affected."

I grimace. I know the feeling. "It's okay, Mom. I just want you to see that we're not so different. And you wouldn't want Popo controlling your life or acting like you couldn't function normally on your own—or like your normal isn't good enough. Because I don't want to have the same relationship with you that you have with Popo. I don't want things to be awkward between us just because we don't agree. And I have to be able to sort through what I'm feeling without you judging me. So maybe stop being so stuck on this November thing, okay? Let me move on from it."

"Is it my fault? Did you learn this from me?" Mom asks quietly.

"I don't know," I admit, because it's the truth. "Maybe. Or maybe we're just wired the same." I gnaw at my words like they're toffee—

hard to get through. "You and Dad never believed in talking to anyone. You know, like a therapist or whatever. You always acted like my being depressed was something I could fix with sunshine and water and exercise. And I think maybe November got so bad because I didn't feel like anybody believed me. I didn't feel supported. I'm not blaming you or Dad, but I'm saying it's sometimes easier to get through the dark moments when someone is there to tell you it's okay, and that there are options, and that everything is going to get better."

"Is that what you want? To talk to a therapist?" Mom asks.

"No," I say. "Because I don't feel like that's what would help me right now. I know it doesn't always look like it to you, but I'm more in control than you think I am. Maybe not of the feelings, but of how to *deal* with them."

"So when you hurt people, that's you in control? That's you making decisions on purpose?" Mom's words twist like a blade in my chest.

My heart starts to pound. "No," I snap, "it's not on purpose. And I'm not the only one who hurts people."

"What's that supposed to mean?" she snaps back, because we're too alike.

"You don't think Dad was hurt by the things you said? All those days he spent trying to cheer you up, and talk you into coming out of your room? I'm sure that hurt him, too." I can feel the fight building up in my chest, and I can't stop it. I feel cornered, and when I'm cornered, I . . . react. "Maybe that's why he's a ghost—because he couldn't deal with someone who didn't want to get help."

Silence.

I swallow the hard lump in my throat, regretting my words immediately.

Hurt people hurt people, right?

But maybe being hurt doesn't make hurting okay. Maybe it's a reason, but it's not an excuse.

"That was mean, Harley." Mom's trying her best to keep her voice even. "I didn't deserve that."

"I'm sorry," I say thinly, trying hard not to let her hear how sorry I really am. Maybe it's stubbornness, or maybe I've been trying so hard to convince her she's mostly wrong that I don't know how to let her be even a little bit right. "Look, tomorrow is a really big day for me. Talking about all of this is just going to throw me off. So . . . can we put this on hold?"

"Fine," Mom says.

"Okay," I say.

I know I should tell her I'm being too hard on her, and that I didn't mean to be cruel. I should tell her that hurting someone else is never okay, no matter what we're feeling. I should tell her she's not someone anyone should have to "deal with," just like I'm not either. Because we're both people, and people can be messy, but the most important thing is that we're trying our best to be better than our last mistakes.

But I don't know how to say the words. I don't know how to give her a little bit without feeling like I'm giving her everything.

Having big discussions with Mom is a balancing act I still don't understand.

After we hang up, I stand outside for a while with my arms wrapped around myself. The happiness I've felt recently is splintering. My hands feel clammy, and I squeeze them against my rib cage just to feel like I'm stable. Like I'm not going to break apart.

And then I take a deep breath, remember how important tomorrow is, and leave my worries in the bushes with the dying katydids.

I have too much work to do.

The dark clouds will have to wait.

CHAPTER FIFTY-FIVE

*P*lease stop pacing. You're making *me* nervous," Vas says, drumming his fingers along the center ring wall.

"I can't help it." I hold up my hands. "Look, I don't even have any fingernails left."

My eyes dart back to the main curtain, knowing any second Simon is going to walk through it and I'll have to perform the best I've ever performed.

This is my chance.

Maybe my only chance, if everyone is right about Simon.

Vas walks toward me and places his hands on my shoulders to slow me down. It works a little too well, and I collapse into his chest.

"Hold me," I say, imitating Princess Leia.

I can feel Vas's silent laughter against my head. He squeezes me tight. "It's going to be okay. You have nothing to worry about. Plus," he adds, "I'll be with you the entire time."

The stairs creak, and I look up from Vas's chest to see Simon making his way toward us. I push off of Vas like I've been caught doing something I shouldn't be doing, even though there are no rules about dating in the circus.

Simon must have seen us, but he doesn't say a word.

Either he really doesn't care, or gossip is not something he involves himself with.

"All right, you two." He sits in the front row, arms draped casually over the seats next to him. "Let's see what you've got."

Vas looks at one of the technicians at the back, who nods beside a wall of controls.

When it was just the two of us training, Vas would lift me onto the trapeze. But we need to show Simon how it would look to the audience, with all the lighting and mechanics.

We need to show him every drop of magic we have to make this work.

I close my eyes and breathe.

The music starts, and Vas and I stand at opposite ends of the room. We walk backward toward the lowered trapeze, like mirror images of each other, stopping before our bodies touch. We reach up, our grips tight on the bar, and it lifts us into the air.

I can feel Vas behind me, moving when I move in the opposite direction. I pull myself up slowly, legs pointed out to the side, holding the pose while the music builds. I take a seat on the bar, grabbing the ropes and rotating like a dancer in a music box, frozen and strong, and then my feet are on top of Vas's, his body hanging below mine like a reflection in the water.

We are opposites, performing bird's nests and meat hooks

and splits on the ropes. And then our bodies become tangled, our faces straining to move away from each other. We hold each other's weight, balance on each other's limbs, swing each other from one move to the next, all the while feeling the fight of not belonging screaming through our movements.

Vas's music fills the room, and I become so lost in the beautiful danger that is our act that I hardly feel like I'm in my body at all.

But I move when I'm supposed to. Feel Vas's skin when I'm supposed to.

I do everything right.

We hold our last pose as the music finishes.

There's a whisper of silence, and then Simon is on his feet, clapping with enthusiasm.

I'm sure I must be dreaming.

"I was not expecting that," Simon says with a hearty laugh. "When you said she was good, I thought you were being polite." He hops over the short wall and reaches us just as we push ourselves off the lowered trapeze. "It was magnificent."

I'm too afraid to smile.

Vas is breathing heavily beside me, his hands on his hips and his neck glistening with sweat. I'm not the only one with their dreams riding on Simon's decision.

Simon nods toward Vas. "And the music was excellent. Beautifully done, my friend." He looks hungry-eyed at the trapeze, his gaze following the lights like he's imagining a bigger picture. "Yes. Yes, I think this will do nicely."

"You mean we get to perform?" I blurt out.

Vas looks almost confused, like this is all too easy. I am too afraid to hope, but too hopeful to doubt.

I squeeze my hands together, desperately waiting for his answer.

Simon smiles and throws his hands up. "I love it. It's perfect. I want you two ready to close the show starting next Thursday."

"What?" Vas asks with a gaping mouth.

"Oh my God," I say at the same time.

"No point waiting for January when you both clearly have an act that's ready to go." Simon claps us both on the shoulders and winks. "Well done, you two." And then he's turning for the door and calling over his shoulder, "I'll ask Betty about getting you both costumes made. Make sure you stop by there before lunch to get your measurements taken."

And then he's gone, and even though I know there are techies in the back who helped with the trapeze controls and the safety net, I only see Vas.

"*Oh my God,*" I repeat. "Did . . . Did that really happen?"

Vas's laugh starts off nervous and restrained, but when he runs his hand through his hair, it turns euphoric. "We're closing the show. Simon is letting us *close the show.*"

"Why do you look so surprised? I thought you said we had nothing to worry about?" I raise a brow, my face wild with joy.

"I only said that to make you feel better," he says. "I never in a million years thought it would go that smoothly. I thought he'd demand changes, or tell me the music wasn't good enough, or . . . I don't know. Something." And then he turns to me with starry eyes.

"It's because you're magic when you're up there. That's why he said yes. I bet he couldn't take his eyes off you."

"Yeah, right." I roll my eyes.

"It's true," he insists. "And the audience won't be able to take their eyes off you either."

My heart flutters, he smiles, and then I'm in his arms again and we're giggling with our noses pushed together, stealing kisses beneath the spotlights.

CHAPTER FIFTY-SIX

The rest of the cast insists on taking us out to dinner. The Terzi Brothers seem almost relieved to have their old slot back. Vivien just seems excited I'm officially part of the show. And Dexi keeps mentioning what a huge deal it is that Simon is going with a plan he didn't come up with himself.

She tells me it means I'm the real deal.

I don't know about that, because I don't feel real.

I feel like a girl with an Infinity Stone for a heart, and any moment I'm going to split in two, again and again, until there's a billion of me, because this is too much happiness for just one person.

CHAPTER FIFTY-SEVEN

*V*as drives the two of us back to camp on his bike. When I slide off the seat and pull the helmet over my head, I realize I haven't stopped smiling since this morning.

When Vas pulls his own helmet off, it looks like he might be thinking the same.

"I don't know how I'm going to sleep tonight," I say with a laugh. "I'm way too excited about Thursday."

Vas pulls off his gloves, his eyes going serious.

"What?" I frown.

When he looks up, his cheeks are pink with awkward embarrassment. "I was going to offer to make you a hot drink, to help you sleep, but I realized it might seem like I'm just trying to get you alone in my trailer."

"I've been to your trailer plenty of times," I point out with a laugh.

"Yeah, but that was before, when we were working." He pauses. "And Jin is . . . sleeping over at a friend's house."

"Oh." My cheeks go pink too.

"But we could go to the Lunch Box, if you'd feel more comfortable. They do hot chocolate and—" Vas starts.

I take a few steps toward his trailer door and motion toward the lock.

His shoulders relax, and he finds his keys.

When we're inside, Vas gets out honey, jam, and a combination of spices from one of the kitchen cupboards. He places a pot on the electric stove, and before long a sweet and spicy fragrance fills the trailer.

"That smells amazing." I breathe in deeply.

Vas grins. "It's called sbiten. My mom used to make it for me when I was sick. I guess I've always associated it with comfort, in a way." He stirs the simmering liquid carefully, his eyes lost in thought.

"What was she like?" I ask.

It takes him a moment to gather his words. "Strict," he says with a laugh. "But kind, too. Her entire life was the circus, but it was such hard work. I think she wanted me to have an easier time with it, which is why she sent me to London to live with Maggie's family. She wanted me to share her dream, but with more opportunities. But I never loved it like she did. I loved the violin." He adjusts the stove a bit. "When I was still in London, I was going to quit my training, but then my mom got sick before I got the chance to tell her. I didn't really feel like I could quit after that. It felt like I'd be letting her down too much."

"I'm sorry," I say.

He nods.

I wonder if he wants me to change the subject, but then he says the words that seem to break his heart all over again.

"She died when I was out here, performing with Maison du Mystère. When I was still partners with Maggie."

My throat knots. "Is . . . Is that why you really quit?" I ask carefully.

He shakes his head. "No. I mean, I'm sure it made it easier. But I was telling the truth when I said I quit because of Maggie." He clenches his jaw, his eyes burning into the hot liquid. "She—she knew my mom died before I did. Her parents called her first, on the morning of one of our performances, because they wanted her to tell me in person. They thought it would make it easier. But she kept it to herself all day—waited until after our performance to tell me." He takes a deep breath, like it's been a long time since he's told this story. I wonder if he's ever told it at all. "Turns out there was a scout in the audience for some big show in New York. She didn't want to risk the performance. She was afraid that when I found out about my mom, I wouldn't want to perform that night, and she needed me."

"Oh my God," I say softly. "I'm so sorry, Vas. That's awful."

"It's not your fault." He looks at me with a weak smile. "But thanks."

"What about your brothers?" I ask, remembering what he told me about them getting into trouble. "Are they . . . ?"

"Dead? No." Vas thins his mouth, and the relief I'd expect from his answer doesn't seem to exist. "But we don't talk. I think they resented me a lot growing up—they thought our mother coddled me. And when she passed away, they wanted me to come back to Russia—help with the family business." He's choosing his words so carefully, I wonder if "business" is just the term he uses in polite conversation. He shrugs. "But I haven't lived in Russia for a long time. It doesn't feel like home anymore. And they don't feel like family."

"It's not . . . too much, is it? Performing when you have so much history? Because if it is, please tell me," I say. "I don't want you to do something if it hurts you."

Vas shrugs. "I don't mind performing. I spent a lot of years training—I've worked hard to get to the level I'm at, and I don't regret that. So no, it's not too much. But sometimes I wonder how far I could've gone if I had put everything into music. I guess maybe some dreams are meant to stay dreams."

He turns the stove off and scoops some of the hot liquid into two mugs before joining me at the small table.

I blow at the steam, testing the side of the mug with my fingertips and pulling them away when they get too hot.

Vas grins. "You're so impatient."

"Character flaw," I say, making a goofy face.

He watches the steam rise, his head tilted slightly to the side. "Have you told your parents about next week?"

My heart stops.

"I know you said they don't support you," Vas says, "but I know what it would probably mean to you to have them there."

I shake my head. "Even if they came, I'd feel like it wouldn't be for the right reasons. I don't want them to feel sorry for me, or obligated to show up. I wanted them to care right from the start.

And, I don't know, I guess I'd rather they didn't come at all than have to beg them."

He nods, taking a careful sip of his drink. I do the same and feel myself overcome with warmth.

"Wow," I say. "I definitely like sbiten."

He laughs. "I'm glad."

When we've finished our drinks, Vas takes the dishes to the sink and starts rinsing them under the tap. And I don't know if it's the curve of his shoulders, or his adorably pointed ears, or even the way his hair is hanging at his temples, but I suddenly want to wrap my arms around him.

So I do.

The faucet creaks, and I feel him press his wet fingers against my hands. He turns, slowly at first, and then our fingers are lost behind each other's necks, our lips closing against each other's parted mouths like we don't care about coming up for air.

I run my hands under his clothes, gripping the hard muscles of his sides, and I guess he's impatient too because he yanks the shirt up over his head and flings it to the floor, lips returning to mine.

When my eyes drift down to the smooth, bare skin of his chest, I see the tattoo trailing down the right side of his ribs.

It's . . . not Chinese characters.

Oh thank God, my mind blurts out.

Vas reads my face anyway, a soft puzzlement in his brow. "What's wrong?"

"Nothing," I say, laughing. "I'm just relieved your tattoo isn't a cliché. I was worried I was going to have to pretend to like it."

He grins. "Well then I'm relieved too."

My fingers follow the black ink on his skin—words and lines contorted and twisted to make the shape of a wolf.

С волка́ми жить, по-во́лчьи выть

"What does this say?" I ask, his breath quickening beneath my touch.

"S volkámi žitʹ, po-vólčʹi vytʹ. It means 'When you live with wolves, you learn to howl,'" he says.

"Is that kind of like 'When in Rome, do as the Romans do?'" I ask.

"A bit. I think of it a little differently. To me, the wolf is dangerous, and the howl is a kind of pain. If you spend too much time around people whose souls are hurting, eventually your soul starts to cry out too." He presses his hand against mine, flattening my palm over the words. "It's a reminder to stay away from people who only bring trouble. One of the few things my brothers taught me."

The ache I hear when he plays the violin is what I see in his eyes now.

"Do you—" I start.

"Want to talk about it?" He smiles, and the ache disappears. "No." He kisses me gently on the mouth. "I'd prefer this."

At some point we're walking backward toward his bed, and he lowers me onto the mattress, his body pressed against mine. And even though we've been this close a hundred times during practice, it's never like *this*.

Like he wants to trace his fingers over every inch of my skin.

Like I'm drunk on chocolate and trees.

Like we want to be contortionists and aerialists and a vanishing act, all at once.

His lips brush against my cheek, and then I feel his breath against my ear. "I don't want to do anything you're not comfortable with." His voice is warm and sweet, like the sbiten we drank together. I can still taste the blackberries from his kisses.

"I'm comfortable doing this," I say, and I turn my face so that our lips meet again.

He presses against me a bit more firmly, his mouth moving against mine like we've somehow rehearsed every kiss, our hands and tongues and bodies in perfect synchronization.

Vas pulls his face back, his breathing growing more rapid. "I just . . . I want you to tell me if anything is too much." He gives me a weak smile. "I don't do this very often. I want it to be perfect. I want it to be right—for both of us."

And then I realize what he's saying. Because he isn't just asking about the kissing, or the staying in his room. He's asking about sex.

I trace my fingers along his arms, trying to ignore the pounding in my chest. Mom's told me enough times that these conversations can be awkward, and that they shouldn't be, but that doesn't make it any easier.

Talking about sex *is* awkward.

At least for me.

"You were the first person I've ever kissed," I say, and the confession feels like it's echoing through the room.

Vas looks genuinely surprised.

And then I feel like I have to clarify. "I mean, *real* kissed, anyway. I kissed someone as a dare in second grade, but I don't think that counts. It wasn't even *my* dare, actually. The other girl didn't want to do it, and so I just—did. I thought I was being helpful or funny or brave or . . . something."

"Yeah, I don't think that counts either," he says with a soft smile, resting his body alongside mine, his head propped up by his hand. Clearly, he knows I like to ramble.

"I know everyone's different, but for me personally, I've never really had those moments where you look at someone and think, 'I can't wait to kiss them.' It always felt like there had to be something more there first. And maybe I'm sappy and romantic at heart, but I always liked the idea of crushing on someone for a long time before a kiss happens. And I guess I've never really had a crush before. Not until you." I take a breath. "But I also don't care as much about the sex part. I know on paper it's a big deal—or at least everyone says it's supposed to be. But I guess I feel like if two people like each other and they both want to do it, there doesn't necessarily have to be a timeline." I twist my mouth, hyperaware that it sounds like I'm giving a speech. "But *also*, I know that sometimes I make decisions without really thinking them through. You know—like the almost-tattoo. And on the off chance I'm being impulsive, I don't think I should jump into anything." I pause. "Not right away. Not until I've thought it through."

Vas smiles gently. "Impulsive? I never would've guessed."

"Oh yeah," I say with wide eyes. "I once spent one hundred and fifty dollars on yarn and crochet needles because the night before,

I decided I was going to open an Etsy store and sell amigurumi Pokémon. All of it is still in my closet, untouched."

His laugh makes his eyes crease, and he takes my hand. "I understand. And . . . I don't want to be something you regret. Not even a little bit."

I smile. "I don't want to stop kissing you, though."

"Well, that's good news," he says, leaning closer. "Because I happen to quite like kissing you."

He closes his soft lips over mine, our fingers unwinding to explore the warmth of each other's skin. When I feel his tongue against the curve of my neck and his fingers trailing up my spine, sparks devour my entire body.

We fall asleep tangled up beneath his blanket.

CHAPTER FIFTY-EIGHT

*E*verything okay?" Vas's violin is tucked beneath his chin, but his bow hangs at his side.

I look back at Mom's newest email for only a second—subject line: The time you fell from the chandelier—before locking the screen and letting my phone drop into my lap. "Yeah, it's fine. Just my mom telling me a story I'd forgotten about."

Vas's violin falls from his neck like he's handling glass. Careful but firm. It's how I should be handling people's feelings, if only I knew where to begin.

Maybe I have butterfingers, but with emotions. Maybe I'm not good at knowing the right things to say. The right way to handle with care.

Which sucks. Because I don't want to hurt Mom. I don't want to hurt anybody.

"Would you like to talk about it?" Vas flashes a smile. "I could make tea."

I shake my head and smile back. "It's nothing serious." Vas sits down beside me anyway, violin and bow draped across his lap. I take a slow breath. "It was about the first time I fell in love with the circus."

"So this is a memory of when you were an embryo?" His grin makes my entire body light up.

I nudge him with my shoulder and laugh. "Okay, well, the first time I *realized* I loved the circus. I was probably four or five. My parents had taken me to rehearsals, and I saw the aerialists with their static trapeze and silk ropes and hoops. It was like watching humans turn into fairies right in front of me. It was like peering into another world only I knew the secrets to." I shrug. "So when I got home, I tried to re-create the act with a jump rope, a Hula-Hoop, and the chandelier that hung above the dining room table. It went about as well as you're probably imagining."

"Did the chandelier make it out alive?" he asks seriously.

I snort. "Nope. It detached from the ceiling, and I ended up on the floor crying my eyes out because I thought I was going to get in trouble. Which, I mean, my parents were upset, but not anywhere near as mad as I expected. My mom was just worried I had hurt myself. And my dad was more concerned with the damage done to the ceiling.

"But then a few days later, my parents took me to the park and showed me how to use the monkey bars. They said if I was going to be an aerialist, I needed to build upper body strength. So I practiced as much as I could, and they never complained about taking me to that park. Not even when I'd want to stay for hours on the weekend."

Vas tilts his head thoughtfully. "So I guess in a way, your parents kind of encouraged you to pursue the circus."

"In a way. Maybe." I blink. "I'd never thought of it that way before. But they've always been so adamant about school. It always felt like they were on one side, and I was on the other."

"Maybe they thought there was room to do both?" Vas offers.

My eyes fall back to his violin. "Like you with music?"

"My parents were strict, and there was no question that they wanted me to pursue the circus over music. But they still bought me my first violin. And maybe it wasn't the support I needed, but it was better than nothing." He taps his thumb against his leg. "I'm sure there are plenty of people who don't get any encouragement at all. Musicians who never find instruments. Artists who never find paintbrushes. Readers who aren't able to find books." He looks up gently.

"And aerialists who aren't given the key to their parents' circus gym." I make a face.

Vas nods. "That too."

"I can't tell if she sends these emails to make me feel guilty, or because she's trying to show me all the different ways she cares," I say. I wonder if that's part of the problem—that I've only ever seen my parents in black and white.

I believe in gray areas. I live in the gray area. But when it comes to my parents, I guess it's always been easier to put them in boxes.

Even though I *hate* boxes.

Because the problem with boxes is that they don't give people any room to grow.

"Maybe she's trying to find a way to be present in your life," he says. "Relationships are like most living things—if you don't nurture them, they'll die."

"No sugarcoating that one, huh?" I raise a brow.

He leans in closely, and I feel my heart thump. "I'm Russian. We like to get to the point." And then he kisses me, and my heart turns to mush.

Nashville, Tennessee

November—Week 14

CHAPTER FIFTY-NINE

On Monday I start counting down the days until our big performance.

Three days to go.

On Tuesday we see our costumes for the first time.

Two days to go.

On Wednesday Vas and I have our final dress rehearsal.

One day to go.

On Thursday I step outside, see the big top in the distance, and
feel all the pieces of my life fitting into place.

Today is the first day of the rest of my life.

CHAPTER SIXTY

*M*y costume is cream and gold, with a seemingly infinite number of sparkles. Vas's is similar, but in black and silver. We are night and day, shadow and light.

The evening star and the morning star.

When I look at myself in the mirror, my hair knotted up in twin buns and my makeup done to perfection, I search for Mom.

Is this what she looked like before a performance?

Did her heart come to life the way mine does?

Was she nervous?

Excited?

Terrified?

I'm almost afraid to know the answer. Because if she felt what I feel now, it makes everything worse. It means she would've known what I'd be missing out on, and she tried to stop me anyway. And if she never felt the way I do? If she didn't love the circus the way I do?

Then I feel bad for her. Because she's lived her whole life

never knowing what this kind of euphoria feels like.

Vas appears over my shoulder, holding a ceramic flowerpot full of miniature bubblegum-pink orchids. He smiles sheepishly, his eyes darkened with stage makeup. "I've always thought it was kind of weird to give someone a bouquet of dead flowers, but it's opening night, so I hope these are okay."

I turn around, frowning. "Dead flowers?"

"I mean, they've been hacked off from their roots. So yeah— dead." He holds the pot toward me. "But these are still alive and well, and they'll last longer too."

I laugh, taking the orchids from him and setting them on the table. "Thank you. I love them."

He nods. "How are you feeling?"

I lock my fingers together and stand up, taking a deep breath and grinning wildly. "The happiest I've ever been."

Vas smiles back, and my heart does somersaults.

When the music starts, my nerves come alive. I feel like my blood is full of a trillion microscopic beads of electricity. I'm pacing in circles, jumping in place, inhaling big gulps of air.

Vas takes my hand and squeezes. "I'd kiss you, but I don't want to ruin your makeup."

I grin. "I'd kiss you anyway, but I don't want to ruin yours."

I can hear the cheering from the audience. The laughter, too. It reverberates through the big top like a stampede of wildebeests through a canyon.

And then it's our turn, and suddenly I can't hear a thing.

I just see Vas, moving beside me like we're both floating toward the center of the ring.

I close my eyes, let everything go, and breathe.

We are light and skin and water and magic. My breath echoes in my ears. I'm sure my heart is hidden there too.

We move together. Exist together. And every second that passes fills me with a kind of power I can't explain.

I feel invincible.

I'm not just a morning star—I'm an entire universe.

And when the audience cheers and I feel myself wrapped up in Vas's arms, I know there is no going back from this feeling.

Because now I know what living feels like.

And it's *dazzling*.

"I'm so proud of you!" Vivien squeals, her arms tight around my neck.

"You were incredible," Dexi says.

"Your chemistry is off the charts," Jin adds.

I make a face. "I mean, that wasn't really what we were going for, but I'll take it."

Jin shrugs. "People see what they want to see."

Vas is standing beside me, looking at me like I'm made of sunlight. Vivien seems to take this as a cue.

"Okay." She skips toward the door, dragging Dexi by the wrist. "We'll see you in a bit." She pauses near the doorway. "Want to go out for ice cream to celebrate?"

I nod giddily. "I'd like that."

Jin perks up, following them out of the dressing room. "Are there drinks involved in this celebration? Because I know a place. . . ."

I turn to Vas. "You're coming too, right?"

"I wouldn't miss it." He steps forward, locking his fingers through mine. "They're right, you know. You were incredible. Everyone in the crowd loved you."

I bite my lip and bounce on my heels. "Do you think so? I know it's weird to be so desperate for a stranger's approval, but there's something about the way they look back at you. Like they want you to *know* when they're happy. Like they're thanking you for giving them something wonderful. And I've always wondered what that would feel like, ever since I was a kid watching other people perform."

"And what does it feel like?" Vas asks gently.

I lean my head back and shut my eyes tight. "Like someone else knows what I've been saying all along—that I'm a good aerialist, and that I belong in the circus." I open my eyes. "I guess I've always wanted the validation."

"I knew you were good the first time I saw you in the big top," Vas says.

I roll my eyes. "Yeah, right. You hated me back then. You were practically sneering the whole time you were playing your violin."

"That's not true! I'm just not good around strangers." He pauses. "Especially cute ones."

I smile, poking him in the ribs to make him laugh. "You thought I was cute?"

He pulls me close to him, folding his hands around my lower

back. "I did. But that's not why I liked you. There was something else about you. This—this kind of focus, I guess. When you'd practice, you'd have this look in your eyes—like it was you against the world, and the rest of us could either get on board or get out of your way."

I make a face. "*That's* why you liked me?"

"I mean, you have really nice lips, too. And eyes," he says, like it's an afterthought.

I shake my head, laughing.

"Ah, there you are." Simon's voice sounds from the doorway.

He's dressed in his suit and top hat, his eyes as mesmerizing as ever.

I'm still smiling, thinking he's here to congratulate us, when I catch the worry in Vas's face. The furrowed brow, the twitch in the corner of his mouth, and the way his shoulders pull back like he's bracing for news.

Something isn't right.

I feel Vas's hands slip away from me. "It's not like you to wander backstage after a show. Is something the matter?" he asks coolly. He knows Simon—he knows his tricks.

I feel my body shrinking and shrinking, until I'm barely the size of an ant.

Simon smooths his mustache with his fingers, searching for his words.

I don't think he has to search very hard. I think he came here knowing exactly what he wanted to say.

"You put on a great show tonight, and you should be very proud of yourselves." Simon's eyes dart between the two of us before landing solely on Vas. "Look, there's no point in dragging this out. There's a new trapeze artist arriving in the morning, and I'm going to need you to teach her the routine. Get her up to speed."

Vas clenches his jaw.

I still don't understand what's happening. Or maybe I don't want to.

"Is . . . Is this for another act?" I ask, my voice cracking.

Simon pulls off his hat, spinning it casually in his hand. "No, she's here for your act. You've done really well, and I don't say that lightly. But I need a professional, and I hired you as a trainee. I'm sorry, but this was never going to be a permanent arrangement."

"But you said I could perform. You said if we—" I start.

"You did perform," Simon interjects. "And you can perform through the rest of the week. But as soon as the new aerialist has the routine down, I'm swapping you out."

My eyes burn hot.

"Don't take it so hard, kid," Simon urges, his voice void of empathy. "There's still a place for you at Maison du Mystère. Just not as the closing act."

Vas clenches his fists beside me. "You tricked us. You manipulated us into coming up with an act knowing full well you would replace Harley."

Simon tuts. "It's business. It's not personal." He turns for the door but looks over his shoulder. "And I'm still keeping your song, so it's not all bad news."

I close my arms around my ribs. Usually I have such a hard

time keeping my words in, but I'm not sure words even exist in my head anymore.

Everything is dark.

Empty.

And I can't breathe.

CHAPTER SIXTY-ONE

I must be balancing on a spinning top, because the world is wobbly and shifting and I can't focus on anything in front of me. Even Vas appears to be swaying, his hands trying to hold me up by my shoulders, but I'm sinking fast onto the floor.

The tears don't stop pouring.

Why did I think I could do this?

Why did I think I was good enough to be here?

I feel like I've learned this lesson before, a hundred times, but never like this. Never so clearly thrown in my face.

Simon is replacing me.

And at first I'm wondering where I messed up, and if my poses weren't good enough or my leg extensions not high enough. I wonder if I looked too much like an amateur on that stage, and if that's why Simon changed his mind.

But he didn't change his mind. This was his plan all along. There was nothing I could have done to make him keep me as a performer.

Because I've never been good enough—not from the start, and not at the end—and maybe everybody knew it but me.

Why did I have to get so carried away?

And why did people let me?

I see my tears fall onto the floor. One, two, three drops, all morphing together to form a puddle.

Vas is trying to call me back to him, but I don't know how to recover. I don't know what to do next. My head is screaming to run forever, through the walls and across water if I have to, to get as far away from here as possible.

But where would I go?

I've burned every single bridge I've crossed.

My chest aches and aches and aches, until I'm not sure I can take another second of it. I'm not sure I can come back from this kind of fall.

My body feels broken. *Everything* feels broken.

I'm squeezing the fabric of my costume because I need to hold on to something that feels real when I hear her voice.

"Harley?"

And then his.

"Are you okay?"

I look up and see Mom and Dad standing in the doorway. But are they real?

And if they are, how are they really here?

In that moment it doesn't matter if they hate me. Because I need my parents more than anything.

I'm on my feet and in their arms, sobbing into Dad's checkered shirt that smells like home. My real, tangible, grounded home, and not the fantasy I've been so desperate to live in.

"I can't do this anymore," I say through sobs. "You were right—I don't belong here."

"Oh, honey," Mom says, kissing me on the top of my head. "I don't understand. What's happened?"

"I just want to go home." I pull my face up and look at them both. "Please, can I come home?"

Mom's face softens. She looks at Dad, who is only looking at me.

He pulls me into his chest. "You can always come home, Harley," he says. "Come on. Let's go get your stuff."

CHAPTER SIXTY-TWO

I'm stuffing all my clothes into my duffel bag when I hear the trailer door fall shut. The noise makes me jump, and I find Vas standing a few feet away, his eyebrows as furrowed as ever and his mouth half open.

"You're leaving? Just like that?" I can hear the hurt in his voice.

But this has nothing to do with him.

I turn back to my bag, shoving the last pair of socks into the corner and pulling the zipper closed. "I don't belong here."

"Yes, you do." He takes a step closer.

"I'm not good enough." I shut my eyes.

"Yes, you *are*." Another step.

I swallow, fighting the tears that begin to pool. "I should never have come here, Vas. This was a giant mistake. I knew it, deep down. I was just too stubborn to admit it."

Vas reaches for my arm, but I spin around too quickly, and his fingers recoil.

I wonder if he knows all the things I wish I could say to him.

If he knows leaving him is just as painful as leaving the circus.

"Please don't go," he says. "It doesn't have to be the end. I'll keep training with you, and we'll get Simon to put you in another act. Maybe the swinging trapeze, or the silk ropes. There are other ways to be a part of the circus."

I shake my head, my voice hollow. "I don't want it anymore."

He looks angry. "That's not true."

"It is," I snap back. "Or at least it will be." I grab my bag and yank it toward me, the weight of it pulling me down. "I have to go. My parents are waiting outside."

I only make it one step before he speaks again.

"I thought you had more fight in you." It sounds like an accusation.

I look up at him, hating how much those green eyes make me want to soften my heart and press myself close to him. They make me feel like they could break me, and I already feel broken. "I've done nothing but fight since I got here. I stayed when everyone ignored me. I stayed when Maggie refused to train me. I stayed when Simon put me on popcorn duty, and even when the only place I could practice was at night when nobody was looking. But I won't stay after this—not after Simon has made it clear that, not only am I not good enough, but I'm not even worth the courtesy of being treated like a person with feelings. It's business, right? Well, I don't like this business, and I don't feel like fighting anymore."

The circus was everything to me. It was magic, and wonder, and life.

But Simon lifted a veil today.

I don't see magic in the circus anymore. I see heartbreak.

"You're not a quitter," Vas says, his jaw tightening.

I twist my mouth, feeling my defenses rise. "You're lecturing *me* about quitting? Come on, Vas. Your heart quit the circus a long time ago, but you won't *actually* quit because you're too scared." I lift my shoulders. "What are you still doing here? Simon is never going to let you write music for this place. He gave you one song, but for how long? You think when he uses all of Teatro della Notte's stolen music for next season, he won't conveniently swap out your song? But sure, you're not a quitter either, right? You'll stay here anyway, while the circus eats up your dreams." I shake my head. "I might be quitting, but at least I'm not letting my heart rot away on a dream I've outgrown."

Vas looks like I've punched him in the chest.

Oh my God, what am I doing? I'm ruining us. I'm ruining everything.

But I can't stop.

"Please don't leave like this. You'll regret it." He swallows. He still thinks there's hope.

But I know better. The words burst out of me too fast. "I regret a lot of things, but leaving won't be one of them."

His green eyes crack in half.

What am I doing? What have I said?

Take it back, take it back, take it back.

"Do you regret me?" I can barely hear him over the pounding in my skull.

"I didn't mean it like that," I say, but it sounds guttural and harsh because I've lost all control of my emotions.

"Did you even consider what it would mean for us if you left? Do you even care?" *Us.* The word twists my insides. His voice is so far away. "I travel eleven months out of the year, in a circus you so clearly never want to step foot in again. Did you even think about whether or not we'd see each other after this?"

I'm shaking everywhere. "I—no." Where are my words? Where is my *mind*?

Vas shifts his jaw. "Of course you didn't. Because that's another character flaw, right? You're always putting yourself before the people you're supposed to love." He hesitates. "Or maybe that was just an illusion too."

"That's not fair," I say, tears streaming down my cheeks. "I'm not trying to hurt you."

"You never are." He shifts his weight. "But you sure do leave quite the body count of hurt people on the way to doing whatever you want." He turns for the door.

"Vas, wait," I blurt out, my heart feeling frantic.

He stops, tilting his chin slightly toward me. "It's fine. I'll get over it. You're doing me a favor, really. Now I know where I stand."

He leaves me alone in the trailer, taking all the color with him.

Las Vegas, Nevada

~~November~~ Week 14

CHAPTER SIXTY-THREE

I've been home for two weeks and have barely spoken a word to my parents. There's a lot we still haven't talked about, and I guess I was in such a hurry to get away from Maison du Mystère that I didn't really think about how those conversations would go.

There's still so much I need to apologize for.

But right now, my heart is too broken for remorse.

It's too broken for anything.

I feel the dark clouds coming back. And I've met them enough times that they should feel familiar, but they never do.

And it's always hard to pinpoint exactly what it is that invited them.

Was it leaving Maison du Mystère? Was it leaving Vas? Or were they already well on their way before then, hovering until they found the perfect opening?

Sometimes I think they're always hovering. Always waiting.

But every now and then I can convince myself I'm happy enough to pretend they aren't there.

I keep reminding myself this isn't the worst it's ever been, but then I think—will it get worse? Is this just the start? And how long will it be until I bounce back again?

Will I *ever* bounce back?

My brain wrestles these thoughts until I'm exhausted and I force myself to sleep most of the days away.

Mom and Dad seem concerned, but they shouldn't be. This is not the part of my life where I needed their concern. This is the part I've already made sense of—by embracing that it *doesn't always make sense*. This is just part of who I am—maybe who I'll always be.

Popo tells me darkness is a wave, and all waves pass eventually.

But right now, in this moment, it feels like it will last forever.

I'm filled with such a crushing amount of regret. Regret that I took Dad's music and gave it to Simon. Regret about hurting Tatya, and neglecting my friendship with Chloe. Regret that I joined Maison du Mystère, and put my trust in Simon.

I regret everything in the last few months.

Everything except Vas.

Until the moment we said goodbye.

CHAPTER SIXTY-FOUR

Relationships are like most living things—if you don't nurture them, they'll die.

All I can hear is Vas's voice, over and over again like he's burning the words into my memory.

Which is pointless, because they're already there.

What have I done? What have I ruined?

I've been ignoring all the people I care about most. The people I love. And why? Because I get too excited and I can't remember to make an effort? Or because I don't *want* to make the effort?

What does that say about me?

I'm not trying to be the crappy half of every relationship, but maybe I am. Not all the time, but when I'm like this? When I stop treating people like they matter? When I take them for granted and assume they'll still be waiting whenever I've finished doing whatever ridiculous thing I'm doing?

I've lost all the friends I care about, and my family may never forgive me.

Hermione Granger used a Time-Turner because there weren't enough hours in the day to do all the things she wanted. But me? I'd use a Time-Turner to do everything over.

I'd take back the mean things I've said. I'd tell people I cared about them more. I'd try harder to make other people as happy as I want myself to be.

Because maybe that's the point I've been missing. Maybe happiness doesn't mean anything at all if I've hurt other people to find it.

Vas was right. Chloe was right. They were *all* right.

It's funny—when I was wrong, I was so certain I knew exactly what I was doing. But now that I want to do the right thing, I have no idea where to start.

CHAPTER SIXTY-FIVE

*E*ventually I find the courage to talk to Mom and Dad. I tell them both how sorry I am. I tell them I don't expect them to forgive me, but I hope they at least believe me when I say I wish I could take it all back.

They don't hesitate for even a second. They tell me they forgive me, and that there's no need to feel guilty anymore. I get the feeling they wanted me home more than they ever wanted the apology.

I'm lucky to have parents who love me unconditionally. I realize that now more than ever.

But this destination I've arrived at—it shouldn't have taken hurting them both to get here. I should've been better.

I'm going to try to be better.

I tell them it's not just that I feel guilty about what I did to them—I'm also humiliated. Because despite all my hard work, I still failed. I couldn't be a trapeze artist, even though I tried as hard as I possibly could.

My parents knew this would happen all along, but I didn't want to believe them.

And the truth is, I feel lost without a dream. Empty.

Maybe it's a good thing they'd never supported me. Because at least this way, they didn't waste anything.

They didn't have to set their hearts on a dream only to watch it break because their daughter *isn't good enough*.

Dad tells me people don't always get what they want, even when they try their hardest. He says that's part of life, and that people aren't entitled to things just because they tried.

Mom points out that this is exactly why she wanted me to have a backup plan, and that I should think about starting school in January if I can sign up for classes late.

Bitterness crawls through me. Because a part of me wants to flinch at their words, to point out that after everything, they *still don't get it*.

But then I remember that I failed. I came home.

My parents were right about everything, and I need to accept it.

I tell Mom I'll think about college.

CHAPTER SIXTY-SIX

I ask Chloe to meet me at our local Starbucks. Despite everything, she agrees. It makes me think our friendship is going to be okay. That I'll be able to repair what I've broken.

I offer to buy her a Pink Drink, but she insists on paying for her own.

I guess it should've been a sign of how the conversation was going to go.

Because when I tell Chloe how sorry I am, she doesn't forgive me the way Mom and Dad did.

She says she told me she was afraid of us drifting apart, and that I let it happen anyway. She tells me I wasn't a good friend to her, that I moved on as soon as something better came along, and that I hurt her.

She says she doesn't know if things can go back to the way they were, because we haven't been friends in months.

She says she's already had time to get used to that, and maybe we're better off doing our own things.

It's a breakup I didn't realize was coming.

I cry at home until my cheeks feel tender and my eyes are swollen, and when I'm staring in the mirror wondering how the hell I got here, I realize it's my fault. I brought this on myself.

Because even if I hate that he said it, maybe Vas was right about the way I've been treating people I claim to care about. I never stop to think how other people feel until it's too late.

I try to remember if I've always been this way, or if I changed the more desperate I became to chase my dreams. And the truth is, I don't know.

I have no idea how many people there are who I need to make amends with. I don't know how far back a list like that would go. I was never keeping track before, because I didn't even realize I was doing it.

But there's one person I *do* remember. One person I know I hurt by accident.

And I know exactly what I need to do to fix it.

CHAPTER SIXTY-SEVEN

*T*eatro della Notte feels like a friend I haven't seen in years. I'm searching its building for quirks and details that will remind me it's the same friend after all, and that nothing's really changed.

But I can't find them. Everything looks different. The black is grayer, the gold paler. Even the smell of the air is different, like dust and asphalt.

It's changed.

Or maybe I've changed, because I can't help thinking how much I miss the smell of popcorn.

The doorman at the back is a stranger, with short blond hair and stern eyes. "Entrance is just around the front, ma'am."

"I'm Kenji and Delilah's daughter," I say, and it feels unnatural.

"Do you have some ID?" he asks, arms folded at his chest.

I start to dig through my bag. "Where's Billy?"

"Who?"

Maybe a lot *has* changed since I've been gone. "Never mind," I say, holding my ID up to him.

He nods, pulling the door open for me.

I find Tatya in her dressing room, still applying her makeup for tonight's show. When she spots me in the mirror, she flashes her megawatt smile, before her eyes seem to hint she remembers what happened the last time we spoke.

"I'm sorry," I say before she gets the chance to talk first. "I should never have talked to my parents about what would happen if you left—not even figuratively. It was a garbage thing to do, especially to a friend."

Tatya turns in her chair, her shoulders relaxing. "Oh, Harley. I forgave you *weeks* ago." She stands up and holds out her arms, and I crush myself against her because I'm just so relieved.

I sit with her while she gets ready, and she asks me all about Maison du Mystère. I tell her all my stories, despite the fact that so many make my heart hurt.

"A little bird told me you were doing incredibly well over there," she says, tracing her eye with black liner. "I was really happy for you, chasing your dreams like that. You're so brave."

I frown. "A little bird?"

Tatya laughs. "I used to work at another circus with Jin Thompson, years ago. Did he not mention it?"

I press my lips together. "No, he didn't." So that's how Maggie found out who I was. And then I frown. "Did you tell my parents? Is that how they knew where I was?"

Tatya shakes her head. "It wasn't me. I didn't even know you were keeping it a secret from them, and they never asked."

I frown. I've been so consumed by my own feelings that I still haven't managed to find out what brought them to the circus. I never told Popo I was performing. In fact, I didn't tell *anyone*.

So if it wasn't Tatya, then who?

"I'm glad you're back," Tatya says, smiling in the mirror. "The circus isn't quite the same without you."

"I'm glad to be back too," I say, but as soon as the words leave me, I realize they're not true.

I barely thought about Teatro della Notte the entire time I was away. And it's not because I don't love it, because I do—even now. Even though it feels different.

But I fell in love with Maison du Mystère. I fell in love with the people. I fell in love with the way their magic was different.

The way their circus *life* was different.

I miss it so much, it feels like there's a knife in my stomach and someone is twisting and twisting and twisting until I want to keel over.

I hope one day I'll love something that much again.

I guess that's one benefit to having a heart that's full of holes—there's a lot of room to love something new.

CHAPTER SIXTY-EIGHT

*D*ad's standing in his office, his violin against his chin, the warm sound filling the room.

There was nothing warm about the way Vas played. His sound would grab hold of your heart and clench hard, making you ache. It was whispers and graveyards and longing for the past.

Dad's sound is friendlier. Softer.

He catches me staring, concern taking over his brow. He drops the wooden instrument to his side. "Is everything okay?"

I take a breath, like I'm coming back to life. "Yeah, fine. Sorry, I was . . . remembering someone."

He nods. This is usually the point he'd turn back to his music, a look on his face that says he'll forgive the interruption but would prefer if it didn't happen again.

But Dad's eyes are still on me. "Did you want to talk?" The words sound strange leaving his mouth. They must taste strange too, because he flexes his jaw and rolls his tongue to the inside of his mouth like he's not sure what to make of them.

"It's okay," I say quickly, starting to retreat. "You're busy."

"No." He sets his violin carefully on his desk, holding a hand toward the small couch against the wall. "I can make time."

Make time. What a strange thing to say. Nobody can really make time—they can only offer the time they have.

But Dad's never offered his time before. Not to me.

I take a seat, my hands fiddling with my pajama bottoms. He sits in his chair across from me, his hands on his knees like he's ready to give a lecture.

And it makes me smile, how obvious it is that Dad has no idea what he's doing.

But at least he's trying.

"What's so funny?" he asks, looking self-conscious.

I shake my head quickly. "You just . . . look like you're about to yell at me for something, that's all."

He looks down, crosses his arms, uncrosses them. Then he's laughing too. "Now I don't know what to do." I laugh harder, and Dad beams. "It's nice to see you happy."

I feel my face falling, but try to hold a smile up to make him feel better. Because "happy" isn't exactly the word I would use to describe myself. Far from it, actually.

Mom and Dad don't understand how someone can laugh but still be depressed. How someone can stop being depressed for a period of time, but still suffer from depression. How someone can appear to be functioning in a way they think is normal, but still be struggling with their mental health.

But I'm so tired of fighting people—even myself—that I don't want to fight about this, too.

So I let him have this one, because some conversations can't happen in a single day.

"I'm sorry about the set list," I say.

"You've already apologized—" Dad starts.

"I know. But it was always when Mom was around. It was never just to you."

He breathes out of his nose, nodding.

I look down in my lap. "I know if it were up to you, you'd probably still be mad. And I'd deserve that, so it's fine. But I want you to know how sorry I really am. If I could go back in time, I wouldn't do it."

His face doesn't change. "You'd stay here? Go to school?"

I freeze like I've been caught.

Dad smiles gently. "That's what I thought."

"I wouldn't steal the music, though," I point out. "But . . . I don't think I would've gone to school."

He sighs, leaning forward so he can rest his elbows on his knees. "You were great up there, you know. Your mom and I haven't said that to you yet, because we didn't want to upset you, but it's true. I was so proud of you. The proudest I've ever been."

The ache in my chest grows.

"Look, if you could go back in time, I wouldn't want you to steal the set list either. But not joining the circus? I don't know if

I'd want that. Because something's changed in you. You've grown up. You've learned lessons—the kind you can only learn by going out and really living. And I think it's been good for you." He holds up a hand. "I'm not saying I'm happy about you running away and ignoring your mom and me for months. But I think it was a good experience for you. I really do."

I'm too stunned to think, so I say the only words I can manage. "But you hate Maison du Mystère."

Dad laughs. "I *dislike* Simon Tarbottle." He pauses. "Well, I hate him now, after what he did to you."

A smile tugs at my mouth. "Thanks, Dad."

"So." He claps his hands. "Since we're in here talking and all, do you want to tell me who that boy was that ran after you into your trailer?"

I lean back and rub my temple, face crumpled. "Not really, no."

"Oh, come on. I can talk about boys with you," he says.

"You're even making *that* sound weird," I point out.

Dad's quiet for a second. "Well, I hope he's nice to you. That's the important thing."

"He is. Was." I drop my hands into my lap. "We aren't in touch."

"I see," he says. "He's a very talented aerialist. I was tempted to offer him a job—poach a performer from Tarbottle and see how he likes it." Dad grins.

"Don't feel like you missed your opportunity. Vas wouldn't have taken it anyway," I say. "He was only performing because of me. He's actually a musician—a really good one. He wrote that song, you know. The one we performed to."

"Did he?" Dad looks genuinely impressed.

I nod. "And if it makes you feel better, he was *very* against using your set list. He wanted to use his own stuff."

"Now I like him even more. Are you sure you don't want to be in touch with him again?" Dad asks.

"Okay, you're really pushing it now," I warn, even though I'm smiling. I stand up. "I'll let you get back to work. I know you're busy."

Dad stands too. "Not too busy for you. Remember that, okay? I'm trying to remember it too."

My eyes start to well up, so I turn for the door quickly. "Oh," I say, stopping myself. When I turn around, Dad is already reaching for his violin. "I almost forgot. I wanted to ask you—who told you and Mom I was performing?"

Dad blinks, feigning confusion.

I raise a brow. "I didn't tell Popo. I didn't tell anyone."

"Huh," he says, and there's a twinkle in his eyes I haven't seen in years. Maybe ever. "It must have been a little bird."

I roll my eyes. "Honestly. You circus people and your little birds." I start to turn, but Dad's softened gaze makes me pause.

"It was your mom," he says gently. "The circus is a small world. She made some calls, asked around, and found out you were going to perform." His face wrinkles into a tired smile. "She wanted to be there. We both did."

The knot tightens in my throat. "But . . . why? Neither of you approved of me joining the circus. You wanted me to go to school."

"We *do* want you to go to school," he corrects. "But we're your parents, and we don't want to miss the big moments. Even the ones we don't agree with."

I nod, and my emotions flood through me.

Dad looks down at the floor and clears his throat. "You know, your mom told me what you said to her. About me being a ghost."

"I didn't mean that—" I start.

He holds up his hand. "It's okay, Harley. I know why you said it. I guess sometimes I get so caught up in my work that I forget to be present. I don't even realize I'm doing it, but I can see why that wouldn't have been fair to you. I hope—I hope I didn't miss out on too many moments with you. I hope I was there for some of them." His eyes well up, but he blinks the tears away quickly. "Maybe if I'd been the dad you needed, you wouldn't have been in such a hurry to run away."

"It wasn't your fault. I made that choice on my own," I say with a shaky voice.

"It is my fault." He gives me a weak smile. "At least a little bit. Because you tried to tell us you weren't feeling supported, and I didn't want to listen. And so I don't blame you for wanting to leave. I really don't. The rest of it, I'll accept your apology for, but that part? That was me failing as your father."

I let my eyes fall to my feet because seeing Dad cry is making me want to burst into sobs.

"There should have been another way to handle everything. For both of us," Dad says. "I don't want anything like this to happen ever again. So the next time you need to talk, I promise I'll listen."

There should have been another way.

It's the lesson I needed to learn most of all. Because feeling hurt is never an excuse to hurt the people I care about.

Maybe family means trying a little harder to understand one another.

Maybe family means there's room to compromise.

"Thanks, Dad," I say, lifting my eyes. "And, for what it's worth, I promise I'll never break into your filing cabinet again."

Dad lifts his brow. "Oh, you don't need to worry about that. I've already changed all the combinations."

I roll my eyes, half embarrassed and half amused.

When I close Dad's office door, I can still hear him laughing behind it.

CHAPTER SIXTY-NINE

I keep expecting to one day wake up happy again. But when my dream of the circus died, it left a hole in my chest. A hole that grows and grows, spilling black onto everything around it.

I don't know how to close it up, or make it stop. So my heart continues to bleed, a little at a time, every day until the world starts to feel too heavy for one person to hold up.

Popo makes teriyaki salmon for dinner, and afterward when Mom and Dad are busy in the office, she asks me to sit with her on the couch.

"You look tired, Harley Yoshi," she says.

"I feel tired," I admit. "But not the kind of tired where you just need to sleep it off. I'm the kind of tired that makes your face hurt and your chest tighten and you want to cry at everything and nothing because your feelings are numb and in overdrive, all at once. I feel like I could sleep for a lifetime and I wouldn't actually feel more awake." I pause. "Sometimes I feel like I don't *want* to be awake."

"Have you talked to your mother about this?" she asks seriously.

"Mom doesn't understand. Not really," I say. "I'd rather keep this to myself."

"But if it gets worse . . . ," Popo starts, and I know what she means.

If it gets worse, she wants me to tell her. She wants me to ask for help, if there ever comes a time when I need it.

"I'm okay," I insist, which is both true and not true. I'm not okay, but not the kind that Popo or anybody else needs to worry about. "But I'll let you know if I'm not."

She nods. "Your mom can be stubborn sometimes. Just like you." She laughs gently. "And maybe that's my fault, for always pushing her to do things she didn't want to do. Maybe she feels like she has to be stubborn, just to have control."

I frown. "Push her to do what?"

Popo's eyes are lost in a memory. "I never wanted your mother to join the circus. I wanted her to be a doctor. She was so good at her academics—I thought she deserved the best job she could get. We fought about it a lot, and after high school she took a job as a trapeze artist for a local circus.

"I gave her such a hard time about it. I never let up, even when I could see that she was so happy. She had just married your father then too. They had plans to join a traveling company, and maybe eventually move overseas. But then one day your mom had a bad fall. She was in the hospital when they told her that her leg was so badly broken, they weren't sure how soon she'd be able to perform again. They also told her she was pregnant."

"What?" My eyes are wide.

Popo's are sunken. Tired. Apologetic. "You were okay, but I made your mom feel so guilty. I told her she was irresponsible, that she could've killed you. I . . . said a lot of things I shouldn't have said back in those days. Things I wish so much I could take back. After that, your mom quit the circus and never performed again."

"I didn't know that. I didn't know any of that," I say.

Popo nods. "I've always felt like it was my fault she gave up on her dreams. And all these years later, I sometimes look at her and wonder if I kept her from being truly happy. I regret the things I said, and the way I behaved. But it's been so many years now—years I can't get back." She closes her hand over mine. "I don't want you to give up on your dreams, especially if you think they're worth holding on to."

"I don't think the circus is for me," I say quietly.

"You're wrong," Popo says with a smile. "From one stubborn person to another, you're very, very wrong." She pats my hand before leaning back in her chair. "Try talking to your parents one more time. I think this time they'll listen."

CHAPTER SEVENTY

*W*hen I dream, I see the circus. I see rings of fire, and distorted mirrors, and extravagant costumes. I see spinning plates, and confetti, and juggling pins in every color of the rainbow. And I see the performers—the acrobats, and aerialists, and contortionists, and clowns. I see the families. I see the children. I see the sparkle in their eyes when they step out of their cars and notice the big top across the grassy field.

And I see me, in the heart of it. Always in the heart of it. Because the circus hasn't left me.

I'm not sure it ever will.

When I wake up in the middle of the night, my memories still blurred with velvet curtains and dancing stars, I know I can't give up on my dreams.

Simon Tarbottle hacked away at them—cut them down so there was nothing to see.

But he didn't kill them. Because my dreams are like roots. They're my foundation.

They give me life.

And nobody has the power to ever take that away from me.

Nobody but me.

I won't give up on the circus.

Just like I know the circus will never give up on me.

CHAPTER SEVENTY-ONE

*M*om and Dad are both in the kitchen, chopping vegetables together like they're part of some kind of couples' cooking show. They haven't noticed me standing in the doorway yet, so their guard is down. They don't have to worry about tiptoeing on eggshells when their daughter with the sad, heavy heart isn't in the room.

I don't blame them for that part, though. I'd be relieved to get a break from me too.

Dad slices off a piece of cheese and holds it up for Mom, whose hands are busy peeling potatoes, so she eats it out of his hand and winks at him.

They're so annoyingly cute. Like when people do photo shoots of baby animals with stuffed animals next to them. You want to roll your eyes, but you can't because it's just too adorable.

Popo looks up from the dining table, her glasses perched on the edge of her nose. She's reading a new book—some crime thriller or another, which she can never seem to get enough of.

"Good morning!" Popo says with delight, even though it's almost dinnertime. She knows I've spent the day sleeping.

Mom and Dad look at me, the relaxed smiles disappearing from their faces. Something tight and restrained appears instead.

"Are you hungry? We're making lemon chicken and potato gratin. Should be ready in an hour," Mom says.

Dad pops another piece of cheese into his mouth and goes back to slicing potatoes.

I wander toward the table and sit down across from Popo. She watches me carefully for a minute, like she's asking if I'm okay. I nod, because sometimes other people need reassurance, even when I'm the one who feels broken. She smiles and cracks her book open again.

"I drove past the university earlier today. They must've had some kind of sports game going on because there was a ton of traffic near the stadium." Mom's still chopping, trying to sound casual. Trying to *fix*. "I bet that'll be so much fun—going to games with your friends. Kenji, don't you think that sounds fun?"

Dad's still eating cheese. "Mm-hmm." He gives her a thumbs-up.

A pressure returns against my chest, pushing down hard. I feel my heart rate pick up. It's even hard to breathe.

"I know it might be too late to get a dorm room, but is that something you'd like? Not that we don't love having you at home, but having a roommate is probably a totally different college experience," Mom continues like everything is normal.

My ribs tighten. My throat tightens.

I feel like someone is wringing my entire body out like I'm

made of cloth, squeezing me until there isn't a drop of life left.

Mom's talking to me, but she's looking around the room like this conversation is for everyone. "Or what about a sorority? I mean, I think they seem like kind of a distraction, but I know there are all different kinds. I'm told it's not just about going to parties. There are academic ones, sports ones, even music or—"

"I'm not going to school."

The room falls silent.

Was that my voice? It felt like thunder.

It felt like *power*.

I keep talking. "Not full-time, anyway. And not to the school you want me to go to."

I'm shaking everywhere, my hands clenched tightly. Mom's eyes are startled and wide. Dad's stopped eating cheese. Popo's face is serene, and maybe even . . . proud?

"I'm sorry," I say, and then the words rush out of me like a wave. "I know how you feel about university. And I know I'm the one who left the circus when I left Maison du Mystère, but the truth is, the circus hasn't left me. Even right now, when I'm hurting and I feel like it's impossible to be happy, I know going to school full-time would be a mistake. Because I love being an aerialist. I love being on the trapeze. It makes me feel whole. And I know if I gave it up—if I traded in my dreams for a backup—I would regret it for the rest of my life." I take a breath. "But, I know school means something to you. And I know your rules about me having to go to school to stay at home. So I'd like to propose a compromise. Community college on a part-time basis, while I continue training on the trapeze."

Mom turns to Dad, expecting him to jump in.

I'm shocked when he doesn't.

He lifts his shoulders. "Would it be the worst thing in the world if we let her train with Tatya? Our daughter is talented. We both saw it."

Mom flattens her mouth, shaking her head. "I know she's talented. I know she's *incredible*." She turns to me. "But what happens if you have another episode like this? What if you quit again and decide you've had enough?"

"If being an aerialist doesn't work out, I can always take more classes. At least this way I won't miss out on training. I'll have a chance to do what I love," I say. "But I know myself, and I'm not going to quit. I mean, I might've still been at Maison du Mystère if you and Dad hadn't shown up. I think I just ran for the easiest exit because I was upset and things had been so bad between us. If I'd had more support from the start, maybe I wouldn't have taken rejection so hard."

"So it's *our* fault now?" Mom gapes.

"No, that's not what I'm saying. It's nobody's fault," I say, trying to steady my voice. "I'm just saying there were other factors involved. And yeah, maybe I'll quit a troupe again, but that doesn't mean I have to quit on my dreams. I can still be an aerialist. I can still find a job somewhere else."

"But what if you don't?" Mom asks, and I wish she would put the knife down because she looks *terrifying* right now.

"Then I don't," I say simply. "But at least I tried. I don't want to stop trying. Not ever. Not when it comes to the circus."

Dad rests his hand on Mom's shoulder. "I know you were always set on her going to school, but maybe we can be flexible. Maybe our dreams for our daughter can be flexible."

She looks up at him with tears in her eyes. "Why are you saying that? Why are you making it sound like it was my fault? You wanted her to go to school too."

"She'll still be going to school—just in a different way than we wanted." He eyes the cutting board. "Honey, could you maybe put the knife down when we're talking?"

She drops it on the counter and holds her hands up. "What, now you think I'm going to *stab* someone too?"

Dad starts to laugh, but she cuts him a look that makes him chomp down on his lip.

Popo's voice breaks through the arguing like a crane soaring over rough water. "I don't think Harley is asking for permission— she's asking for your support."

Mom looks at her and drops her arms. I think the two of them share unspoken words before she finally opens her mouth. "Why did you give her that photograph?"

"Delilah—" Dad starts.

Mom holds up a hand, still staring at Popo. "No. I haven't asked because I didn't want to fight, but I want to know. Why would you show her that? Knowing everything that happened? Are you trying to hurt me? Punish me? What is it, Ma?"

Popo removes her glasses and sets them on the table. "I

shouldn't have kept you from the circus. I know that now."

"I'm not talking about the circus," Mom snaps, and Popo's face rumples. "I'm talking about Harley almost dying. Isn't that what you told me? That she almost died? That I almost murdered my own daughter?"

Popo stands, shakier than usual. "I'm sorry for what I said. It was wrong of me. And that's why I'm trying to show you I learned from my mistakes—so you don't make the same ones."

Mom crosses her arms, shaking her head angrily. "You have no right to interfere. You had your turn raising a daughter. This is my turn, and I'm doing it the way *I* think is best."

Popo looks ashen. She's probably never heard Mom speak to her like this before.

Dad tries to take Mom's hand, but she swats him away. She's a volcano that's already erupted. I don't think any of us can calm her down until she's finished letting out the fire.

She's yelling about all the things Popo did wrong, and all the things she's trying to do right, and some of it is so personal and raw, I feel like I'm eavesdropping on a conversation I shouldn't be.

But the more I watch Popo, the more Mom's voice starts to fade in the background.

Popo looks . . . confused.

Scared.

And like she isn't listening to Mom either.

"Popo?" I ask quietly. "Are you okay?"

It happens fast.

Popo makes a noise that sounds like a grunt. She grabs her left arm. Her entire face crumples in pain.

And then her frail body falls to the floor.

I've never heard a person sound so truly afraid until the moment Mom screams for her mother.

CHAPTER SEVENTY-TWO

*W*e follow the ambulance to the hospital, Dad driving because Mom is choking on her tears, asking, "What have I done?" over and over again.

It feels like we're in the waiting room for hours. Maybe we are. Dad refuses to leave Mom's side, so I make a couple coffee runs, trying to be helpful.

Mom won't drink anything. She won't look at me either, and I'm terrified for Popo, but also terrified this all happened because of me.

Why did I have to bring up the circus and school? Why did I have to make everything worse?

And even though Dad is usually terrible at noticing what's going on in front of him, he does notice me.

"This isn't your fault," he says when Mom is in the bathroom.

I look at him with tired eyes. "Then why did you wait until Mom was gone to tell me that?"

"Because I know your mom, and if she realizes you're blaming yourself, it will make everything worse. She's feeling guilty enough right now," Dad says. "But I promise you, your mom doesn't think it's your fault either. Not even a little bit."

I nod. "Do you think Popo is going to be okay?"

"God, I hope so," Dad says, and even though the words leave him like they're supposed to lift some of the weight off of us, it just feels like the room gets heavier.

The doctor says Popo is in recovery. She's going to be okay.

The light coming in from the window makes Popo look pale. She's resting in the hospital bed, her eyes closed and her hands folded on her stomach. If it weren't for the fact that she's attached to a monitor, it would look like she's been prepped for a coffin.

"Are you sure she's alive?" Dad says, because clearly we have the same lack of filter when it comes to words.

Mom swats him on the arm. "That's not even a little bit funny."

When she's walking toward Popo's bed, Dad looks at me and pinches his fingers at the air like he's asking if maybe it was, *a little bit*.

I nod, and we both pack our smiles away before we get back in Mom's vantage point.

I sit in one of the chairs—Mom and I both at Popo's sides—and Dad's hovering behind me.

"Hey, I bet Popo will be hungry when she wakes up. Maybe I could run out to McDonald's and grab her some breakfast?" Dad offers.

Mom makes a face. "Kenji, she just had a heart attack. She can't eat McDonald's."

"Ah. Right." Dad hesitates. "Well, I could at least run to the store, grab her a few things she might need. Like a toothbrush, or a comb . . ."

"I think the hospital has that stuff," Mom says, rubbing the side of her head tiredly.

Dad nods slowly, looking up at the ceiling. Then he lights up. "What about her book? She'd probably love to read that when she wakes up."

Mom opens her mouth to shut his idea down, when something makes her stop. Something Dad must be mouthing to her. But when I turn around to look, Dad's smiling awkwardly at me.

"That would be great. Thank you," Mom says.

Dad walks around to the other side of the bed, pecks her on the cheek, and hurries out of the room.

"Okay, what secret conversation did I miss?" I ask.

Mom smiles softly. "He thought maybe we should talk alone. Just the two of us."

I look down at Popo, who is still sleeping.

"I'm sorry." I swallow the knot that's been in my throat for hours.

"You," Mom says seriously, "have *nothing* to apologize for. Nothing. This was my fault. I shouldn't have gotten so worked up."

I look up at Mom seriously. "Don't you think Popo would say it wasn't your fault either?"

Mom's eyes water, but she wipes them away quickly.

"You were telling her how you felt, which is what I was doing to you. And if you had had a heart attack instead of Popo, would you have wanted me to blame myself?" I ask.

A laugh escape's Mom's lips. "When did you get so smart?"

I smirk. "I've always been smart. That's why I don't need school."

Mom narrows her eyes, and I roll mine.

"I know. *Not funny.*"

Mom tucks her hair behind her ears and crosses her arms. "It wasn't all her fault, you know."

I make a face. "I didn't think anyone would blame Popo for her own heart attack."

Mom shakes her head. "I mean about the circus—about why I quit."

"Oh." My heart thumps.

She sighs, staring at Popo for a long time, searching for the courage to say her story out loud. "It's true Popo said a lot of harsh things to me after I almost lost you. But they were all things I had already been thinking myself. And I chose to quit not because of Popo—but because in that moment, I knew I loved something much more than I ever loved the circus." She looks at me seriously. *"You."*

"You could've still gone back to the trapeze," I offer.

"But I didn't want to. Not after the fall. I didn't want to risk getting hurt again, but I also changed. My priorities were different," she explains.

"And you wished you would've had a backup," I finish for her. "Look, I know you're worried I'm going to end up feeling like you did, but that's for me to find out. It's my life, and right now I just don't see myself ever changing my mind. Besides, it's not like you didn't end up having a backup. You opened an entire circus, for crying out loud!"

Mom bites her lip, and I realize she hasn't finished telling me the truth. "I was only able to open Teatro della Notte because I had your father's help. His . . . financial support."

I frown, not understanding what that's supposed to mean.

Mom's cheeks darken, like she's ashamed. "I felt like I owed your father *so much*. More than I could ever pay back. And I didn't want that for you. I didn't want you to feel like you had to depend on someone, or owe them anything. I wanted you to have the freedom to make your own choices without struggling. The choice to travel, or change jobs, or . . . leave."

Leave.

I feel sick. "Are you saying you want to leave Dad?"

Mom shakes her head quickly, the tears building again. "No. I mean, not exactly. Not anymore." She shuts her eyes and presses her lips together. "It's complicated."

My blood starts to heat up. "Does Dad know how you feel? Does he know you want to split up?"

"I do not want to split up with him," Mom says, and she does actually sound certain despite her previous words. "But your dad and I have been best friends for most of our lives. I know you called him a ghost, but for me he's been an anchor. He's always been there for me, just like I've always been there for him. And that hasn't changed. We are still best friends, and we love each other. But . . . well, all I'm saying is that I didn't feel like I was allowed the choice to fall out of love with him. Romantically. Because by that point we had a daughter, and I depended on him for everything—even all the physical care that was required after I broke my leg—and I just felt trapped. Like, the more he did, the more I couldn't do. I'm not saying any of this is his fault— it's nobody's fault—but I wanted something different for you. I wanted you to be independent, so you always, always had options. More than I felt like I had."

I don't know how to comprehend what she's saying to me. Mom and Dad always seemed so in love. So perfect together.

It doesn't make sense she wouldn't want it. She was a *part* of it.

"It's complicated," Mom says again. "And I know it's confusing to hear. But sometimes love changes. Not necessarily to something less, or more, but just—different. But how much we both love you? That's never changed. I love you the most you could possibly love anyone, and it's been like that since the moment I knew you were in my belly."

I hear her words and let them sink in.

"I'm not telling you this for any reason other than that I just want you to know *why*," Mom says quietly. "Maybe it will explain why I sometimes pushed too hard."

"Okay," I say.

She smiles, relieved. "Okay."

I raise a brow. "This doesn't change how I feel about the circus. But thank you for telling me."

Mom laughs. "I figured that. And I suppose community college isn't the end of the world. But promise me that if you change your mind, you won't be too stubborn to tell me? Because if you ever wanted to take more classes . . ." Her voice trails off and she smiles.

I hold up a hand. "I swear, if I decide I'm missing out on dorm and sorority life, you will be the very first person to know."

She wipes her tears away and sighs, frowning. "So does this mean you don't want the university hoodies I bought the other day? Because I got one for me, too. And your dad."

I laugh first, and then Mom follows, and we don't stop until a nurse sticks her head in the room because she heard all the noise and worried something was wrong.

CHAPTER SEVENTY-THREE

*I*t takes a while before Popo is feeling better. But in that time, I realize I've been feeling better too.

The clouds still linger, but they aren't as black. Sometimes I forget they're there at all.

Popo says she's proud of me for staying true to myself, and that she's sorry she took all the attention away from my big moment.

I don't know if Mom tells Dad what we talked about that day at the hospital, but their relationship goes back to the way it's always been. Which I guess is different from what I thought, because now I don't see two people with an epic love story.

I see two people who love each other deeply, who work hard at loving each other, but relish their friendship over everything else.

And that's okay. I want to believe it's okay.

Because I want my parents to be happy as much as I want to be happy.

And I won't judge them for the choices they make to find that happiness.

Hopefully they'll treat me the same.

I'm sitting between my parents on the couch one evening watching a movie, the smell of the buttered popcorn in my lap dragging me deep into memories that still feel like wounds, when I realize I've been so concerned about trying to make pieces of me fit together that I failed to see how they *already* fit.

They fit here, with Mom and Dad.

I'm their daughter. I'm parts of Mom. Parts of Dad. Parts of neither, and both. Some parts belong to just me.

But I will always be home here.

My *parents* will always be home.

It doesn't mean I have to stop searching for family, or another place in the world where I belong.

But it does mean that if I don't find it—if life has other plans— that I will always, always be able to come home.

And maybe I've been so busy chasing this idea of belonging somewhere that I've been failing to see what's right in front of me. I have parents who love me. It's a privilege not everyone has.

And maybe belonging isn't like arriving at a destination—it's about cherishing and nurturing relationships over time.

Following my dreams isn't how I'll find my family. It isn't how I'll find my home.

Family comes from the love I put into the world around me.

And home is my parents, who forever live in my heart.

Which means home is always with me.

Six Months Later

CHAPTER SEVENTY-FOUR

I fall into the chair at my dressing table, my skin still tingling with the adrenaline of being onstage. I don't even realize I'm beaming until I look in the mirror and see my own face. I hardly recognize myself with all the makeup and glitter, but I know I'm in there somewhere.

Mom's here too, in the photograph I have taped to the glass. It's her on the trapeze, all those years ago. Before she had me. Before she even knew she wanted me.

I have a bit of Popo here too, in the form of the hóngbāo she gave me for Chinese New Year—a bright red envelope with shiny gold writing on the front, and eight dollars inside.

It's a present Popo has given me every year for as long as I can remember, but this year was different. This year the luck worked.

Because look where I am.

I still have dark days, even though my world is bursting in yellow, but I'm learning to manage them better. I'm getting better at sensing when they're coming—like watching the tide roll in from a pier.

I don't think they'll ever go away, but I'm here and I'm trying my best and I think that matters more.

Tatya pokes her head around the corner. "I'm taking off. See you tomorrow at the gym?"

I smile. "Yeah, see you tomorrow."

She disappears, and I turn back to the table, scouring the pile of stage makeup for face wipes. I know they're here somewhere, because I just used them last—

The entire world spins when my eyes fall to the pot of flowers sitting on the edge of my table.

Bubblegum-pink orchids.

My heart pounds like it's signaling the opening of an act.

A shadow moves behind me, filling the space in the mirror. I close my eyes, not sure I want to look.

I'm scared I might be wrong, and hope is already lifting me out of our atmosphere.

I breathe chocolate and trees, and every color in the world fills my soul.

My eyes flash open, and he's there in the mirror, his green eyes filled with nervous joy, his beautiful honey-brown hair shoved to one side.

Vas.

"Hello." I didn't know I could miss a voice so much until just now.

"Hi," I say, my own voice barely above a whisper. I turn around in my chair so I can see all of him—the *real* him.

"You were amazing out there," he says, hands stuffed in his pockets.

Sparks ignite all over my skin. "You saw the show?"

He nods. "Someone was kind enough to give me a ticket, so I thought I'd better not waste it." He pauses. "And I was hoping to run into you."

I want to scream "I've missed you" at the top of my lungs, but I'm working on my self-control. So instead, I go with, "It's really nice to see you."

He looks down at the floor, and I suddenly don't think it matters what I'd said. We're like dance partners who've never met before, trampling on each other's feet and trying to figure out a rhythm.

We're out of sync.

"How are you?" I ask after a long pause.

He looks back up, sighing into a smile. "I'm okay. A bit jet-lagged."

"Jet-lagged from Denver?" I make a face, recalling the last place Vivien told me they were.

"I see you're keeping tabs," Vas says playfully. "But no. I flew in from London."

I nod like this is all perfectly normal, even though it most definitely isn't.

Vas is in my dressing room and we're making *small talk*.

What happened to us?

And then I remember. *I* happened to us.

"I'm sorry," I say, my brain feeling like it's about to collapse.

"For everything I said. Most of it was just coming out wrong, but I handled the whole thing terribly. And you didn't deserve that."

"No," he cuts in. "I did deserve it. I was interfering with something that had nothing to do with me. There's no scenario in the world where it's okay to want your girlfriend to stay at a job she hates just because you don't want to lose her. That was me being selfish, and I'm the one who's sorry."

Girlfriend. We'd never used titles out loud before. Hearing him say it in reference to the past—to our breakup—makes my chest quiver.

He sighs. "And everything you said to me was true. About being a hypocrite. But everyone needs to be called out on their bullshit now and then, right?" There's a twitch in the corner of his mouth.

I try to smile, even though my face feels heavy. "I appreciate the apology, but there's really nothing to forgive."

He looks at me like there's so much more he wants to say.

The feeling is definitely mutual.

"So," I say. "You're here. In Las Vegas." I'm trying—and failing—to hide my excitement.

He bounces on his toes, nervous again. "Uh, yeah. I have a job offer, actually."

"Really?" I'm standing now, one hand clutching the back of my chair because I'm worried his news is going to make me topple over.

I knew this was a possibility, but seeing him right here, in front of me . . .

I'm unprepared.

He nods. "Here. At Teatro della Notte."

I feel dizzy with hope.

"Your dad got in touch and said he loved the song I wrote. The one we performed to. He asked if I had any more material—said he was looking for an up-and-coming composer to mentor, because he's been thinking about slowing down his schedule." Vas smiles gently. "He said he wanted to spend more time with his family."

My heart tumbles and tumbles and tumbles.

"I haven't officially accepted the job yet," he explains while my brain is still processing that he's really here because of my dad. Because of what I asked my dad to do. "It didn't seem right to accept without asking your permission first."

"You should take the job," I say, like everything about this is simple. I'm trying my best to look surprised, but I don't think it's working.

Vas watches me, a glint appearing in the corner of his eye. "Did you have anything to do with the job offer?"

And because there's no point in lying to Vas about something he clearly knows the answer to, I say, "Yes."

"Why?" The word vibrates through my core.

What kind of question is that? Why do I want Vas here? Why do I want him to be happy? Why do I want to make things better between us?

Why implies he doesn't have a clue.

Maybe we've grown further apart than I realized.

"Because you deserve this," I say at last.

"I thought—*hoped*—it was because of you," he says quietly. "I'm glad I wasn't wrong. I would've felt pretty silly right about now if you'd said you didn't know a thing about the job."

"Why would that make a difference? It's a great job. My dad is a great . . . composer." I make a face. It's impossible to hide how awkward I feel.

"But we'd see each other a lot. Maybe even most days."

I shrug like it isn't a big deal.

"And I'd basically be colleagues with your dad. Maybe even friends." Vas looks at me seriously. "I might even get invited over for dinner sometimes."

Is he trying to make a joke out of this? I roll my eyes. "It's not like we haven't done the whole 'stay on your side of the big top' before."

He frowns. "Why would we stay on opposite sides of the big top?"

"You know—so we can stay as far away from each other as possible and not make this more awkward than it needs to be," I say exasperatedly.

The muscle in his jaw tightens. "Is that what you want?"

I sigh. If he's asking, I might as well tell him the truth. He'll see it in my face sooner or later anyway.

I'd rather he reject me now and get it over with.

Preferably before my dad invites him to dinner.

"No, of course not. I've missed you. I've missed you so much, it literally makes my heart hurt to think about you. And I do—often. And I know you're only here because of the job, and that's fine. When my dad said he wanted to hire someone, I told him about you because I knew you'd be perfect for it. And because once upon a time you went out of your way to give me a chance. I wanted to return the favor. But there are no strings attached here, and I don't want you to feel like I expect anything at all. Not even a hello, if that's what you want. I promise you that I will not make working together weird. Because you deserve to have your dreams come true, Vas. More than anyone I know."

There's a long silence between us, our eyes flitting back and forth, trying to understand each other.

And then Vas's face softens. "It's true that I'm here because of the job. But I would've been here *months* ago if I knew that's what you wanted. I only stayed away because I thought I was supposed to."

His words tug at my chest, prodding my heart to hope.

"I still feel the same way about you as I did in November," Vas confesses. "But if you don't feel the same, just tell me and I'll—"

"I do," I blurt out.

He raises his brow, the corner of his mouth slightly curling. "You do?"

I nod.

"So . . . I should take the job, then?" He's grinning.

I smile back, and it feels so much like relief. "Yes. *Please* take the job."

Vas takes a step closer, letting his hands fall to his sides.

"Wait," I say with wide eyes. "Does this mean you get to give Simon a resignation letter?" I'm not going to lie—imagining the look on Simon Tarbottle's face when he loses his double trapeze act is bordering on thrilling.

"There's no need. I quit Maison du Mystère the day after you left."

I feel like I'm spinning again.

I've noticed for months that Vas's name never came up in any of my conversations with Vivien. I assumed she was trying not to open old wounds, but now it makes sense.

Because he wasn't even there.

"I . . . didn't know that."

"Don't be too hard on Vee and Dexi. I made them promise not to say anything," he says with a grin. "Which was probably really hard for them, because I kind of made a scene."

"You?" I laugh. "I don't believe it."

He nods. "I may have set your dad's sheet music on fire. In front of Simon's trailer."

"What?" My mouth hangs open.

"I admit, it was a bit dramatic," he says sheepishly. "But I didn't want him to have your dad's set list. Not when you'd already left. And I didn't want him to have our act, either. That was your story to tell, not anyone else's."

The ache in my heart returns, but this time it's in the best way possible.

"Thank you, Vas."

I close the gap between us and let my fingers brush against his. The moment our skin touches, he takes hold of both my hands and stares tenderly into my eyes.

"Would it be possible for us to start over?" he asks.

"I would love that," I say.

It's the circus, after all. What *isn't* possible?

Everyone backstage rushes toward the doors, all crowding together because the finale is always chaos. Every performer has to be fast getting to their marks. The aerialists especially, because the technicians have a schedule to follow too, and there are plenty of us that need to be in the air when the timpani roll ends and the fanfare plays.

Us.

Because I am a part of the big finale too.

It's a small part—barely a part at all. Most of the audience probably wouldn't even notice there was an extra cast member in the air.

But to me it's *everything*.

Tatya squeezes beside me, flashing her teeth happily while we listen to the ringmaster thank the audience, and the band, and then . . .

The performers rush toward the stage.

It's too dark for the audience to see what's going on, save for the burst of shadows and the strategically placed spotlights zigzagging across the floor like wild fairies.

I find my spot near the violins, lift my hands, and close my fingers over the metal bar. I know Tatya is on the opposite side of the orchestra, doing the same.

The percussion takes over, drowning out the sound of the wires raising the trapeze.

And then the fanfare.

The lights turn on, a scattering of colors bursting across the room like a luminous, Technicolor rainbow. Confetti pours from the sky, glittery and marvelous. Clowns charge through the audience, waving in gratitude. Contortionists are balanced on top of each other like a house of cards. Jugglers are tossing colorful pins into the air while they balance on unicycles. Three aerialists are in multicolored silk ropes, high above the audience. And there's me and Tatya, sitting on two static trapezes like mirror images of one another, doing barrel rolls and side planches and front balances and splits in the ropes.

The circus swirls around me, full of life and wonder and magic.

And below, the audience cheers.

ACKNOWLEDGMENTS

I feel like the luckiest person on the planet to be sitting here writing the acknowledgments for my third book. I don't know how this is real life, but I'm so immensely grateful to every single person who helped make this possible.

An enormous thank-you to my agent, Penny Moore, who has been such a champion for my books and my career. You are a superhero in so many ways, and it's an honor to be on this journey with you.

To my editor, Jennifer Ung, who has the most incredible ability to sense the story I want to tell, even when I'm failing through early drafts. Your support and passion for the stories you help bring into the world is incredible, and I'm so overwhelmingly grateful we get to continue working on these books together.

A huge thank-you to the team at Simon Pulse who helped make *Harley in the Sky* a real book: Mara Anastas, Liesa Abrams, Chriscynethia Floyd, Christina Pecorale, Emily Hutton, Lauren Hoffman, Caitlin Sweeny, Nicole Russo, Lauren Carr, Michelle Leo, Chelsea Morgan, Rebecca Vitkus, Stacey Sakal, and Sara Berko. And a special thank-you to designer Heather Palisi and artist Sarah J. Coleman, who created such a breathtaking cover.

Another big thank-you to everyone at Aevitas Creative Management, and Andrea Barzvi and Sandy Hodgman at Empire Literary.

And to every wonderful person at Ink Road, for publishing my last three books in the country I now call home—thank you. I am forever grateful that readers in the UK have had a chance to meet Kiko, Rumi, and now Harley, too.

To the amazing book community who has shown so much support, and in particular to the people who have, for reasons I'll never understand, been so kind to me: Eric Smith, Rachel Strolle, Brandy Colbert, Samantha Shannon, Sara Barnard, Samira Ahmed, S. K. Ali, Rebecca Mix, and Alice Oseman.

To every reader who picks up a book of mine—thank you. Whether it was your kind of book or not, I appreciate it more than you could ever know. And a special shout-out to some of the readers who've helped make the last few years so special: Tasha, Taylor, Cody, Samantha, Jemma, Charlotte, Emma, JM, and Avery.

Thank you to my agency siblings, who are seriously some of the best people in the universe. And an extra special thank-you to Nicki Pau Preto, for not only being my publishing twin and friend but for also being one of the main reasons I haven't permanently curled up into a ball these last few years. When people talk about finding a good writer friend, they mean people like Nicki. You are amazing, and it's an honor to call you my friend.

A very special thank-you to my critique partner, Adalyn Taylor Grace, for reading all of the worst early drafts and still finding something good in them.

And a massive thank-you to every single member of the *Harley in the Sky* Street Team. You have made these past months an absolute delight, and I have enjoyed getting to know all of you. You work so hard at everything you do, and I am forever grateful to each of you for giving your time and energy to help this book. I couldn't have asked for a better street team to help send *Harley* out into the world!

To my family and friends who've been so supportive—thank you times infinity.

In particular, thank you to my dad, for being the person who will read first drafts, last drafts, and sometimes even the versions in between. And to Grandma and Grandpa, for sharing your history with me, and to Popo, the real Chin Choy "Jane" Soong, for letting me borrow your name. Somebody once told me that we're remembered until we're forgotten. I hope this book lets a small piece of your story live on.

And to my kids, Shaine and Oliver, and my husband, Ross: thank you for being my family. I love you all more than I can ever truly explain with words, but if I tried, I'd say it's definitely more than you can fit in the *Millennium Falcon*.